I0713855

KINGS of SCREEN
Between
TAKES
MORGANA
BEVAN

Copyright © 2021 by Morgana Bevan

All rights reserved.

Between Takes is a work of fiction. Names, characters, places, and incidents are all products of the author's imagination and are used fictitiously. Any resemblance to actual events, locals or persons, living or dead, is entirely coincidental.

No part of this book may be reproduced in any form or by any electronic or mechanical means, including information storage and retrieval systems, without written permission from the author, except for the use of brief quotations in a book review.

ISBN: 9781919609119

ISBN (Alternate Cover): 978-1-916719-00-2

Cover Design by: Lily Bear Design Co.

Editing by Kristen Susienka

For Amy, one day we'll spill all the tea.

Between TAKES

MORGANA BEVAN

CHAPTER ONE

"*M*ona? Are you there?" An American voice asked, desperation leaking into her cheery tone.

I couldn't have heard her right.

She couldn't have actually offered me a job as an actor's assistant. Because why would she do that? I'm not even remotely qualified. My sister was an agent too, and I'd learnt plenty from her drunken rants when one client or another got a bit out of hand. But that didn't equal experience.

But what if I hadn't misheard?

"So I'm clear: you want me to babysit an off-the-rails actor for six months?" My light Scottish accent deepened with my confusion.

Sherry chuckled. "That about sums it up. But if he asks, you're his assistant."

Fuck! She *was* serious.

I let my head fall back against the sterile white wall behind me. The jolt of my scalp lightly scraping against the brick stung, but it did nothing to ease my racing heart.

"And my sister thought I was qualified?"

"I know this would be your first assistant job, but Isla was certain you were my girl, and frankly, based on the tales she's told me, I agree with her." Her words ran at a mile a minute, stressed but still cheery as she tried to reassure me.

Isla, my talent agent sister, had abandoned both me and Edinburgh for rival Glasgow almost six months before. Why would she think I could wrangle difficult stars? It still didn't make sense.

My background was in *marketing*. Although, I must have sucked at it because no way should I still be struggling to enjoy the job after two years and three attempts with different companies. I didn't know the first thing about managing *an actor*.

Logically, I knew that was a huge issue here. And yet a stupid thrill continued working its way into my brain.

It would be something different, something challenging.

"What tales?" I asked, remembering Sherry was still there.

"She told me how you got MJ Harris on the stage during your college Freshers Week."

My eyes fell shut, trying to suppress the memory of an itchy rapper who wanted to do nothing but snort his freshly delivered coke and skip out on a room full of drunk first years screaming his name.

He didn't get the coke, and he didn't skip out.

Only because I snapped a photo of him with the bag before snatching it and racing into the bathroom with it. He hadn't been prepared for a fresh-faced second-year Fresher's Helper stepping in and swiping his precious drugs. I'd dangled that tiny bag over the toilet with my phone in my other hand, poised to post it all over social media. His eyes had bugged out, but he gave in.

When the show ended, I was there, waiting at the side of the stage to return his prize. I didn't care if he destroyed his brain cells with it. My job had been to get him on that damn stage. After that, he was someone else's problem.

"I really need a repeat, Mona. Shaun is trying to dig

himself into a hole. I've spent too much time making that man, and I won't let his sorry attempt at self-destruction ruin it now."

Okay, but a drug-addict rapper wasn't the same as an award-winning TV star. Falling from grace or not, he was a big fish, and I was a tiny minnow. He'd stomp me into the ground without breaking a sweat.

"I need you, Mona. I'm desperate," Sherry whispered, the words strangled with disgust. "He's going to tank *Mystery Lines*, his latest TV project, and destroy my reputation. There's an eye-watering amount of money riding on him getting to wrap, and I need a badass who won't take his shit."

Silence fell between us as I let her words sink in.

I'm a badass? Funny, I didn't feel like one these days. I felt like a floundering failure who couldn't figure out which way was up half the time.

"Please say you're in on this!"

Despite myself, I grinned. Someone thought I could whip the golden boy of television into shape. Who cared if that person was my sister? Someone believed in me.

"Did I mention that I'm desperate and there's a hefty pay cheque waiting for you?"

"How hefty?" I asked, pursing my lips to hold in any rash responses.

Pay at my current job wasn't great. It was enough to cover the day to day, but I didn't want to live pay cheque to pay cheque. I hadn't been able to save very much and that wouldn't change, not even with my frugal ways. Thankfully, I didn't have student loans to worry about – one pro of being born Scottish: university was free. Even a slight increase would be huge.

My eyes bulged at the figure she quoted. If I planned it right, I could buy a house outright at the end of the contract with that kind of cash. "When do I start?"

"Oh, thank fucking god!" She sighed, and I could easily

imagine her slouching down in an insanely expensive swivel chair. "Monday. You start Monday."

It was on the tip of my tongue to agree when my brain connected the dots.

My eyes widened. Today was Friday. I would be giving only a few hours' notice.

True, I'd had a lot of trouble finding a job I actually liked, but I'd never up and quit with no warning before.

"Mona?" Sherry's cheery voice pulled me out of my panic spiral. She'd been talking, and I'd zoned out.

"Sorry. I missed that."

"I said, because you're coming to my rescue at the last minute, I'll include a relocation bonus."

I stared at the white wall above the stairs, frowning.

Relocation bonus. Why did I need a relocation bonus?

"The job's not in Glasgow?" I asked, my words slow and measured as I tried to put the pieces together.

"No, dear. Shaun's in Cardiff. I need you in Cardiff."

Silence met her clarification. Quitting a job I hated with a shit supervisor was one thing. But packing up my life and moving four hundred miles down the country without notice? That needed a bit more thought.

And I had to do it all in a weekend.

"On Monday," she repeated, concern diluting her upbeat tone. "Is that a problem?"

Was it a problem?

Isla had clearly given her stamp of approval. She wouldn't miss me. My brother was in London and my parents had retired to Cornwall nearly a year ago. In Cardiff, I'd be closer to all of them. The fact was, there was nothing holding me in Edinburgh. I didn't need to worry about leaving anyone behind. My life here was boring and predictable at the best of times.

"No problem at all. I'll get everything sorted at my end."

Once the words left my mouth, a heavy weight lifted off

my chest. That is until I realised that I now needed to walk back into the office and give my dickhead of a supervisor three hours' notice of my departure. I was nervous – hands-shaking nervous. I had no idea how he would take it. He'd either be gleeful or downright mean about it.

"I'll arrange everything here too," Sherry said, the edge in her voice raising my eyebrows. "I'm going to contract you with the agency rather than Shaun directly. If you run into any problems working for him, let me know immediately and I'll jump in if you need help."

What problems should I be expecting?

"By the time you arrive on Monday, the production team will have your passes ready. I'll text you the details you need and send over the contract by the end of the day." She cleared her throat, hesitating over something. "Do you have questions for me?"

Aside from what the hell am I getting myself into?

"What exactly does an assistant do?"

"Keep him on track, dear," Sherry said, some of the tension draining from her voice now. "He's in a weird place and following through with his commitments is sometimes challenging for him. Keep his schedule up to date, make sure he's attending all his meetings – especially with the producers – get him to set on time, remind him to memorise his lines, manage his communications, run errands. Try not to piss him off." Sherry chuckled at that. "But that'll be nigh on impossible, so I'd ignore his complaining if I were you."

The process sounded easy enough on its own, but throw in a volatile actor and it might not be as straightforward as it appeared.

I swallowed hard. It would be fine.

Besides, I was a badass now. I could handle anything.

❄

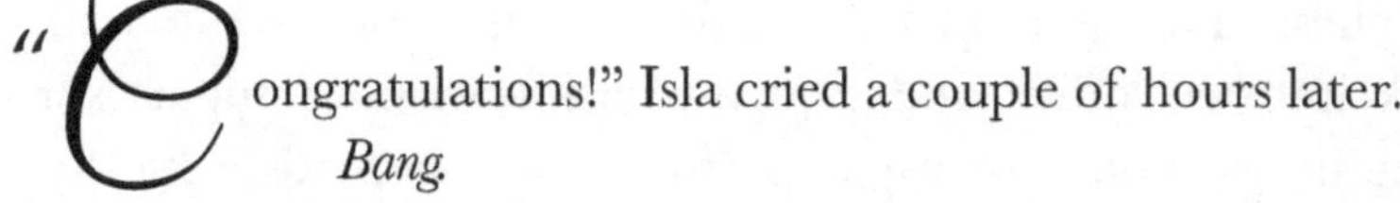

"Congratulations!" Isla cried a couple of hours later. *Bang.*

I jumped as she popped the cork on the bottle of champagne she held. I pulled my short pink hair back into a small but messy ponytail and sighed. I had two days to pack up my life and move. There was no time for hairbrushes or showers or make-up.

There was also no time for champagne and getting very, very drunk, but Isla wore a huge grin I couldn't refuse. The pride shining in her eyes was my undoing. It had been a while since I'd felt deserving of it. Besides, a move like this was huge. Why shouldn't I celebrate a little?

Despite my frazzled state, I accepted the glass with an answering smile of my own.

I'd found Isla in my flat with packages of flat-packed cardboard and alcohol when I got home. Now, we stood surrounded by boxes, most of them empty. Assembling them had been a sweaty feat that came with a lot of swearing and one too many paper cuts. Who knew you could get a paper cut from a cardboard box!

"How did quitting go?" Isla took a seat on the arm of my sofa.

I pulled a face and stuffed a wrapped plate into the box.

"Did he blow up?" Isla chuckled. "Oh, please tell me he made an absolute fool of himself?"

"Is, get real." I rolled my eyes and continued wrapping kitchenware. "He was gleeful, belittling me and my life choices. I bit my cheek and waited through it. It was all pretty smooth sailing after that."

Isla blinked at me, a frown forming between her brows. "No comment on the work you'd be leaving unfinished."

"I offered to do a handover, but he didn't want me to finish up any of my projects because, and I quote, my 'work ethic would make a mockery of his highly respected clients'." Read: tiny pet shop fronting a puppy mill.

Isla leaned back, absorbing the surprising turn. I'd been expecting a lot worse too.

"I'm just relieved to be free of such a mind-numbingly boring job." I smirked, remembering how I'd exited the building. "I might have skipped through the foyer."

Amusement twinkled in Isla's gaze when she met mine. "You didn't?"

I nodded. "My feet left the ground and everything. Security watched me go with a bemused smile. All I needed was a dye job, a pair of killer red heels and a yellow brick road, and you could call me Dorothy."

But alas, I was rather attached to my pastel-pink shoulder-length cut. It stood out in stark contrast to my sister's more conventional long honey-blond tresses. We shared our mother's sharp features, which made us look younger than we actually were. Isla was two years older than me at twenty-seven, and even she got ID'd half the time.

"I'm so proud of you." Isla raised her glass to the air in toast.

Funny, I thought I'd packed the glassware already.

"I've done nothing yet."

"Nonsense. You're taking a brave risk and I couldn't be happier for you." Isla took a seat on my sofa and sipped her bubbling glass. "You watch. This will be just what you need."

I didn't doubt I needed a change of pace. Something was very definitely lacking in my life, and nothing I tried fit. I wasn't delusional; I knew this would be a challenge, but it felt right.

Right or not, my grin wilted at the edges. "Even though I only got it because of you?"

"Sweetheart, getting into this business on your own is really bloody hard." She shrugged, taking a sip of champagne. "The entertainment industry is a nepotistic business. Do you know how many friends, siblings and children I've seen filter through my agency because they're connected to one person or another?"

I shook my head. Isla worked with five other agents. It couldn't be that many.

"At least a hundred in the last six years." She shrugged, her eyes glinting with mischief as mine widened. "But I was one of them, so I'm definitely not complaining, and no one is going to bat so much as an eyelash at you."

Isla tapped at her phone, her forehead creasing in concentration while she searched for something. The matter closed for her, and maybe it should be for me too. If it was normal, why should I care that I lacked experience? I'd been perfectly capable in uni. I'd managed people and schedules at the student union for most of my degree. Surely that counted for something?

I wrapped another plate in newspaper and moved onto the next, my jaw tightening as I watched my sister type away. She was supposed to be helping me. The contents of my entire one-bed flat needed packing and hauling an hour down the road to her flat in Glasgow in the morning. If we didn't want to be up until 2AM, there needed to be more wrapping happening alongside the celebrating and distracted texting.

I didn't think I had a lot of stuff, but it was hard to avoid the facts when faced with packing it all up and storing it. The truth was: I owned a lot of unnecessary shit. What single person needed twelve plates or twenty mugs? Yes, they were all pretty designs, but I didn't have any friends left to entertain. It was all wasted money and space.

My smart speakers kicked in thanks to Isla, blaring "That Don't Impress Me Much" by Shania Twain and scaring the bejesus out of me. Isla wrestled the plate from my grip, a huge grin spreading across her face again. Then she took my hands and pulled me away from the boxes.

When we were kids, we used to dance around the kitchen

to this song. One of us was always tripping up our parents as they made dinner. An answering smile tugged at my lips.

"I told Sherry you were a badass, and you are. You just need to be reminded of it," Isla shouted, jumping up and down to the music, her hair flying in all directions and her hazel eyes flashing with mirth. She used her grip to force my body to twist, but with at least two inches on my five and a half feet and considerably more muscle mass, she didn't need to try too hard.

We collapsed onto the sofa as the song ended, laughing too hard to breathe. For a moment, I blocked out the practicalities and leaned into the excitement. Monday I'd be in a new city, with a new flat, a new job and new experiences. I didn't know what was coming, but the uncertainty held its own thrill.

Isla pulled out her phone and started typing again. She dropped it in my lap before picking up a pile of newspapers. I glanced down at the phone, frowning. A striking pair of green eyes stared up at me from the screen.

"I'll get some of these boxes filled. You do a little digging on your new assignment."

Assignment. I snorted. That made it sound like I was a spy and he was my next target.

I scanned the page of articles that a search for "Shaun Martin" generated. The first couple of hits were from gossip websites, and I rolled my eyes at their clickbait-y titles.

THE TYLER–MARTIN BREAK NO ONE SAW COMING

WHO'S TO BLAME FOR SHILY SPLIT?

DRUGS, SEX, ALCOHOL AND ROCK-N-ROLL: TOO MUCH FOR SHAUN MARTIN?

SHAUN MARTIN CRASHES OUT. LILY TYLER TO BLAME?

On and on the headlines went. Some insinuated that Shaun was violent and that's why Lily kicked him to the kerb after twelve years. Others suggested he'd only stuck with her for the fame. All of them quoted anonymous "sources" close to the couple. I knew enough about Isla's job to not put any stock in some anonymous prat taking a pop at his or her friends. If they were even friends.

"Have you seen some of these?" I asked Isla, disgust heightening my voice.

She nodded. "I had a glance before I gave Sherry your number."

"'Acclaimed celebrity actor Shaun Martin crashes stunt car two weeks after pop-rock sensation Lily Tyler ends long-term relationship with him. Is this his cry for love or a cry for help? Sources close to Martin tell *New Hollywood* Tyler pulled Martin out of an abusive childhood home and gave him a career. After the breakup, he's worried his career is going to slip away without her. He was going out with a bang, they said.'"

I glanced at Isla, dropping her phone on the sofa. "How can they print things like that?"

"It's a tabloid paper." She shrugged, not even pausing as she piled my DVDs into a box. "They print whatever they like and keep a staff of lawyers on retainer."

The whole thing left a foul taste in my mouth. The man was hurting. Maybe he needed a little room to breathe without the world avidly watching him for the smallest crack.

CHAPTER TWO

*J*uggling a coffee cup while power walking across a busy, sprawling studio lot was my worst idea today. But it was only 8AM, and there was still plenty of time for bigger fuck-ups – not that I was planning to fuck up. It was just the kind of thing I was braced for after Sherry's cryptic warnings and my internet searches.

It's not like I didn't set six alarms last night. I even skipped my morning coffee. All to make up for the fact that I woke at 7:15AM to the shouting of my new flatmates returning from some bender of a night out. I'd missed every single alarm and lost any time to dawdle with my own drink and sooth my jumping nerves.

In under an hour, I made it out of the shower, dressed, drove across Cardiff, picked up my security passes, and stopped to pick up his coffee order, as Sherry directed, from the Craft Services table at the studio. I didn't really have time for it, but considering I wanted to make a good impression my first day, I stopped. Maybe it would sweeten him up and save me a lecture from Mr Hotshot actor on tardiness.

Although he definitely couldn't talk.

Sherry's extremely lengthy briefing email made it crystal clear that my real job was to keep him on time and out of trouble.

Skidding to a halt, I barely avoided getting run over by a rack of clothes. The wardrobe assistant scowled at me, her eyes fixed on the large soy milk mocha I held dangerously close to her treasures. She barrelled on and I blew out a relieved breath. Pretty multi-hued pastel hair or not, I didn't want to mess with that death glare.

When the coast was clear, I snuck a glance at my watch. *Fifteen minutes to make-up. Fuck.*

I took off at a run – which, let me tell you, is not easy on grass; adding in ballerina pumps and a full scalding-hot cup of coffee was asking for trouble. But by some miracle, I didn't spill it, and I even made it through the maze of identical-looking trailers. I followed a hunch that his would be the biggest, and I wasn't wrong. I stopped near a trailer with a laminated sign of his name to catch my breath and compose myself before I approached the lion's den and knocked.

My heart was still in my throat, but at least when I banged on the door, I was certain words would come out of my mouth.

Seconds stretched into minutes as I stared at the door. We didn't have time for more of a delay, and I really didn't want Shaun to be late to set my first day. What a failure that would be.

But knocking was gaining me nothing but bruised knuckles.

Sherry had been clear: Shaun was never on time these days. No way had he already left for make-up. Plus, I could hear the quiet buzz of a TV. The hotshot was in there, and he was ignoring me.

I've never been great with people ignoring me – just ask my brother. Call it youngest child syndrome if you want, but the fact is I learned how to make people give me their attention at a young age. And right now, some uppity TV star crashing to earth was not getting in my way.

With renewed vigour, I slammed my hand against the door repeatedly. It stung, but it was effective. The trailer rattled with my thumps.

Heavy footsteps raced towards the door and I stepped back. It narrowly missed my nose as it flew open.

"What?" Shaun Martin shouted, glaring down at me with hard eyes.

For a moment, I lost my words.

I'd seen pictures, of course, but nothing could prepare me for the real deal. The fire in his eyes proved he had a mammoth temper. With all that animosity centred on me, my brain stuttered.

But after a few breaths, I snapped out of it. I'd allowed no one to have that kind of power over me. Not my teachers, not my boss, definitely not my ex-boyfriend. I certainly wouldn't start with Shaun Martin. If he wanted to glare at someone, he could look in a mirror.

I pushed my shoulders back, cleared my throat and offered my free hand. "Mr Martin, I'm Mona Baines. It's nice to meet you."

The glare went up a notch. *Okay, so killing him with politeness isn't going to work.*

"May I come in?" I asked, trying for a sunny smile.

Somehow his face darkened further. He crossed his arms – his very muscular arms – and blocked the doorway.

"I have your mocha." I offered the cup, forcing my smile back in place.

His face softened as his eyes dropped to the coffee, and I thought for sure that would be my in. But he didn't ease his stance or so much as twitch towards the cup.

"Sherry said soy milk mocha was your drink." I frowned

down at the cup. Come to think of it, why did I believe his agent actually knew him? My sister had a file on all of her clients, but that didn't mean Sherry was as diligent. "Never mind. I can get you something else from Craft Services."

"Why is my agent telling you my coffee order?"

"She didn't tell you?"

His eyes narrowed, and I took that to mean no.

My bravado slipped along with my smile. "I'm your new assistant."

Silence followed my declaration. I had to give up on winning this asshole with kindness. Every time I smiled, his face darkened.

"Not a chance," he muttered before swinging the door shut in my face. A distinctive click of locks followed.

I blinked at the plastic door. "Well, that could have gone better."

"You did what!" Shaun roared from behind the door moments later.

I flinched. It was loud, okay? *Maybe I should check in with make-up and let them know he'll be late. Find myself a headset too, just in case anyone is looking for him.*

Before I could move more than two steps, the door flew open. I froze, my wide eyes fixed on the handsome man using his striking green gaze to turn me inside out.

"You!" he shouted, pointing a long finger at me. "Just to be clear: I did not hire you. I don't need you."

He held the phone away from his ear as a shrill voice blared from it. I stood over six feet away, and even I could hear Sherry tearing into him.

"It was one time." He forced the words out through gritted teeth. "They can't get their knickers in a twist over one late start."

It was actually five in two weeks. Sherry was a very talk-ative person, and then her briefing notes gave even more detail. Probably not great business practice, spilling your client's secrets in writing, but right now, I was grateful.

"I don't need a babysitter. I'm handling it." He dragged his hands through his thick brown hair, tugging at the ends a little too hard.

Someone is stressed.

"That's ridiculous," Shaun muttered. "I'm the star! They wouldn't."

They so would – or so Sherry said.

Apparently, he wasn't the easiest person to handle on set. Just two weeks into a gruelling six-month schedule and Shaun had already alienated half the crew. The producers had been amicable to start, but now they'd started to see that their chosen star was driving them into the sun.

The fight drained from Shaun's shoulders and the tension bled out of him. Moments later, he slumped against the door-frame. His eyes scanned slowly up my body, and something about his unfocused but softening gaze made goose bumps break out along my arms.

My boss was checking *me* out.

It lasted for all of five seconds, and then my spine stiffened and I folded my arms across my chest. With a leisurely pace, his eyes rose to my hard face. He smirked before focusing his attention back on Sherry.

"Fine. But it's a trial and when I say it's done, it's done."

I was fairly certain Sherry wouldn't agree with his estimations. He tensed and I barely stopped myself from smiling in triumph.

Take that, Hotshot!

"Are you fucking serious?" His eyes fixed on me, eying me like whatever threat Sherry had issued was entirely my fault. Given her desperation to get me here, I was fairly certain it was a threat. I glared right back at him. "Pretty sure *I* employ *you*, Sherry. Are you enjoying the beach house my fee earned you?"

Oh yeah, entitled asshole alert. Somebody had forgotten his roots.

My research said Shaun Martin didn't come from an acting dynasty. He grew up in a small working-class South Wales town, went to a secondary school. If the critics were to be believed, he was a natural talent. He'd never had acting lessons, no Sunday drama clubs or drama classes in school. With all that, you'd think he'd be a bit more humble.

"I'm telling you this won't work, but whatever." His lip curled like a sullen child's. All he needed to do was stomp his foot and the image would be complete. He grumbled one more time then hung up.

Shaun clattered down the steps and sauntered towards me. I tensed and eyed him like the shark he was. He took the coffee from my rigid hands. I was rather proud of myself for keeping the damn thing intact all this time.

"What did you say your name was?"

This close, I had to tip my head back to meet his eyes. I wasn't short by any stretch of the imagination, but he made me feel tiny and vulnerable. Not a thing I'd ever wanted from a man. And I wouldn't start wanting it now.

"Mona."

"Fine, Mona. It looks like you're my PA." He sipped the coffee, pulling a face when it hit his tongue. I hated lukewarm coffee too.

He lowered the cup and fixed me with a glower meant to make me sink into the dirt, I'm sure.

"Ground rules: Stay out of my way and we'll be fine. Take my calls. Your number one job is to keep the producers and my agent away from me. Clear?"

Not bothering to wait for a reply, he turned around and walked back to his trailer. I followed him, disbelief and outrage warring for control of my mouth. Outrage won.

"No dice. I'll do my job." My firm tone caused him to spin around, a quirked eyebrow raised. "I'll keep you on track and that includes keeping you out of a bottle and attending creative meetings with the producers who took a massive gamble on your falling star. My job is to get you through this show in one piece and make sure you're still hireable."

"Now, wait——" he started, but I raised my hand, cutting him off. His mouth hung open in shock.

"You may not like me. Or the situation," I continued, raising my voice to discourage any more interruptions. "But I'm what you've got. It's me or a huge fee .when you fail to complete this show and maybe the end of your career as you know it. You have no choices left."

His lips flatlined as my meaning sank in. If he didn't get his act together soon, he could kiss his A-list status, and all the perks that came with it, goodbye. If he fucked up this show, he'd be too much of a liability for any of the big studios or production companies to take the risk.

With my speech done and my position clear, I waited. And waited some more. He observed me. His hard gaze bore into me, searching for a crack. I didn't so much as flinch.

"Fine. It's you. Now do your job and leave me the fuck alone." Shaun spun on his heels and bounced up the steps.

The door swung shut behind him again.

Oh no, he didn't. I stomped up to his door and slammed my fists against it. Not looking for a repeat of the last time, I backed away fast. Taking a deep breath, I squared my shoulders and put on my best "don't fuck with me" mask and waited.

The door flew open, slamming back against the trailer.

"What!"

"You're in make-up in five minutes." I was rather proud of my cool, calm tone.

"Then I'll go in five."

"No. It'll take you five to walk there. You leave now."

His eyes skimmed my body before returning to my firmly set face.

"You're a hard-ass. Anyone ever tell you that?"

With a grim smile, I crossed my arms and waited.

At that, Shaun Martin sighed and clattered down the steps before following me to make-up like an obedient dog.

But I wasn't fooled.

CHAPTER THREE

When my phone rang the next morning a little after 3AM, I didn't need to read the screen to know who it was. No one rang me before 8AM. Ever. My family valued their lives, and I wasn't close enough to my old friends to call any of them at any hour. That meant it could only be one person and he was calling me before our ridiculous call time.

"Yes, Shaun?" My words might have been a little slurred. If he asked why, I'd blame the lack of coffee and the fact I was sat in my car in the studio car park with my head pressed against the steering wheel, wishing it were a pillow. *Honestly, on what planet is a 4AM call time, okay?* I'd felt sick just texting times over to the driver the production had hired.

"Why the fuck is there a driver at my door?" He didn't so much as pause for pleasantries. Lucky for him, beneath his angry moaning I could hear a croak of tiredness.

"You have to be on set in an hour." I forced a note of understanding into my voice. After all, I didn't want to be awake either. "Make-up and wardrobe are expecting you in fifteen minutes."

"Why did you let them call me this early?" he grumbled. "Tell them I'll be there at ten."

And that did it. My patience ran away from me and I gritted my teeth.

"I'll tell them no such thing. Get in the car and do the job the producers are paying you a pretty penny to do."

Without another word, I hung up and went in search of coffee.

I might have admired his pretty face and ripped body for a moment, but the man had a stick up his ass. I wouldn't let myself forget that.

"*Y*ou're Mona, right? Shaun's new assistant?" A tall, bearded guy stopped beside me while I mixed my second coffee of the morning. His lilting Welsh accent took his friendly smile up a notch. He wore a headset similar to the one hanging around my neck. "I'm Brian, the first AD."

"What's an AD?"

He frowned. "Have you ever worked on a set before?"

I shook my head, refusing to feel even the smallest twinge of doubt. I didn't need to know the lingo to keep a firm handle on Shaun.

"Assistant director. I'm the guy in charge of set, the one who keeps this train on the tracks." He pointed to a raven-haired woman pinning something to the wall. "That's Leanne. She's the crowd second AD. Talk to her if you've got any issues with the SAs." He paused, his cheeks reddening slightly as he took in my pinched expression. "Sorry, habit. Support artists, or extras, as the wider world knows them – just don't use that term where they can hear you. Leanne deals with getting them to set and keeping track of continuity."

He spun around, his gaze scanning the wide-open space.

"Hey, Aidan!" he shouted, his voice clanging in the morning hush.

Yet another tall, good-looking man. What were they putting in the water around here?

Aidan's gaze shifted from Brian to me. Although friendly, there was definitely an assessing light to the once-over I got. He was younger than Brian. I'd place Brian in his early thirties, but I'd hazard a guess that Aidan was younger than me.

"Aidan's my right-hand man, my third AD. He handles the runners and directs the background most of the time. If you run into any issues with Shaun's schedule or wardrobe, talk to me or Leanne. If it's transport- or accommodation-related, check in with production."

I scanned the bustling space as Brian explained how I should use the radio mic if I needed to reach people, and which channels to use. I nodded along while I watched people scramble about the space. Some positioned furniture and set pieces on the sound stage, while others checked equipment and adjusted lighting.

"All you really need to know right now is to stay out of the way. The rest you'll pick up pretty fast." He pointed towards a small group of people who looked younger than Aidan. They wore headsets and had radios clipped to their belts. "The runners can help with basic things, and if you ever get too busy, we can have them handle shepherding Shaun to make-up and wardrobe."

I studied their fresh faces. They seemed innocent, like they might cry if Shaun inflicted yesterday's stunt with the trailer door on them.

Before I could respond to Brian, Shaun arrived on set, baring his teeth and barking at anyone who dared cross his path. Brian snapped to attention, and everyone sprang into action. The sound stage cleared and an older man dropped his script, jumping to his feet with exuberance and open arms. He guided Shaun through the scene while a couple of extras –

em, SAs – in everyday clothes positioned themselves around the living-room set.

Despite the early-morning phone call, I'd been feeling a wee bit optimistic. Shaun had been on his best behaviour after our rocky introductions yesterday, sitting through make-up without arguing and accepting criticism without snark. I thought I was home free, that Sherry had exaggerated.

"Can you get a fucking move on, Carys?" Shaun snapped at his beautiful co-star. Her mic kept playing up and the sound assistant struggled to fix it. "It's not a hard scene."

My jaw dropped open. Carys's character was supposed to have found her mother's mangled body. She needed to be highly emotional, but every time she started crying, he'd roll his eyes and shout, "Again." It might not have been a hard scene, but the person acting as her brother was an utter dickhead. I'd struggle too.

They hurried on, but that didn't appease Shaun. He really had a bee in his bonnet today. If even one member of the cast missed their cue, he muttered beneath his breath, causing the whole thing to reset. Eventually, muttering became too much for him and he resorted to growling.

Who the hell actually growls at people? TV stars, apparently.

Safe to say, the entire thing put the crew on edge, but it didn't faze them. Production rolled forward despite the tense atmosphere.

I took to periodically feeding Shaun, figuring it was a regular low blood sugar thing and he was tired. Every time the director called for a break, I stepped in with a plate of cut-up fruit. Shaun scowled at it the first time, but eventually, he silently picked up a piece of apple and kept moving.

You'd think I'd enjoy the silence. Hell, I thought I'd enjoy it. All the better to appreciate his rock-hard body and gorgeous face. When he wasn't speaking, he was rather nice to look at. He didn't have a resting prat face, so I easily forgot the venom he could spit and found myself softening.

Of course, it never lasted.

He'd open his mouth and I'd scowl at myself for forgetting that beneath the pretty veneer lay a vile, bitter man. He shouldn't have held the smallest iota of my attention. Yet my eyes always drifted back to him, caressing the ridges of his broad shoulders and his tapered waist with far too much interest.

Thankfully, or not, his bad attitude quickly escalated to shouting at the crew and his co-stars. One of the runners delivered him coffee and the glacial atmosphere went from frigid to deadly. The kid couldn't have been older than twenty. He tried to hold a smile, but even from the sidelines, I could see the fragile edges slipping.

Shaun accepted the cup with a grunt, took a sip and spat it back out. The runner's smile collapsed as his face turned ashen.

"Are you trying to poison me?" Shaun shouted, his voice cracking like a whip.

Silence swept across the sound stage. All eyes turned to watch Shaun, equal parts dread and fascination on their faces.

"The entire fucking production knows I'm lactose intolerant! So why the fuck are you giving me this?"

The runner flinched and backed away. Brian winced, but otherwise did nothing.

"I-I didn't know," the runner stammered.

"You didn't know?" Shaun repeated, his voice deceptively calm. The runner nodded, his face frozen in terror. "If you're too stupid to retain basic information, you're not cut out for this business. Get off my fucking set!" Shaun roared, his voice echoing around the big space.

What the hell was wrong with these people? He was attacking a kid for an honest mistake and they were just standing back and letting it happen. He was out of line; he had to be stopped.

"Shaun!" I yelled.

"What!" he snapped back, his eyes flashing as they focused on me.

The runner staggered away, shaking and breathing hard. A red-haired woman about my age placed her hand on his shoulder and led him out of the warehouse.

"We all know you're a hotshot. You don't need to be a dick to the crew," I shouted across the space, turning the tables on him. I power walked across the stage, anger fuelling my clipped and loud steps.

"If he wasn't properly trained, he shouldn't have been allowed near my coffee."

"That's fair, and I'm sure the production team is correcting it now, but you could have handled it better."

Shaun stepped back as I jabbed my finger into his hard chest.

Damn! How much muscle is he carrying?

"He's just a kid. He made a mistake, and he definitely didn't deserve to be publicly belittled for it."

Shaun ground his teeth. "He could have killed me."

I snorted. "We both know that's not true."

Shaun stared at me, irritation shining from his hard eyes. He took a step towards me until our chests almost touched, and I had to crane my neck to meet his annoyingly attractive gaze. We were too close. I itched to wipe that smug smirk from his face.

"It would have set the production back."

I shrugged. "I'd have found you some lactase, and you'd have gotten on with it."

"It's not that simple."

I laughed. It wasn't an amused sound. It was a sarcastic "give me a break" chuckle that I'd dredged up from the bottom of my patience barrel.

"It *is* that simple. You've been baring your teeth at people all day, but flying off the handle at an inexperienced kid… seriously, Shaun?"

Shaun crossed his arms and widened his stance. He glared at me, his eyes promising retribution.

"They all know you're an arse, but they also know you're hurting. They make allowances and give you space. You snap at Brian, but he's too nice to tell you to fuck off. So, consider me their human shield. Leave the fucking crew alone, Shaun, or I swear you won't have to worry about a young runner slipping milk into your coffee."

As threats went, it was lame, but if he was really concerned about ruining his movie-star image by shitting himself in front of the crew, I'd happily help that anxiety along.

"You work for me," Shaun said, invading my personal space until our faces almost met. His breath reeked like a distillery.

Drunk. He's fucking drunk on set.

I was sure he'd been sober when he arrived. Where had he gotten it? A problem I'd deal with at another time.

"Only for six months," I reminded him, "and I have a very clear mandate for that time. You can't fire me, so show me your worst! But if you so much as scowl at another runner, I promise you'll wish you'd never met Sherry. I will make your life a living hell."

We glared at each other, neither of us willing to break eye contact or back down.

If I were a less intelligent woman, I'd think that light in his eyes was appreciation. I knew better.

CHAPTER FOUR

The next morning followed the same routine, minus the early-morning phone call from Shaun moaning about his call time again. Exhaustion had gotten the better of me, and convincing myself to walk the extra hundred feet to Craft Services was just not happening.

I'd thought that being the star of the show would mean he'd get a fancy trailer, but beneath the leather and drapery, it was still just a caravan. Call it a honey wagon if you want – the crew did. I still couldn't shake the image of the caravans we'd stayed in as kids.

It was divided into three spaces. In the front, a leather-upholstered sofa took up one wall and a solid oak dining table sat opposite. In the middle and opposite the door was an open-plan, fully functioning kitchen with a breakfast bar I'd never seen Shaun use (apart from the coffeemaker). A door led off the kitchen and into a double bedroom and en suite.

I helped myself to the coffee on the bar. One sip of his trailer stash sealed the deal. This was going to be how I started every morning from now on. Yet addictive taste or not, all the coffee in the world couldn't keep me lively.

I was resting my head on his table when I heard the door

open. Without lifting my head, I pushed the mocha towards him. It didn't go flying off the table. That took skill.

He didn't comment on my coffee delivery. Instead, something crashed on the table and I jolted upright. A white box sat on the surface inches from where my head had been. I glared at the smirk curving his lips.

"I didn't peg you as the violent type," I said.

He scowled before turning his back on me. "I'm going to head over to make-up."

"Okay. Give me a sec and I'll walk over with you." I snatched the box off the table – it was a shiny new tablet; no way was I leaving it behind – and shoved my chair back.

"I'm good." The words were bit out.

I eyed his rigid back. "Are you definitely going to make-up?"

He huffed and barrelled out the door. It slammed back against the trailer, shaking the ground beneath my feet.

Maybe he would go straight to make-up. Maybe it would all be fine. I still wasn't naïve enough to believe it.

I raced after him, the box with my new tablet tucked safely under my arm.

"I said I was good," he muttered when I caught up to him.

Today I'd sensibly chosen to wear trainers. All the better to run after angry actors. My ankles definitely thanked me for the lack of sprain.

"I heard you." I slowed from an outright run to a jog to keep up with his long strides.

"And you didn't believe me."

"Why the hell should I?"

"I'm your boss?"

"Ah, yes. Lauding that over me isn't going to win you anything in this situation. I didn't understand why Sherry was so insistent on her chain of command when I took the job." I peeked at him from the corner of my eye. He wore a face like thunder. "Didn't take you long to clear it up. Thanks for that."

Shaun stiffened. "I can still fire you."

I shrugged. "Not without a fight, I'd wager. Face it. You're stuck with me. I know it, you know it, the tablet knows it."

"You make a habit of anthropomorphising objects?" He studied me like I was a very weird bug following him around.

"Hardly. I meant you giving me a tablet means you know you're not getting rid of me."

He humphed.

"Speaking of the tablet, thank—"

"Don't thank me."

"But—"

"Jesus, Mona. It's just a work tool!" He stopped outside the make-up trailer. His smirk returned as I gripped my side, trying to put pressure on the stitch my mad dash after him had created. "Don't make it into something it's not."

"I'm not!"

His brow quirked, and I took a firm grip on my squeaky voice.

"I'm not," I repeated, my tone more even and serious. "I was raised right. It's rude not to thank someone when they give you something or help you."

His expression shut down. He stared at me with ice in his gaze. They hadn't exactly been friendly before.

What the hell had I done now?

"Then don't do me any favours 'cause you won't be hearing those words from me." Shaun took the metal steps into the make-up trailer two at a time, our conversation apparently finished.

"Well, I'm still grate—" The door slammed shut before I could get the words out.

We hadn't exactly been getting on, but that was a definite backslide. I sat on the bottom step, frowning at the shiny white box and its glossy image of a tablet. *Maybe he isn't all that bad.*

Instead of worrying about the changeable idiot, I powered up the tablet and focused on crosschecking my notes from a meeting with the producers. It had been preloaded with most of Shaun's appointments. I could immediately see that a good chunk of them were missing, and set to work programming it while make-up transformed him.

The door creaked open fifteen minutes later. A sigh sounded behind me.

"You could have gone back to the trailer."

I forced myself to stand. My butt was numb and I could barely feel my fingers. It might have been June, but the mornings could still be pretty chilly.

"I'm alright here," I said, my voice light and a sunny smile plastered across my face.

Shaun rolled his eyes. The man really didn't like people being happy. Duly noted, I amped up the cheer while I checked the time on my tablet.

"We should get you to wardrobe."

Thankfully, their trailer was only a couple doors down because if I had to shuffle Shaun across the site, we would definitely be late to set.

I skipped off down the wide path, nodding my head as people shouted good morning. Their smiles dried up as they spotted Shaun trailing after me, but I refused to let it dent my charade.

"Are you going to do that all day?" Shaun grumbled as we stopped outside the wardrobe trailer.

"What? Be happy?"

"No." He frowned, crossing his arms. "Yes. It's annoying."

"Then yes."

"Why?"

"Because it annoys you." I grinned wider, enjoying the flash of disbelief I could read in his eyes.

"*I* just got home, Shaun."

The "what the hell do you want now" remained unspoken. I was still on a cheery kick. He'd stomped off growling so many times throughout the day that it had become a bit of a game, one I'd enjoyed far too much.

"I forgot my boxing gloves at the trailer. I need you to bring them to me."

I sighed. My bed was so close. It was only 5PM, but I'd been up since 2AM. Unlike my robot of a boss, some of us needed a full eight hours of sleep to function.

"Can't it wait until tomorrow? We'll be back in less than eleven hours."

"No. I need them now," he barked before the line went dead.

Grumbling, I picked up my handbag from where I'd unceremoniously dropped it on my bedroom floor. My phone pinged with a text. An address that was definitely not Shaun's.

SHAUN

Drop them off here.

I stared at the screen, narrowing my gaze. *Where is he sending me?*

"Bloody dickhead actors and their ridiculous unreasonable needs. *I'm an idiot, Mona. Mona, I can't remember where I left my shit. Be a dear, Mona, find this thing I put down two days ago. I don't know what it was or where I had it last, but it's important.*"

I was still grumbling and swearing at Shaun when I pulled into the studio car park.

As I searched his spotless trailer, it occurred to me I hadn't asked the most important question: why did he have boxing gloves in his trailer? No bag hung in the front space, and there definitely wasn't one in his bedroom. The frame couldn't have handled the weight, anyway. If he had a space set up on site, I'd have heard about it by now.

Well, somebody had better give me a heads up before they install one. I do not need to walk in on Shaun topless and sweaty. Oh my god. Where the hell did that thought come from?

Way to torture myself. I froze on my hands and knees in what made up the bedroom section of his trailer. Why did he need a bed anyway? It wasn't like he slept. I'd seen his schedule. He couldn't blame his alcohol consumption if he dropped dead. The man needed to slow down.

I found the gloves stashed at the bottom of his wardrobe with an assortment of sporting goods that boggled my mind. There was even a hockey stick buried in there!

With the gloves in hand, I locked up and got out of there before I lost my mind trying to make sense of Shaun's actions. I needed to sleep tonight. Fixating on the things he chose to store in his trailer and why was not going to help achieve that. Besides, there was no earthly reason I should care!

The address turned out to belong to one of those stripped-back gyms plopped in the middle of industrial sites. In this case, the gym sat wedged between a tyre garage and a windows supplier. Metal bars crisscrossed the windows and a red steel door that could sustain a ram raid led inside. The car park was packed, but the sight didn't sit right with me.

This wasn't where A-list celebrities worked out, surely. It was too bare and purpose-focused. No one would hand him fancy water bottles or fluff his towels. Did they do that? I'd never set foot in one of those super-expensive gyms, so I didn't know.

The outside matched the inside – bare concrete floors, mats scattered about with patches duct-taped and giant weight machines lining the walls. A huge boxing ring took up the bulk of the room.

I wrinkled my nose at the stench of stale sweat. While scanning the space for Shaun's familiar presence, I resisted the urge to plug my nose.

Someone flew into the ropes surrounding the boxing ring.

He bounced back and continued sparring his partner at the other end.

I narrowed my eyes at the figure. He was topless and the way he moved fascinated me. He was graceful, dodging almost all of his sparring partner's blows. The muscles in his back danced in a mesmerising rhythm, making the tree of life on his upper back pulse and flutter. Sweat made his tanned skin gleam, and I lost myself for a moment, tracing every dip.

Was it getting hot in here, or was I just losing my mind over a ripped stranger?

Then I paused. He was the right height and build. Tufts of familiar brown hair stuck out around his head guard. But it couldn't be Shaun. This guy had gloves. Surely Shaun wouldn't have sent me back to the studio if it wasn't, in fact, an emergency.

I winced as a punch caught him beneath the chin and he barrelled backwards into the ropes. They caught him, holding him up until his feverish green gaze clashed with mine.

Oh my god.

I was lusting after my boss.

Mortification raced through me, and my face heated.

Shaun straightened, his eyes never leaving mine. "Let's take five," he said, his voice perfectly normal and not intrigued. Nope, that was all in my imagination.

Before he could climb over the ropes and join me on the ground, I shook the gloves at him. I averted my eyes and placed them on the boxing ring floor.

Without a word, I rushed towards the exit, my eyes fixed on the doors and the cool air waiting for me outside. Distantly, I heard Shaun swear and the muffled slap of his feet hitting the mats surrounding the ring.

"Mona, wait up," he called, catching up to me far too quickly.

I couldn't look at him yet. My skin was still overheated,

and my body ached in all the right places. He'd take one look at my face and see it all.

He grasped my arm, spinning me around.

"What, Shaun?" I snapped, my eyes carefully fixed on his sternum. His glistening, very muscular sternum. I swallowed hard and forced the snark to take over. "Do you have another pointless errand for me to run?"

"It wasn't pointless when I called. Lewis had a spare set."

"So, you couldn't call me and tell me that?"

"I meant to."

My hard gaze flicked up to meet his. He was frowning down at me, his eyes scanning my face and his bare chest a little too close for my over-stimulated mind. I pulled free from his grip, taking a step back towards the door, and crossed my arms.

"Next time, make the call."

I slammed out of the gym before he could respond. I needed distance, a cold shower, and a reminder that he was my prickly asshole of a boss. He was most definitely off limits. I'd dealt with enough self-entitled pricks to know better.

CHAPTER FIVE

The next day, it was like nothing had happened. Shaun turned up on time wearing sunglasses. Considering the sun hadn't even risen, I grew suspicious.

"What the hell are you wearing, Shaun?"

His mismatched shoes and wrinkled shirt also added to my frown.

The only reply he gave was a grunt. He collapsed face down on his sofa and stayed there, unmoving for long enough that suspicion gave way to concern.

I put the tablet down and went to check on him. Standing over him, the stench made my eyes water. I turned my head away, taking shallow breaths.

"Did you stay up drinking all night?"

Again, he grunted.

"You need to be on set in less than an hour."

His words were muffled by the sofa, but they sounded suspiciously like "deal with it." He cured me of my concern without lifting his head. Hell, this stunt would cure me of any lingering lust too. *Small mercies.*

My hands landed on my hips. "Get your ass up now!" I shouted, relishing the hiss of pain that exploded from him.

Placing a hand on his shoulder, I pulled him back until I could see his face. I gritted my teeth against the fumes that hit me. "You're supposed to be a professional. Professionals don't turn up on set too drunk to read their lines. Get in the shower and sober up."

His sunglasses slipped off as he flopped onto his back, and he winced. "Can you close the blinds?" he asked, covering his eyes with his arm and ignoring my orders.

"No, I can't."

"Mona," he groaned.

"You've got a job to do."

"Just tell them I'm sick."

I snorted, and he peeked at me from beneath his arm.

"What's so funny?"

"Thought I was dealing with an A-lister, not a has been." I shook my head. "Sure, Shaun, I'll tell them you're sick." He relaxed into the pillow, a satisfied smile curling his lips. This time, it did not liquify my insides. "Then you can kiss your career goodbye. Of course, it doesn't matter to me. I'm only tied to your sorry ass for six months. The world's my oyster after that. You will just have to deal with the rumours that Shaun Martin let a girl destroy his promising career."

Shaun stared at me, his jaw working as he ground his teeth.

"Weren't there talks of Oscars before you trashed that car?" I asked, my voice honey sweet.

He launched off the sofa, grumbling beneath his breath as he stomped to the back of the trailer and the shower.

Grinning like I'd won Wimbledon, I picked up my radio and notified the crew we were running late. I couldn't care less about the late part right then. I'd bested Shaun Martin. The king of screen thought he had the upper hand, but he'd just confirmed his weakness, and I had every intention of using it against him to suit both our needs.

"Can you stop with that look?" Shaun asked thirty minutes later while the wardrobe mistress laid out his costume in the changing area.

"What look?"

"This smirking business." He circled his finger in front of my face and I swatted it away. "I don't like it."

"Why? It's your preferred expression."

"I don't walk around looking like I'm better than everyone."

"And you know how to make them bend to your every whim?" I snorted, and he shook his head. "Oh, boy. Are you delusional or what?"

His scowl barely diminished his polished good looks. How was that even fair? To make it worse, he tore off the fresh t-shirt I'd shoved at him when he stepped into the main area of his trailer wearing nothing but a towel. He was getting over his hangover and in the process, he'd decided that it was "test Mona day". I would not let him win.

"Something wrong?" he asked, amusement dripping from his words.

"Not at all." My eyes fixed on a spot just to the side of his gloriously naked chest.

Moira, his wardrobe mistress, continued pulling items from the rack at a leisurely pace. Couldn't she tell I was desperate for an out here?

"Maybe you should wait outside if you can't handle a naked man."

My eyes narrowed at the challenge in his voice. I couldn't leave now. The bastard would think he'd won!

"I've seen plenty of naked chests," I said, tutting like he was boring me. "Yours doesn't quite compare. Maybe start lifting weights instead of throwing your weight around a ring. It might buff you up a bit."

Please don't start lifting weights.

I made a show of studying all that exposed skin. How I kept a straight face and didn't float off into dreamland is beyond me – at least I think I maintained my detached, scientific expression. I'd definitely need to get laid before I could keep working with him.

His eyes narrowed. "Your deflections are hilarious, but honestly, Mona, you're not fooling anyone."

My gaze snapped to him. He wasn't going to bring up last night. Surely not. I thought we had some unspoken agreement. I held my breath and waited for it. He grinned at the sight.

"You were licking your lips last night. You like my body as it is, and you're not going to convince me otherwise."

I crossed my arms and glared at him. He was right, of course, but I wasn't going to confirm that. He didn't need to know he was right. He just wanted to lord it over me and add it to his manipulation arsenal. I saw right through that pretty-boy smile of his.

"Keep dreaming, Hotshot."

"I don't think it's *my* dreams you need to worry about."

And with that smug pronouncement, he disappeared behind the curtain of his changing room. Why had I made him get up this morning? It was peaceful while he lay face down, suffocating himself. Sigh. I didn't know what was good for me until it was too late.

"*I* could murder a Welsh cake right now," Shaun said, his tone wistful.

It felt like I'd been sat on the equipment case – or flight case, as they said around here – for hours. There weren't really any seats on set, just the director's chair and seating for main cast, but flight cases seemed to ease the burden for everyone else.

Shaun leaned against the equipment case next to mine while we waited for the stage to be reset. *Guess the actor's chair wasn't that comfortable.*

"You're not allowed flour or sugar."

"There're raisins in them. Surely that cancels out the bad?"

I pushed a plate of fruit towards him without taking my eyes from my tablet. "Eat a grape, Shaun."

"I don't want grapes," he whined. "I want a Welsh cake."

"And I'd like a boss who doesn't throw tantrums like a child, but we can't all have our way," I muttered, too distracted to give it my all.

He wanted to change all of his personal trainer sessions. He thought he could snap his fingers and it would be done. No sweet-talking his usually very sympathetic trainer. No checking if the new schedule worked. "Just do it, Mona" was all he'd snapped when I'd pointed out that it may not be that easy. Trainers had other clients and their own schedule. Well, I'd been proven right because Shaun's PT was putting up a fight and I was on the verge of using his credit card to bribe the man.

CHAPTER SIX

*S*unday rolled around quickly, and I was deliriously happy to turn the alarm off when I went to bed the night before. Because Shaun had a day off from set, that meant I had a day off from him. I had plans. So many wonderful plans. I was going to unpack my room, go shopping, read a book, pamper myself. All the things I'd neglected for my first week in the city.

I was going to enjoy a day without the rollercoaster that was Shaun Martin.

So, why then did my phone start buzzing incessantly before I was good and ready to get up?

HOTSHOT

Need U 2 pick up suit from dry cleaners.

HOTSHOT

Interview @ 10. Need it b4.

HOTSHOT

Mona! SOS.

MONA

It's my day off, get your own suit.

HOTSHOT

U don't get day off until I do.

MONA

You're joking with this text talk, right? What are you, 12?

HOTSHOT

Ur hilarious. Now move!

I dropped the phone on my bedside table and rolled over, burying my face in the pillows and cocooning myself in the duvet. It was my day off. He could fend for himself.

Almost instantly, my phone started buzzing again, and this time it was the consistent drone of an incoming call.

I could ignore him. It was my right after six gruelling, nonstop days playing his errand girl. Sleep deprivation was quickly becoming my normal and I did not like it. Sherry had warned me about his mood swings, but would it have killed her to prepare me for the absurd hours? I was getting up crazy early to beat him to set, and he was robbing me of the benefit of early wraps. Then I had to stay up late dealing with his latest crisis.

I hadn't even ignored the call yet and already I felt guilty. Could I actually enjoy my day off if this was hanging over me?

I should just do it, and then I'd have the entire day to myself…

That thought had some merit.

Sighing, I rolled back towards the annoying sound and answered.

"Yes, slave driver, how can I help you at this ridiculous hour of the morning?"

"Get up. I was being serious about the suit. Audrey Harper is due at ten and my best suit is at the dry cleaners."

"Why does Audrey Harper need you in a suit at ten AM on a Sunday?"

"You really know bugger all about my world, don't you?"

Shaun scoffed. He didn't wait for a reply, choosing to give me a screen education – could I call it a screen-a-cation for short? Oh geez, I was definitely too tired if that was popping into my head.

"She's the top entertainment reporter in the US. The fact she's flown over to interview me is a big thing. I thought both Sherry and the producers would have mentioned it."

They hadn't.

Neither had he, not once in the last week. It also wasn't on his calendar.

"You couldn't have planned for this, oh I don't know, yesterday?"

"I forgot, alright?" His tone was mildly sheepish. Not sheepish enough for me to forgive him for hijacking my day off. My phone buzzed against my ear. "I just texted you the owner's number. They're closed today, so you'll have to sweet-talk him. I know you're capable of it; I've seen you with the crew."

Wait, was that envy in his voice? I laughed. "Aw, poor Shaun. Doesn't know the difference between sweet-talking and genuine kindness."

Shaun growled. "Will you pick up the suit or not?"

"Yes, but that's it. I drop it off and then I leave. I am not sticking around. No more texts until tomorrow."

"Fine," he ground out. "Just get here well before ten."

The way he said it… did I really want to know what time it actually was?

No was the answer. A thousand times no.

He'd called me at 7AM. Yes, I know it's not an ungodly hour to most people, but we're talking 7AM on a Sunday after six days of back-to-back early starts. I deserved a lie-in!

He also hadn't prepared me for the mountain of clothes waiting for me at the dry cleaners.

"Where have you been getting clothes all week if your entire wardrobe was at the cleaners?" I asked when he opened the door to his flat.

I couldn't see him from behind my towering burden. The doorman had to open the door for me and call the lift. I was shocked I'd made it without losing something.

"I've got plenty of clothes left."

"You own more clothes than me," I muttered, my shock muffled by the mound of plastic floating in front of my face.

"Why are we talking about clothes? Where's my suit?" The haphazard stack in my arms started to shake.

"Uh, Shaun, can you wait until I put them down?"

"There's no time."

"Yeah, I got that, but they're heavy enough and they aren't really stacked—"

He pulled a bag free with a triumphant, "Aha!" The entire pile slid from my grasp until the only thing left in my hands was a pair of denim jeans. I stared at them with growing horror.

"You pay someone to dry-clean jeans?" It was such a gigantic waste of money. They did perfectly fine in a washing machine.

Shaun walked off, none the wiser of my disgust. He had his suit and a crisp white shirt in hand. Nothing else mattered in Shaun Martin-land.

"Aren't you going to help me clean up your mess?" I called after him, knowing full well I wouldn't get an answer.

Muttering beneath my breath, I started gathering what I could safely carry. I wandered into the flat, my eyes skidding from polished surface to polished surface.

Everything seemed so... *white*.

The front door opened into a spacious living room decked out with white walls, light hardwood floors and white furniture. Seriously, even the sofa was white. I'd be terrified to sit on the thing. Floor-to-ceiling windows made up the outer wall spanning from the living room to the top-of-the-line white kitchen. The view of the bay was breath-taking, but somebody needed a serious splash of colour in his life.

"Shaun, where do you want all these clothes?"

"Bring them in here," he called from somewhere beyond the kitchen.

I found a staircase that led up to a mezzanine and a master bedroom. This space broke the mould on the floor below. A plush charcoal carpet spanned the floor, and the bed was made up with emerald-green sheets. The walls were still glaringly white, but with the promise of a view of the bay from bed, I'm not sure I'd care either.

"Just hang them up in the wardrobe. I'll unwrap them when I need them," Shaun said, his voice sounding behind the only closed door in the room.

I did as I was told, trying not to gasp at the size of his walk-in wardrobe. I didn't know we had these in the UK.

On my fourth trip with the last of the clothes, Shaun stepped out of the bathroom. Any words I might have spoken dried up on my tongue. The man looked good in black. Far too good.

"You could have helped," I muttered, using the bite of irritation to remind me I did not like him; lusting after him wasn't sensible.

"Boss." He pointed to himself and then to me. "Assistant."

Haha. Asshole.

"Well, in that case, your assistant is taking her day off. I'll see you bright and early tomorrow morning."

I was nearly out of his bedroom door when I thought I heard him mutter my name, but that couldn't be right because he'd agreed this was it. He'd promised me the day off. Hadn't he?

"Did you have any big plans?" Shaun asked, his voice louder.

I paused in the doorway and slowly turned back to him. "What does it matter? It's my day off. I can do whatever I want with it."

He dragged his hand through his hair. "Remember when I said you don't get a day off until I do?"

I scowled. That was not a thing.

"I'm not getting a day off and I need my assistant's help with this interview."

"Why?" I drawled, suspicion dripping from every letter as I eyed him. Shaun didn't give praise. That sounded like lowball praise. I wasn't buying it.

"It's a big interview and it would help if I wasn't worrying about other stuff."

"Stuff like what?"

He blinked at me, clearly unprepared for a battle. Too bad for him I could switch it on with little effort.

"Answering the door, coffees." He scrubbed his hand down his cheek. "I don't know – stuff. Things come up. I can't plan for everything."

I snorted. "I wouldn't say you plan for anything."

He nodded. "That's… fair."

It was my turn to blink. He'd agreed with me without a fight. What the fuck was going on here? I was missing something, surely.

"Is there a reason you don't want to be alone with this reporter?" I kept my voice level and free of any kind of judgement. If he'd hit on her and led her on, he wouldn't catch flak from me. Not out loud, at least.

He bit his lip, indecision playing over his features. "Lily used to help me with them."

His quiet words were like a sharp turn on a rollercoaster. I didn't know what to do with them. We were just arguing, right?

"Did you tell Sherry?" Surely, she'd have stepped in if she thought it was that simple. "Maybe she could be here to help you with interviews."

A sneer distorted the curve of his lips, shattering the momentary vulnerability. "Last I checked, you were my assistant, not my handler. Just do your job, Mona." Pushing past me, he jogged down the stairs, and I followed, my steps slow and reluctant.

My scowl returned. I hadn't agreed yet, but could I even say no now? Pretty sure this wasn't the kind of issue Sherry wanted to hear about, and really, at the rate of pay, could I refuse? He was more than paying for overtime, and I wasn't ready for this new chapter to end too soon.

"I think we should set up here. Can you clear all of this away?" Shaun asked, gesturing to a pile of books, throws and general debris that littered his sofa and coffee table.

Or maybe I want it to end right now.

"I'm not your cleaner."

"I'm aware, but they aren't due until Monday." Shaun's expression was unreadable, fixed in a masterful display of arrogant boredom as if he hadn't dropped an image-altering bomb upstairs. "So, you're all I've got. Audrey and her crew will be here in twenty minutes."

If there was one thing I seriously hated, it was time limits, and in the same vein, deadlines. The people who set them always underestimated how long a task would take, which always resulted in my panicking as the clock ticked down. Something similar occurred at Shaun's. I cleaned his living room for my sanity, not because he told me. Maybe I should have refused and left, but then he'd just call Sherry, and she'd already taken enough of a chance on me. I really didn't want to give her a reason to question that, even if I was pretty sure my contract didn't list cleaning as part of my duties.

I greeted the reporter's crew, made drinks and backed out of the way until it was all done. How an interview could roll on longer than an hour was beyond me. By the time I shut the door on Audrey Harper and her camera crew, it was after 2PM. At least an hour had been lost to her blatant attempts to flirt with Shaun, and another hour on questions Shaun refused to answer. Next time he booked one of these interviews, I'd be in control and it wouldn't happen on a Sunday during my day off.

I escaped his flat without further comments or demands. At least I'd get some of my day to myself.

❄

*M*onday - 2200

HOTSHOT

Bring PT ses fwd tomoz.

MONA

Done

HOTSHOT

Good. Think calendar is wrong. Fix it.

MONA

Tomorrow. Anything else? Or can I go back to sleep?

HOTSHOT

Not rn.

MONA

What the hell does that mean?

*T*uesday - 1730

HOTSHOT

Cancel 2nite IV. Sumthing's come up.

MONA

Do you want to rearrange?

HOTSHOT

No.

MONA

Done.

ednesday - 2300

HOTSHOT

Need U 2 pic up new shoes tomoz. Ask 4
Ceci @ Frasers.

MONA

Okay, I'm putting you in an English recovery
group. These texts are getting ridiculous.

HOTSHOT

Get me lunch frm Lola's.

MONA

Fine.

hursday - 1900

HOTSHOT

WTF is this?

HOTSHOT

[Photo attachment]

MONA

Tofu?

HOTSHOT

Wat is it doing on my plate?

MONA

It was on your meal plan.

HOTSHOT

No it's not.

MONA

[Photo attachment] See the highlighted section. Satay and peanut braised tofu with rice.

HOTSHOT

I didn't approve that!

MONA

Talk to your PT.

CHAPTER SEVEN

"That for me?" Shaun asked, tipping his head towards the coffee cup in my hand. For the first time in a week, a calm smile graced his lips, and my words and common sense ran away. No wonder the world had fallen in love with him. He was too much to handle when he focused that smile on you.

He didn't wait for a reply. He plucked the cup from my hands and walked away.

Shaking the fog from my mind, I chased after him. Telling him I didn't drink milk either had been my biggest mistake. Keeping a cup of coffee to myself was near enough impossible now.

Trotting alongside, I swiped my fingers across the tablet and brought up his schedule.

"You've got one more scene to film today, and then you've got a meeting with the producers at Harry's. If the day keeps running behind, I'll have your car waiting."

He grunted but kept his eyes forward as he stalked through the sets with a singular focus.

Shaun pushed open a solid fire door, revealing stacks and

stacks of equipment boxes. He wandered over to a short flight case and lifted himself onto it.

"What?" he asked, his tone defensive. My confusion must have shown.

"You have a perfectly nice trailer. Why are you in here?"

"No one thinks to look for me here."

His tone was subdued, and my guard eased.

"What is this place?" I placed the tablet down and lifted myself onto the flight case, grateful for my Pilates habit.

Shaun glanced around. "It's an equipment store. They put all the empty crates for the kit that doesn't get moved around that much in here." Despite the helpful explanation, there wasn't much life in his voice.

"Have you always been like this?"

"Like what?" Shaun asked.

"I've known you for two weeks. Even I can see that you hate your job."

"I don't hate my job," he scoffed.

I snorted. It wasn't ladylike, but who cared? He was such a liar.

"I don't!" His tone hardened and my eyes flew back to his face. "And while we're having this heart-to-heart, let's get something straight: You're my assistant. Not my friend. Not my therapist. Chew me out in front of the crew, but stay out of my personal life."

Stupid, Mona. As if you could actually help the idiotic man.

He didn't deserve my help, anyway.

"Fine." I jumped down from the box. "They want you back on set."

Shaun's feet landed on the concrete with a hard slap before I could take more than a couple steps.

"Oh, and I don't need you at the producer's meeting. I don't need you showing me up in front of them." With that he stalked out of the room without so much as a second look.

I stared after him, my brows furrowed with confusion.

What the hell had I done to provoke that? "Nothing" was the answer, and dwelling on it wouldn't get me through the day.

The crew had made up time and flew through Shaun's remaining scene. The car was waiting and the producers had called to confirm the meeting at Harry's. When they wrapped him, I handed over his phone and nodded goodbye with a relieved smile. I was dead on my feet and liable to fall asleep on the dirty studio floor if I didn't find my way home soon.

I was on my way to my car when my phone rang. I frowned as the number of Shaun's driver lit the screen. *Why is Tom calling me? If Shaun needs something, he'll text me.*

"Hi Mona, do you have an ETA on Shaun?"

"He should be with you already. He left half an hour ago."

Tom groaned. "I've been out front for the last hour and I haven't seen him."

The top of my head prickled as I listened. I'd watched Shaun collect his phone and wave goodbye with that nice smile that had made me think all was well.

And then he'd snuck away.

I blamed the smile. It was far too good at turning me inside out. It addled my suspicious brain. I should have walked him to the damn car.

I promised Tom I'd find him and hung up.

Maybe I wasn't cut out for this job. Clearly I was already complacent. Add another five and a half months of reduced sleep and... I didn't want to consider how disastrous that would be. Staying ahead of him took work.

Throwing caution to the wind, I walked back on set and found Brian. One look at my face and he held up his hands.

"Has anyone seen Shaun?" Brian shouted before I could

open my mouth. His Welsh voice projected and echoed through the open space.

Everyone froze, all eyes flying to us. I must have worn a murderous expression because some of the younger members of the team backed away. Others laughed. When no one answered, Brian put a call out over the radio.

Almost instantly, I had my answer.

Face darkening, I stormed out of the studio and down the hall. I tried not to call myself an idiot for not immediately checking. Even so, I should have fucking known.

❄

I found Shaun laid out on the dusty floor of the equipment store. Shaun stared up at the ceiling. A bottle of whisky sat open by his side. His face was wet, and as I watched, another tear fell. Some of my anger cooled at the sight of his sadness.

He was so lost in his own head he didn't hear me approach. When I stood over him, his eyes widened in alarm. He swiped at his face and sat up, knocking the bottle over. He righted it with a fumbling hand.

I hated myself for feeling so much as a pang of sympathy for the ungrateful sod.

"I thought you would have gone home by now," he grumbled, the gutted look of a man who'd had his heart ripped out replaced with the scowl I knew too well.

I kneeled down, mindful not to touch the floor with my bare knees. *A sundress was a stupid idea.* "Tom called me before I got in my car."

He nodded, his eyes fixed on my face, assessing me, waiting.

"Did you agree to this show because you thought it would distract you?"

His shoulders slumped and he lay back down. "What did I

say about getting personal?" he grumbled as his face hardened.

I kept going. "I looked you up after I accepted the job. Wanted to know what I was getting myself into."

He grunted but otherwise remained silent.

"It's been a year since Lily left and you went off the deep end. Considering how much you cost the last production, I was surprised you got this job."

"Yeah, well, don't let anyone convince you that studio execs are smart." Bitterness dripped from his voice.

"You could have said no."

"And let the world think I'm too hung up on a girl to work?" Shaun laughed, a surprisingly painful sound. "The press would have a field day with that one."

If I'd proposed to my partner of twelve years and got dumped instead, I'd be torn up too. Not sure I'd have taken it out on the people around me and put my career at risk, though. I'd always thought the drama surrounding a celebrity breakup was exaggerated, blown out of proportion by the press and their love of clickbait headlines. Looking at Shaun, though, maybe there was some truth to it after all.

"Stop looking at me like that," he growled, dragging me out of my head.

My eyes narrowed. I viciously squashed the pangs of sympathy gathering inside me. "You're not doing a stellar job of proving them wrong."

Maybe it wasn't all about losing Lily Tyler. Maybe it was actually about losing super successful Lily Tyler. The pop princess and frontwoman of The Brightside, whose very existence netted Shaun all the publicity he'd ever needed to win awards and pull in audiences.

"I'm trying, alright?" He threw an arm over his eyes.

"You're lying on a filthy floor with a half full bottle of whisky, hiding from your assistant and dodging a meeting with already cranky producers. You couldn't even be bothered to go to your lockable and comfortable trailer." My eyes hovered over his pity party for one. A mixture of disgust and disappointment dripped from my words "This is what you call trying?"

When my ex and I had finally broken up, I celebrated. Had the worst hangover of my life, but I embraced my new singlehood with relish. Shaun's prickly bear, woe-is-me routine was a grating contrast. Who was the actor here?

Shaun groaned and focused that brilliant green gaze on me. It wasn't fair. Someone so handsome shouldn't have the power to cut you in half with a look. He was disarming. But this time, I wouldn't let my guard down.

"What would you have me do, Ms Perfect?" His hard eyes drilled into me, daring me to contradict him. "I'm here. I didn't want to be, but this is what I get for letting friends decide what's best for me."

Maybe this had been a bad idea. Nobody had prepared me for this man. My armour wasn't thick enough to withstand six months of barbs. The thought of telling Sherry she'd been wrong to trust my sister's judgement made my stomach hurt, but Isla would understand. Once she knew the kind of man she'd pitted me against, she'd beg me to move home.

"Well?" he drawled, staring at me in challenge. "Finn, Jackson and Nathan think they know it all too, but the three of them are on the other side of the world while I'm stuck here with you."

All I had to do was get him to the meeting. After that, I could call Sherry and tell her it wasn't going to work. I could bare my soul for imminent freedom.

Sighing, I leaned my squatted weight against a flight case and prepared myself to open a painful compartment.

"When I dumped my ex, he and all of our friends expected me to fall to pieces. My sister knew better, but to them, failing at a relationship after four years of effort was supposed to devastate me." I swallowed, the memory of my ex's parting smile front and centre. It had been full of pity. He hated the fact I beat him to the punch, but he still thought that splitting up would finally break me, that he'd win. "And it did, but I'm not a girl who buries herself in a duvet and takes my heartache out on everyone around me."

I forced myself to meet Shaun's gaze. At some point, he'd sat up. He leaned towards me, avidly hanging off my words. He was such an enigma.

"Instead, I carried on as normal. I was polite to him when I saw him but avoided him whenever I could. I hung out with my family, had fun, partied with my sister, talked so loud no one had a hope in hell of shutting me up. I held onto the me he'd tried to snuff out, and I made sure the world at large knew that losing one man hadn't changed a thing."

"And it worked?" Shaun asked, his voice hoarse.

"He was pissed." I grinned. "I pretended I was fine and happy until I believed it. Once it became a truth for me, it didn't matter if anyone doubted my smile."

He wiped his hands over his dusty jeans, his eyes focused on the movement. Silence held us in its grip, and my thighs started to burn. If he didn't get a move on soon, I'd be walking like I'd done a thousand squats.

"Losing Lily was a pretty big blow for me," he whispered. He peeked at me from beneath his lashes, assessing my reaction but braced to share all the same.

I'd been his lackey for two weeks, dealt with every single jibe. This was only the second time he'd looked at me with that uncertain edge. It was confusing the first time and I still didn't know what to do with it. I schooled my features, forced the discomfort to the back of my mind and settled in.

"Not in the way the media seems to think. I owe her for my career, but her impact on my work fizzled out years ago. I've proven myself. I don't need a woman, even her, to get me jobs." He swallowed, his subdued gaze fixing on the shelving unit opposite us. "My dad wasn't a pleasant person to be around. He didn't believe I'd amount to anything, especially not in something as soft as acting." His sharp gaze caught mine before skittering away. "His words, not mine. Sorry, I don't really talk about this anymore."

"I get it. Family's hard sometimes. You don't need to tell me."

He shook his head, rubbing his eyes. "Lily was the only person who understood, who believed in me. Or at least that's how it felt. So, I didn't just lose a girlfriend. I lost my best friend and my crutch."

"So as a result, you drink yourself stupid and self-destruct your career?"

His eyes narrowed as he considered my blatant disbelief. "Come on, then. Seeing as you understand me so fucking well, what would you do?"

I ignored the harsh bite in his tone. "Weren't you listening, Hotshot?" I wasn't sure if I was teasing him or baiting him. The whole situation unsettled me. I didn't know what to do with a wounded Shaun. At least when I thought he was nothing but an asshole, I could resist him. "I'd prove them all wrong and win something bigger and better."

The arrogance fell from Shaun's features, leaving me with a clear view of his insecurities.

"What if I can't do it?" he asked, his voice quiet and hesitant.

"You're an actor. Act."

Shaun wore a bewildered but thoughtful expression, and something inside me caught fire. I'd done something good for a guy who'd given me nothing but a hard time. I should have felt ill for helping him. Instead, something about the softening lines around his eyes filled me with warmth.

Certainty emboldened me. I stood and held out my hand to him.

"Come on. You can start showing the world the new you by showing the producers you mean business."

Shaun stared at my hand, his lips pursed. I wiggled my fingers, silently taunting him. He grabbed hold and climbed to his feet, putting no weight on me – a good thing too. I'm fairly certain he'd have pulled me over if I'd truly had to support him.

He slung his arm over my shoulder and together we walked off set. I escorted him to the meeting and sat myself down at a table nearby to make sure he didn't make a run for it.

But one heart-to-heart between us did not equal trust. He was still on my shit list. The fact he hadn't scoffed at me or belittled my story and had shared some of his with me helped a little – although not enough to stop me quitting. He could flutter those green eyes at me all he liked. But once this meeting ended, I was done.

CHAPTER EIGHT

I tried to quit. I said the words. Multiple times, in fact.

Unfortunately, Sherry had selective hearing when it came to the word "no." Instead of quitting, I somehow ended the call with a pay rise and tickets to a BAFTA award show. I'm not sure it was a good trade-off – my sanity for money and chumming with a bunch of celebs. I didn't like the celeb I had. Why the hell would I want to hang out with more?

That argument also fell on deaf ears. *So, I still have a job. Sigh.*

I might have stumbled into the one job I couldn't quit. Wouldn't that be a nightmare?

If there was one thing I didn't need after the last two weeks, it was Shaun Martin trying to take my door down at 6AM on my day off. It wasn't a particularly nice door, cracked and peeling and in desperate need of a clean. At least my flatmates got to experience an early wake-up call for once. Maybe they'd learn to use the day for something productive, like dishes or – god forbid – finding a job.

Back to the six-foot-three chiselled masterpiece in running gear glaring at me in my tiny galley kitchen. The moment he'd barged his way into the flat without so much as a "Hello, how are you at this awful hour?", I made a beeline for the kitchen and coffee. If I was being forced to stand upright at this hour, I needed caffeine immediately.

"This is not what I expected," Shaun muttered, his lips pulled back in disgust. His eyes roamed the small space, taking in the layers of grime and grease that only industrial bleach would fix. The sink overflowed with my flatmates' dishes, and they'd started to breed, spreading out across the counter. Tomato sauce splattered the cooker, crusted and most likely growing – I didn't want to get close enough to confirm that.

I shrugged. It was cheap and nothing more than a place to sleep. I didn't even have to cook here; all of my meals were provided by catering at the studio. I could deal with it for six months, especially if it meant saving a nice chunk of change.

"You tried to quit?" Shaun asked, the words ground out between his teeth.

My eyes dropped to his mouth with a frown. Maybe I should look into a mouth guard for him. It wouldn't do his career any good if his teeth turned to dust.

"Mona!" He lifted my chin. "Eyes up here."

Huh, when had he gotten so close?

"I thought we agreed to a truce yesterday?"

My frown deepened. "When did that happen?"

Shaking his head, he paced the short length of my kitchen. I leaned against the counter and glumly watched him stalk the space. Coffee would have to wait.

"We had a moment, you – uh – fuck." He ran his hands through his hair and stopped in front of me with an imploring look for me to, what, put him out of his misery? No chance!

"I'm not good at this sort of shit."

I quirked my eyebrows and waited.

"You helped me. With your story. And you didn't have to, so I thought that meant you got it."

"Got what?"

"I'm not the asshole you think I am," he said, his voice and face soft, pleading.

"Tragic past aside, I've yet to see evidence of that, Shaun."

He frowned down at me, and the intensity in his green eyes was too much for me at this hour. I busied myself making coffee now that I could safely remove mugs from the cupboard and pour boiling water. He stopped me before I could so much as lift the kettle.

"You don't want to drink that."

"Why the hell would I not want caffeine when you dragged me out of bed before the sun's fully risen?" I happily used my voice as a whip, but he didn't so much as wince. Maybe the effect was wearing off. His lips pinched at the edges and his eyes laughed at me.

"Sherry said you don't have any friends down here yet."

How did she even…? Oh. My sister had better hide.

"I'm taking you out, so go put something…" His eyes wandered down my body, and for a moment, the amusement fled and something heated replaced it. In the confusion, I'd forgotten that all I wore was a pair of thin pyjama shorts and a strap top. He swallowed.

"It's my day off, Shaun." I crossed my arms over my chest and glared at him.

"I'm offering an olive branch. Meet me half-way, at least?" His eyes latched onto mine like a lifeline.

Barging into my flat on my day off and dragging me out of bed was a pretty shitty olive branch. Still, if Sherry wouldn't accept my resignation, it would be nice to not have to worry about Shaun growling at me.

"Where are we going?" I asked with caution, trying to keep the possibility of backing out on the table.

"Smoothies."

The hope in his eyes stilled me. It would be nice to not hate my boss.

"Okay, I'll be right back."

Before I could retreat farther, his hand shot out, grasping my arm. It felt like I'd touched a live wire. The shock reverberated through my body in delicious ways. He snatched his hand back, and had I not been fixated on the sensation, I'd have laughed at the colour staining his cheeks.

"Something you can work out in," he added. "We're running first."

I nodded. It was all I could manage in that moment.

*W*hy hadn't I pitched a fit? Me, running? Not bloody likely.

Yet I went along with it. I blamed the tiredness. Clearly, I'd still been half asleep when agreeing to this.

Half an hour, forty-five minutes, an hour – hell, I didn't know how long he tortured me. It felt like an age. But sometime later, we finally slowed to a walk outside a little smoothie hut in Cardiff Bay. Sweat dripped down my face. My t-shirt had moulded itself to my torso. I was very glad for my ponytail, but it just wasn't cutting it. While he ordered our smoothies, I ripped the bobble out of my hair and scraped it back into a very messy bun. I couldn't deal with the hair sticking to the back of my neck any longer. I didn't care how it looked.

When he returned, my berry smoothie in hand, he took in the change but chose not to comment.

He'd also lost his t-shirt.

It was tucked into the waistband of his shorts and his bare skin glistened in the early morning sunlight. Sweat trickled down his neck and my gaze dipped, tracking it as it slid down his defined chest. My mouth went dry while he sipped his bright-green smoothie. Heat flooded me and I tensed.

He's your boss and, tragic past or not, he's a dick.

Hoping he hadn't noticed, I peeked at him from beneath my lashes. He was staring out at the sea before us, a small smirk tugging at his lips. His eyes shifted, catching mine. My stomach dropped at the amusement there, and I turned away, tugging on my straw, trying to control the warmth engulfing my face.

"Now do you want to tell me why you really dragged me out of bed?" I asked after swallowing a good mouthful of smoothie, pretending I wasn't checking him out. Considering we had another four days of 4AM call times, I was sour about the whole thing. "If you say it was to watch me suffer, I might have to pour this delicious smoothie over your head."

"Hey, you did well. You kept pace with me."

"Don't lie to me."

He laughed, but the sound tapered off when the scowl didn't fall from my lips. He took my arm and guided me to the steps of Roald Dahl Plass. It was a wide-open concrete area that stepped down to the jetty, surrounded by thirty-foot pillars and a mixture of old and modern architecture. It also had a direct line of view out to sea and very few places to take shelter from the breeze.

"I wasn't lying. You were great." He sat down on the cold stone, gesturing for me to follow suit.

"I've had some very detailed phone calls and emails from your personal trainer in the last two weeks. I know how much you work out, pal. Don't lie to me."

He placed his smoothie aside and leaned back, the picture of ease. His discomfort was clear in the pinch of his eyes. "We didn't get off to the best start."

"Stating the obvious much?"

At his sharp look, I wisely shut my mouth and leant back on the stone to bask in the morning light. The area was almost deserted, but then it was a Sunday morning and most people were sensible enough to still be in their beds.

"When Sherry called last night to lay me out, I was surprised. You're the first person to try and relate to my situa-tion. I know what I said, but talking to you helped, and something clicked yesterday. For me, at least." He eyed me like I was a puzzle and he couldn't find the missing piece. "You're more than my latest babysitter."

Latest? There had been more assistants? Lovely how Sherry failed to disclose that.

"Did you run the rest of them off too?"

"Yes. Most of them quit on the first day. I expected you to run for the hills with tears in your eyes after I nearly took your nose off with the trailer door."

My head snapped around to meet his sparkling eyes. "You did that on purpose?"

I don't know why I was shocked. He had a volatile reputation.

Shaun looked away, remorse softening the edges of his face. "Yeah, sorry about that." He sat up, bumping my shoulder as he went. "My point is, I'd like us to start over. I misjudged you, and – I don't know – maybe we could be friends." He shrugged, gifting me a sheepish smile.

"Friends with my boss?"

"Why not? It's not like anything you do for me could be construed as normal."

He had a point. If I'd taken any other boss to task like I did him, I'd have lost my job on the spot. There wouldn't have been any bribes.

"Friends get involved in each other's personal lives." Did that sound bitter?

The smile overtook his face. "I'm an ignorant dickhead?"

It wasn't news to me. I crossed my arms and waited.

"You were only trying to help. I shouldn't have lashed out." Shaun's sincere gaze bore into mine, imploring me to forgive him. "In my position, it's hard to trust and easier to push people away. It's a bad habit, and I'm sorry I inflicted it on you. I'll try to do better."

I wasn't naïve enough to believe it wouldn't happen again. Still, the optimist in me hoped for an overnight change.

Maybe it won't be so bad, being his friend.

He sounded sincere. And other than dragging me out of bed and making me jog, he'd actually been nice all morning. *Maybe it could work.*

"Okay, but on two conditions," I muttered, taking a sip of my melting smoothie. He bit his lip and gestured for me to get on with it. "I get Sundays off." He opened his mouth to argue and I pointed my finger at him. "Uh, wait. I get Sundays off. You don't text me or call me unless it's a genuine emergency and you're bleeding to death. Understood?"

He nodded, another smile playing at the edges of his lips.

"And quit waking me early on down days or I'll take back my offer of friendship."

He laughed, and I mean really laughed. It was a beautiful sound that I needed to hear more often.

CHAPTER NINE

It was a bizarrely quiet day on set. I shouldn't have been surprised, but I hadn't really understood what a closed set meant until my entrance had been accompanied by the clanging of metal: sex scenes were rolling, and that meant cast, crew, and access were limited. I'm not sure if they really locked the door, but a runner had been stationed at the soundstage entrance to vet every single person who tried to open it. He looked like he was enjoying himself.

"Mona, do you have a minute?" Alys, the production coordinator, asked, her voice hushed, pulling my gaze from the steely-faced runner mimicking a bouncer.

She stood a little away from my flight case, rocking slightly on her feet as she studied me with an expectant expression. Her kind blue eyes begged me to say yes to anything she asked. The stress lining her face spoke louder as she chewed her lip.

My eyes jumped to the intimate scene unfolding behind a screen on the soundstage. There were maybe five members of crew, plus me, in the entire building. My remit of work had drastically decreased today, and I'd already cleared Shaun's inbox.

I nodded. "They're going to be at that for a while."

She didn't so much as glance in the direction I indicated. Honestly, a couple of hours ago, it had been hard to ignore what intimate meant. The thought of watching Shaun pretend to fuck someone was not on my to-do list for the day. I still squirmed at the jealousy I felt tugging at me.

How real were these scenes? Were they actually naked? I'd seen the wardrobe mistress go in with robes, so it was likely.

Now and then a moan would rent the air and my entire body would freeze, straining to figure out if it was real or fake.

Why the hell did I care? He was my boss. This wasn't a porno, so it was definitely faked, and again, *he was my boss*. Feelings of jealousy towards him were not welcome here. Neither were the other ones that made me squirm in my seat. So we'd shared a bit of a moment in the bay? It was just one-sided and I needed to smother it or get laid. One of those options would work.

A groan came again. My entire face flamed and my body tensed.

I need a distraction badly.

Before me, Alys relaxed. "Our production secretary quit yesterday and we haven't had time to find someone else. I need help. Badly." Her gaze flicked to the screen. "Do you think Shaun would mind if you gave us a hand this afternoon? If you want to, that is?"

There was a glint of hope in her eyes that hadn't been there before. How could I say no to that?

"Sure, I've got nothing else to do but twiddle my thumbs at this point." I jumped down from my case, landing on my toes to stop the wedged heel of my boots making any noise and earning me the ire of Gary, the director.

For the first time since she'd approached, Alys smiled. "You're a lifesaver. You have no idea."

I shrugged. Truth was, she was doing me a massive favour.

If I stayed here, there was no telling what I'd do when I saw Shaun step out in a robe and not much else.

I eyed the radio as Alys walked away. She needed me now, but I should really tell Shaun where I was going. I reached for it and stopped. The radios would be silent in there.

Closing my eyes, I braced myself for what I was going to have to do. Forget maybe running into Shaun in a robe. I was going to have to go in there. My stomach flipped at the thought.

On reluctant feet, I walked towards the break in the screens blocking the set. My heart hammered in my mouth.

What if I go in and they are in the middle of a scene? Maybe I can just leave a note.

I paused outside the screen, arguing with myself, daring myself to stop being a chicken and get it over with. It was his job. My job.

Before I could make a decision, a hand latched onto my wrist and pulled me through the gap. Shaun stood before me in a white robe, looking totally at ease in the thin material. My eyes skimmed over his body before I could get them under control. They stopped at his knees, and the material gapped slightly across his chest, giving me tantalising glimpses of the mouth-watering, ripped muscle I'd seen at the boxing ring.

His smirk taunted me when I focused on his face.

"Why are you lingering outside the screens?" His voice sounded crystal clear and not the least bit hoarse like I knew mine would be. "If you wanted to watch, you just had to ask," he whispered, a teasing glint in his eyes.

My face flushed, and that was enough to knock some sense into me. His being almost naked in front of me made me nervous. *So what? Shove it in a box and move on.*

I straightened my spine and narrowed my eyes at him. "I was coming to tell you to call me on the radio if you need anything. Production need help, and seeing as you don't need me…"

I glimpsed an unmade bed in the corner of the room and my thoughts stalled. An art department assistant was remaking it while the skeleton crew reset for another shot.

Were they going to do it again? Oh god, I couldn't take listening to anymore of those sounds.

My eyes latched onto his. "I'll be in the production office for the afternoon. Call if you need me." Information given, I rushed out, backing out of the space.

Shaun watched me go with a slow, knowing smile.

Nightmares. I was going to have nightmares about this entire thing. Oh, who was I kidding? They'd be anything but nightmares.

The production office was nothing more than a shipping container with plastic foldable tables and chairs. Two huge printers took up the far corner and a table was laid out with piles of call sheets and script sides. There were only two other people in the room. One typed furiously and the other hissed into a phone, talking in firm tones to someone who I'd guess wasn't doing as they'd been told.

I didn't know what they did here. The fear that she'd throw some completely foreign task, like formatting a call sheet, at me filled me with a dread I hadn't experienced in years. Not even working for Shaun had made me that uneasy.

"That's Heather, our production manager." Alys pointed to a dark-headed woman with streaks of grey peppering her hair. She nodded towards the woman on the phone, a small smirk gracing her lips as she took in the scene. "And the woman with the acidic bite is Cassie. She's the second AD. Have you guys met yet?"

"In passing, I think. I'm not in here a lot."

Alys nodded before pulling out a chair next to Cassie. "I'll set you up here. There's a laptop for you to use for the day. It's our only production laptop. We all use our own normally."

I took a seat and powered it up while Alys went around the other side and sat down next to Heather. They'd pushed two tables together, making it easier to talk across the space.

"You know we're shipping out for some location filming in a couple weeks, right?"

I nodded, and Alys's shoulders relaxed a little more.

"Our accommodation arrangements just fell through and I now need to find an alternative."

It was my turn to sink into my seat. Hotels. I could book hotels.

"Okay. How many rooms?" Surely they wouldn't take all the people I'd seen on set.

"Sixty."

My eyes bulged. Sixty hotel rooms in West Wales? Were there even hotels that big in West Wales?

"Three of them need to be premium suites for Shaun, Carys, and Gary," Alys continued as if I wasn't having a minor panic on my side of the table. "Try and find something near Pembroke Dock and St Clears. It needs to have loads of parking. If we can be all in one hotel, that's preferable. A tall ask considering it's six weeks away, but try."

"Does that include breakfast?"

"Don't worry about breakfast. We'll rarely be at the hotel late enough for it, anyway."

Of course not. The land of 4AM starts right here. If that wasn't a mood dampener, I didn't know what was.

Alys laughed. "You'll get used to the hours. I promise."

"I'm not sure I believe you," I said, eying her smiling face critically.

❄

*F*ive PM rolled around, and I finally hit an ah-ha moment. I'd blame the replay of Shaun's wicked smile for how long it had taken, but then there were a lot of possibilities to sort through. Thankfully, there was an estate just outside Tenby that could house the entire crew and provide catering for our insane hours.

Alys sat taller in her seat as I filled her in. The furrow between her brows from whatever she'd been staring at for the last hour finally cleared too.

"That's perfect," she said. "What rate did they quote?"

"£125. I know it's too high. They said they might offer some kind of a deal."

While I spoke, Alys pulled out a calculator and started tapping away.

"Not necessarily too high if they could come down to say £95 and supply a VAT receipt. We work without VAT anyway." Alys focused on the calculator, her smile slowly widening as the numbers came together. "What do you think, Heather? We could avoid catering overtime and have this place provide breakfast for all waves of the crew."

Heather glanced at the calculator, her glasses slipping down her nose. "Sounds good if they can actually do it."

"Do you want to call them back and see if that deal will work for them?" Alys asked, her grin becoming infectious.

There was a thrill here I'd never experienced. I'd solved what appeared to be an impossible problem, and they were all actually happy about it. In all of my other jobs, someone would have been displeased that I'd found a solution. Someone always wanted you to fail so they could take your place. This felt different. Solve one problem and the entire team wins. It gets crossed off a collective list.

Yes, the hours were crazy. From what I'd seen and Alys's comments, it didn't change from production to production.

Yet here I felt more fulfilled in three hours than I'd ever had at another job or as Shaun's assistant.

What if this was it, the sense of direction I'd been looking for? I could go back to Scotland in six months and work on drama in Glasgow. Studying Alys, I couldn't help but wonder if she felt like this at the end of every job. If she did, I understood why she'd deal with the hours and the stress. It was addictive.

CHAPTER TEN

"Do you want a coffee, Mona?" Shaun asked the next day.

The director had called time while they reset for the next scene. It was a crowded day on set and a huge contrast to the silence of the one before. I couldn't get my bearings with this production. One day I'd see the same faces, and the next there would be fifty new ones and a trailer full of SAs.

Today was one of the full ones. I'd found a place out of the way to watch the action while keeping on top of Shaun's emails. Prior to starting my job, I never had any idea the type of shit actors like him received daily. Only ten percent of it was viable communication. The rest was nothing but pages and pages of one girl or another offering herself up to him. Some of them included pictures. I'd almost thrown the tablet across the set when I'd first opened one of those images. Now it was like a game. Who could shock Mona into smashing a light? If I went down the production route, I'd be saved these visual scars at least.

My eyes flicked to the line of SAs crowding the craft table.

Coffee sounded great, but fighting my way through that didn't appeal to me.

"I'll grab you one from your trailer," I said, hopping down from my flight case.

I pushed past the crowd of girls waiting to fawn over Shaun. The smug bastard had joked that I'd give myself eyestrain if I kept rolling my eyes at them. I couldn't help it. If they'd be less obvious, maybe I'd be able to resist.

I'd escaped through the studio doors when a hand landed on my shoulder, spinning me around. Off balance, I fell face first into a muscular chest. Shaun's hand landed on my hip, steading me and stealing my breath.

"If you wanted a hug, you could have asked." Shaun laughed, stepping away.

He isn't serious. Is he?

He chuckled as I studied him, seemingly unaffected by the brief touch. His smile wasn't right, though. There was something strained about it.

"I didn't mean go fetch me coffee, Mona."

Huh?

My eyes fixated on his mouth. The moisture on his lips and the way he kept dragging it between his teeth... I shook my head, struggling to clear the fog.

It seemed one touch from him and my common sense vanished.

With a finger beneath my chin, he tilted my head back until I met his amused gaze. It roamed my face, latching onto my lips and leaning forward. If I didn't know better, I'd think there was interest in those green pools.

"How do I get a repeat of this? I think I could get used to you speechless."

I shook my head, his words freeing me. I made a face at him, using attitude to pour cold water over the flames his big hands had fanned.

"You can let go of me now."

"Are you sure?" He smirked. "You still feel a bit unstable to me."

His fingers flexed against my hip, but with a reluctant nod, he released me. I put as much distance between us as would be considered normal – meaning, I scuttled six feet away and watched him through narrowed eyes. I could still feel his hands on me, sending electric waves across my skin.

I almost wished prickly Shaun would make a reappearance. I could protect myself from that version of him. This one was too much to handle.

"So, coffee?" Shaun asked, barely covering the quiver of amusement in his voice.

"Coffee. Yes, I think that would be a good idea." I turned on my heel and marched towards the line of trailers.

"Mona?" Shaun called after me, his confusion audible.

"We're ready for you, Mr Martin," Leanne, the crowd second AD, called out to him.

With my back ramrod straight, I forced myself to walk away without a backwards glance, my neck itching like someone was watching me. Wondering whether it was him, I picked up my pace, power walking to the trailer before my restraint crumbled. I'd have coffee waiting for his next break. And in the meantime, I'd find my bloody cool and put out the fire he'd lit.

"Thank you," Shaun said thirty minutes later as I handed him a tall mug of mocha. I froze, scanning his face as mild shock plastered mine. He wiped his mouth with the back of his hand. "What?"

"You said thank you."

He shrugged. "Thought I should make some new habits."

Because of me? Surely not.

An irrational slither of guilt hit me. It was tiny. Why did he have to be nice when I was thinking about my next move?

He settled in beside me, forcing me to shuffle over on my flight case. He took a sip and let out a contented sigh.

"Okay, so you're right. The coffee in my trailer is better than that stuff." He gestured towards the craft table hidden behind a crowd of SAs.

I stared at the crowd, my eyes widening in horror. There were more of them. It wasn't my imagination. They'd bred! Where were they going to put them all? The set wasn't that big.

"Earth to Mona." Shaun snapped his fingers in front of my eyes.

"Sorry, did you say something?"

"Depends. If I don't repeat it, do I get a free pass?"

I studied him. "A free pass from what?"

"You know that benefit dinner Sherry signed me up for?"

I nodded, my stomach cramping. The benefit dinner for refugees that was a month away and had sold out, tripling in capacity purely because it had been widely reported that he'd be in attendance.

"I need you to get me out of it." He said it like it was nothing more important than a trip to the cinema. Thousands of pounds' worth of donations, and it meant nothing to him.

"Why?" I tried to swallow the disbelief. I shouldn't have been surprised, but dammit, I was. I thought I'd glimpsed the real Shaun, the one who took his assistant out for smoothies because he felt guilty for making her life difficult.

"I don't feel up to it."

The disappointment crashing into me was unwelcome. So, he'd lulled me into thinking he'd turned over a new leaf. Why should I care that he'd been lying? And yet, the pressure in my head said I did care. In fact, I cared so much I was angry.

With a tight nod, I hot-footed it to the bathroom trailer before I lost my temper. He'd been nice to me for five minutes, and suddenly, I didn't want to tear him apart in front of the crew. I'd gone soft.

What was that all about?

It wasn't until I tried to slam the restroom trailer door that I realised he'd followed me. I'd been so focused on escaping his bullshit that I hadn't heard him.

Muttering to myself, I gave up trying to shut the door. I turned on the sink's cold water and splashed myself. I hoped it might give me a moment to breathe.

It didn't.

"What's wrong?" Concern trickled from his words.

I whirled around to face him and his eyes widened. Water dripping from my face didn't help reinforce my take-no-shit armour.

"Why are you here?"

"Pretty sure I asked first." He shut the door and flipped the lock.

"You followed me into the women's toilets. How is that normal behaviour, Shaun?"

He crossed his arms and settled in with an arrogant smile. His expectation that I'd roll over and do whatever he said was written clearly across his face. My blood boiling, I pulled my shoulders back and channelled the old, unaffected Mona.

Sod feeling guilty. He didn't deserve my bloody loyalty. And what difference would it make, anyway? It wasn't like I had a job with him after *Mystery Lines* finished.

Forcing a hard smile to my lips, I shut down his ridiculous expectations. "I'm not cancelling the charity dinner. You're going to put on your best tux. You're going to smile and take pictures with all the women who bought tickets to be near you." In the flow, I jabbed my finger into his chest, staring up at him with disgust. "For one fucking night, you're going to pretend that you're a decent human being who actually cares that people are dying while you swan around with your self-centred attitude." I sucked in a breath, fighting for air in the stale space.

His fingers wrapped around the one I'd pressed into him. I tried to pull my hand back, but he held firm.

I frowned at his hand. "Let go of me."

"No."

"What do you mean 'no'?" I tugged at my hand until it hurt. "Let me go."

"Would you stop and listen to me?" he asked, exasperated. "I didn't think, okay? You're right. It would be a shitty thing to skip, but you've seen the schedule, Mona. That week is going to be hell. I told Sherry not to book PR during filming, but she ignored me. I can't win either way, so cancel and I'll deal with the fallout."

"No."

"What do you mean 'no'?" He threw my words back at me with a scowl. His face darkened, and I remembered I was locked in a trailer with him.

"It's good enough for you to keep touching me, but I can't throw it back at you?"

I gave a pointed look at the fist holding my hand to his chest. He released me so fast you'd think I'd burned him.

"It's not the charity's fault you don't have control of your agent. It's not their fault that you can't keep an assistant longer than a day – present company excluded – but I wouldn't hold your breath. It's not the refugees' fault that you're going to have a long day and be tired."

"Do you want my work to suffer, is that it?"

I laughed in his face at that. He wore such a serious expression. He actually believed that his performance suffering was worse than ditching the event.

"Enlighten me, Mona. Why is that funny?"

"You get up extra early to batter your body with physical exertion and then you roll yourself into make-up every single morning for them to cover the dark circles under your eyes."

"And?" He crossed his arms in a pitiful display of defiance.

"You don't sleep, Shaun. In just over two weeks, I've learnt how to recognise when your energy is dropping and I'm there with caffeine or food."

Some of that annoying certainty drained from his face.

"If your performance was going to suffer from exhaustion, the entire production would be behind schedule. They'd be playing catch-up trying to get one good scene from you."

"What's your point?"

"They aren't behind; they're ahead. You've got no issues functioning on limited sleep."

Silence followed my observation. Shaun stared at me with a frown, but an understanding light entered his eyes. He knew I was right.

"You're going to the benefit. We're not talking about it anymore."

I stepped past the shell-shocked actor, unlocked the door, and clattered down the steps. As I did so, I took a deep breath and smiled. With the hot sun on my face and a new lightness in my chest, I felt so much better.

Aiden, the third AD, was wandering around outside with a lost look on his young face. When he spotted me, the tension slipped from his shoulders.

"Have you seen Shaun? We need him on set," he said, rushing to catch up with my clipped pace.

"Try the ladies' toilets."

CHAPTER ELEVEN

"Hey Mona, wait up," Shaun shouted as I headed across the car park the next evening.

I stopped mere feet from it and shut my eyes. Maybe I'd imagined my car. Maybe he wasn't chasing me down for god knew what reason after wrap.

"Where are you going?" he asked, slightly breathless as he stopped at my side.

All around us cars pulled off. Everyone who could escape on wrap was. Production and the AD team would be here for at least another hour, finalising tomorrow's plans and anything they could beyond this week.

"Where do you think I'm going after 7PM on a Thursday, Shaun?" I didn't even bother to contain the bite of snark. *Don't ask me stupid questions after a painful day.*

Nothing had gone right today. Shaun had arrived late to set through no fault of his own. Some dumbass reporter decided to run over on his telephone interview. That had set the entire schedule back, but Gary was determined to wrap on time and cover the same number of sides. He'd skimped on breaks, which had set the crew on edge and stressed a couple of cast members out to the point where they'd forgotten their lines entirely.

At this rate, I would miss the opening act and I'd been looking forward to doing something other than work all week.

"You're not going home."

I quirked a brow, focusing my ire on Shaun. "How do you know that, Sherlock?"

Had one of the ADs ratted me out? I was meeting Tilly, the wardrobe assistant, at Axel's, a small rock music venue in town. One of Tilly's favourite local bands was playing and she'd invited me. My first friend in Wales and an outing. I wanted to end the day on a good note, not with me glaring at my shifty-eyed boss.

He studied me, a pucker between his brows. "You're dressed differently."

I glanced down at my simple black Candlemakers t-shirt and blue skinny jeans. It was hardly a big change from my sundresses. I wore band shirts to work sometimes. They were super laid-back on set, and given the hours, the focus was more about comfort than style or impressing anyone.

"So where are you going? Can I come with you?" Shaun asked in a rush. I stared at him, bewildered.

Who is this?

"You want to go to a gig with me?" I asked slowly. Maybe I'd misunderstood.

"Yeah, let's do that."

He stepped around me to approach the passenger side of my old Ford Focus, wearing the easy grin of a man who got his way without even trying. My feet stuck to the concrete as I blinked at him.

What the hell have I done to deserve this?

"You know it's a small venue, right?"

"Don't care."

"But it's not your style."

He shrugged. "Beats going home to an empty flat."

A fist squeezed my heart at that. Still, I wracked my brain for a way out. I wanted a night off, not a night on crowd control.

"But people will recognise you."

"I'll deal with it." His eyes dropped to the car. "Are you going to unlock it or are we going to keep chatting while you miss the first act?"

Growling, I pressed the button and the locks popped. There was no way out. I mean, I could have tried harder, but that hopeful look gutted me. A million questions sat on the tip of my tongue.

Why didn't he want to go home? Was it because of Lily? Did his flat remind him of her? Was he lonely?

I swallowed them all and drove.

The bar was packed. From the relief that crossed Tilly's face when she met me outside, the opening act hadn't long started. Or they could be nearly done. She wouldn't care which it was, as long as she got up front for Lover's Knot.

She'd frowned when she'd first spotted Shaun but said nothing, which was a relief. I did not feel like fielding twenty questions over this little outing. She tried to drag me into the crowd until we both noticed the uncomfortable look on Shaun's face. I'd sent her to claim her spot and confined myself to watching from the side of the room.

A narrow stage took up the bulk of the front wall. Black walls and burgundy curtains provided the only decorations. A sound booth took up one side wall with a merch stand opposite. Pillars held up the second level, framing the bar at the back of the room and a row of cocktail tables and stools. The top level was closed off, keeping the crowd condensed and ramping up the atmosphere.

"You don't like live music," I shouted at Shaun, struggling to be heard over the thump of the drums.

His gaze dropped to mine, his expression oddly blank, like he was controlling his responses. I frowned at that.

"I like it well enough."

"Liar. You're all tense. Not a single inch of you enjoys this." I nodded towards the mixed crowd. Their attention was avidly fixed on the stage and the band giving their all to this performance. "Every single one of them is smiling, nodding their heads or tapping their feet. They're enjoying it. You are not."

Shaun shrugged rather than responded, which was fair considering it took effort to be heard.

"Why are you here?"

He studied me, considering his answer. Or which lie to spin next. "Today sucked, and I needed to do something other than go home and get drunk," he shouted, leaning towards me to be sure I heard him, or that no one else did. "And I wanted to get to know my assistant."

I frowned at the last part. Why did he have to come to a gig to get to know me? And while I was thinking about it, did he regularly get drunk at home alone? All the things that were inappropriate for me to ask my boss, but really, I'd positioned myself out of the normal box from day one.

I nodded. It was fine; he was just being friendly and it looked like asshole Shaun had gone into hibernation. I could handle this.

"Does it have to be this loud?" he asked, his lips brushing against my hair. My heart just about burst from my chest with surprise. A shiver raced down my spine, adding fire to the desire I had been trying very hard to tame.

"Oh geez. Have you never been to a gig before?"

Shaun studied the ground.

"How? I thought you and Lily were involved before she took off. Surely that involved gigs?"

"They were a bit more civilised than this."

I snorted again. "She's a pop-rock sensation. I don't believe you."

"I went to one in the very beginning and absolutely hated the crowds. Unlike my friends. After a while, the venues got bigger and separate areas were set up for family and friends." He glanced back at me, a genuine smile tugging up the edges of his lips. "And they had earplugs."

I chuckled and fixed my attention back on the stage. *Earplugs? No, thank you.*

The band was a local group led by a female singer who was kicking ass up there. She was also gorgeous, and from what I could see, most of the front row comprised of men. Tilly must have had a hell of a time claiming her space.

I glanced at Shaun slyly from beneath my lashes. He didn't look the slightest bit interested. He wasn't even looking at her. Instead, he seemed too busy glaring at the soundie in the sound booth.

Unbelievable.

I nudged him and he lowered his head towards mine. "The soundie can't help you," I shouted. "Just enjoy the damn show."

"He's the one looking at me." His attention dropped to his beer, and he grimaced. "And I would if this beer didn't taste so damn flat and my feet weren't sticking to the floor."

My gaze flicked to the soundie, and right enough, he kept glancing at Shaun every few seconds. *Uh oh. He recognises Shaun.* I scanned the crowd. No one was sneaking glances over their shoulders, but that meant nothing. How long did we have before we got mobbed? Would they mob him? Sweat prickled my skin at the thought. Why hadn't he brought a bodyguard?

I forced my attention back to Shaun. "The floors aren't sticky and the beer isn't flat. It's just not up to your one-hundred-pound-bottle-of-whisky standards."

The band wrapped up and the volume dropped, replaced

with a playlist of studio recordings. People made a rush for the bar and toilets, while I just tried not to get swept away in the crowd. I wouldn't have been surprised if some people actually left, only turning up for their friends and favourites. Shaun caught my hand and pulled me to him, sheltering me from the crush. Tucked under his arm, I couldn't ignore the heat of his body and the alluring scent of his cologne.

On stage, the band's friends helped swap out instruments. The opening band plucked up their equipment and helped clear the stage for the next act. Soon, the chatting level off stage rose, anticipation building.

I spied Tilly's multi-hued pastel hair through the crowd. *She got her front row, at least.*

"Are you okay?" Shaun asked as someone bumped into us with no apology.

I glanced at him and nearly touched his nose with mine. His face was far closer than I'd anticipated. I shrank back, trying to keep my distance while nodding.

"Is it always like this?"

"This is my first gig down here, but yeah, this seems pretty normal."

At least in Glasgow it was. Music venues in Edinburgh were few and far between now, forever getting gutted by big companies until you could count the good ones on a single hand.

His grip on my waist tightened as someone wobbled dangerously close to me. The feel of his fingers almost digging into my soft skin conjured images I'd have preferred stay buried. One involved our clothes on the floor and a sound-track to rival the fake ones recorded on set.

"Someone could get hurt."

I studied him from the corner of my eye as his gaze travelled the room and glared at anyone who got too close. A buzz of energy licked at my nerve endings and made it impossible to ignore the press of him. Did he feel it too?

With the way he bared his teeth at people and seemed not even slightly flustered, I'd hazard a guess that the answer was no.

Pushing my shoulders back, I stepped away from him. His fingers dug in, trying to stop me. His head whipped around to me, his eyes questioning me with concern.

"Too hot," I lied.

He seemed to accept it with little thought.

His attempts to keep people away backfired spectacularly. The lights were up, and people were now rubbernecking to confirm the whispers of their friends. I really hoped they didn't start approaching him. I was tiny compared to some of these people. Even a good number of the women rocked stilettos, giving them a three- to four-inch height advantage on me. I didn't stand a chance.

"We can leave if you want?" I really didn't want to, but it was a far better alternative to getting caught up in a crowd vying for his attention.

Shaun frowned, his eyes fixed on me. "Do you want to leave?"

I shrugged. "Not really, but if you're uncomfortable, I'll—"

"I'm fine. You've had a hard week too. Ignore the stares; you've earned tonight," he said, his voice low but strong.

My eyes roamed his face, an odd mix of shock and pleasure freezing me to the spot. His tone was yet another sign of appreciation, but combined with the furnace of aches his hold had inspired and the earnest light in his eyes, it took on a deeper meaning. A meaning I had no business reading in my boss's words.

"Hello, you wonderful people. Have you missed me?" A lilting and cocky Welsh voice asked, his words floating over the quickly hushing crowd. I tore my gaze from Shaun and turned to face the stage, every inch of me tense and hyper aware of how close his arm came to brushing mine.

Murmurs of half-hearted agreement flickered across the crowd.

"I can't hear you! Did you miss me?" The crowd roared an affirmative, and the singer grinned. A chorus of sighs ricocheted through the room. "We're Lovers Knot, but you already know that, and tonight we're going to rock your world."

CHAPTER TWELVE

I swayed for hours on my feet and my voice grew hoarse from singing along, but I wouldn't have changed last night for the world.

Tilly had worn sunglasses in the wardrobe trailer when we'd turned up this morning, and Moira, her boss, took delight in rattling around the small space. Nothing would wipe the silly grin off her lips, though. Hungover or not, she was still riding a high from last night.

Hell, even Shaun seemed in a good mood, and he'd claimed to hate gigs. An SA had come up to him on set for an autograph, and he'd actually smiled at her. Cue shock and horror.

After checking in with the production office on Shaun's schedule, I retreated to his trailer for a breather, and maybe a brief lie down. He'd been fending off groupies for at least nine years; he could handle a couple hours without me.

Resisting the lure of his super comfortable sofa, I poured myself a gigantic mug of coffee and settled in at the table. *First thing's first: rejig Shaun's calendar against production's tweaks.*

Shaun found me hours later pinching the bridge of my nose. Staring at a small bright screen might not have been my best idea of the day – particularly not after a late night and with a stomach full of nothing but coffee.

Then a deliciously fragrant bowl appeared in front of my nose, and the headache eased its grip.

I stared at him. "What's this?"

Shaun pushed my tablet aside and placed the bowl in front of me along with a set of cutlery. He'd brought me curry and rice. I stared at him and the meal. *Why is he bringing me food?*

"Eat, Mona," Shaun ordered, taking a seat across from me.

I didn't move, and he chuckled.

"I swear I didn't poison it. It's just a butternut curry." I met his wary gaze, shock written plain across my face. He shifted in his seat, his eyes dropping to the bowl. "I know you don't drink milk, but I wasn't sure if it was for health reasons or because you're vegan. So, I got the vegan option to be safe." He sighed at my continued silence. "I didn't see you at lunch."

I glanced at the time on my tablet, surprised to find that time had flown by and I'd definitely missed lunch.

"Thanks for this." I picked up the cutlery and dove in.

"Just look after yourself, please? I don't want you getting sick because of me."

I met his concerned eyes, but trepidation held my voice hostage. He was being nice. I had no defence against Nice Shaun.

"When I eat, you eat. No exceptions. If I have to eat every meal with you, I'll do it."

I laughed. "You won't do that."

He didn't so much as smirk at my disbelief.

"You're going to come home with me every night and cook me dinner?" I was joking, but he nodded, his mask of seriousness intact.

"If I have to, then prepare for a dinner guest."

As threats went, it was potent and confusing. Why the hell

should my boss care if I ate? He barely cared about how his actions affected others. My eating habits shouldn't have piqued his interest. At least during the workday, I'd be able to uphold that. An image of my grimy galley kitchen flashed before my eyes, and I grimaced. I did not want to cook real food in that place.

Thankfully, someone knocked on the door before Shaun could force the matter. Muttering beneath his breath, he opened it to a fresh-faced runner. He stared up at Shaun with wide, nervous eyes. His throat worked but no sound emerged while his face reddened.

"I'll be there in a sec," Shaun said, his tone much softer than his usual biting exasperation with the junior staff.

The runner's eyes widened further, the change in Shaun setting the kid on edge.

"We're not done." He turned to me with a smirk that said, "See? I can't control how people react to me."

"Do you need him on set?" I asked the runner.

The guy's eyes latched onto me and his face relaxed marginally. He nodded.

"Stop playing with the boy and go." I climbed to my feet and approached him. He watched me with a shuttered expression. I didn't understand the look, and if I'm honest, I didn't want to think about it. Who knew where my mind would go after last night?

"I've got work to do. Go!" I pushed him out the door and down the steps.

I expected him to resist a little, but he didn't put up a fight and I went flying down the stairs after him. Before I hit the floor, Shaun caught me. I must have squeaked as I lost my footing.

Electricity swept through me as we connected, making me shiver. With the press of his hard chest against mine and his concerned green gaze scanning my face, I almost forgot he was my boss and currently made up of sixty percent asshole.

"Are you okay?" He held me to him.

I nodded and swallowed against the flutter of my pulse pounding in my throat. I'd never rush him again.

"I didn't have you pegged as clumsy." Shaun set me back on my feet at the base of the stairs. He released his grip slowly, watching for the slightest wobble.

"Thank you for catching me," I whispered, my voice hoarse. "I'm fine. They need you on set."

Shaun hesitated, his grip on my arms tightening while his intense gaze kept searching mine. With a reluctant nod, he dropped his hands and backed away.

Both shaken and puzzled, I sank down on the step and watched him walk away. There had been genuine concern in his eyes, and some stupid part of my brain insisted that it was more than worry for an assistant he didn't even want.

But he paid attention. Despite his busy schedule and people feeding him a constant stream of information, he listened to me. No one had ever noticed if I'd skipped a meal or two when work got busy. He paid attention to what I said as well as what I didn't.

Shaun was different in so many ways, but he seemed to accept me as I was. I'm sure he'd love it if I relaxed my control, yet I was almost certain he didn't actually want me to change. And that meant an awful lot to me.

All the same, if I couldn't shake off this fascination, I'd need to move on faster than planned. Working with a man I was hot for wasn't great to begin with, but add the boss factor and we were on thin ice. I couldn't let it happen. I had to beat this.

And what if you can't?

A fraction of me didn't believe I could resist, and if that fraction grew, then I'd need to say goodbye to the money and find something else to do. Whether I liked it or not.

CHAPTER THIRTEEN

I poked my head out of the trailer just in time for wrap and got hijacked before I reached Shaun on set. It was one hundred percent worth the delay. Alys and Heather caught me on my way past the production office and invited me for crew drinks in a couple weeks. I left them walking on cloud nine, the ground so far beneath my feet I never wanted to come down.

It's been a while since I've had anyone but my sister invite me places! This'll be fun.

My friends had pretty much faded into the background while I'd been with my ex, and then of course his friends had disappeared in a puff of smoke as soon as we split. No surprise. For years I'd been stagnant in Edinburgh, but I just couldn't see it. Moving had been the best decision of my life, and no one would make me regret it.

I arrived on set to find Shaun gone and the crew tidying up. Glancing around the darkening space, I decided to just head home.

I turned back to Shaun's trailer to collect my things and got stopped a dozen times with people marvelling at the change in him. All of them thanked me, but I shrugged off the praise. One person couldn't change someone's shitty attitude. He had to pull himself out of his hole.

A good thirty minutes had passed by the time I got back. I swung the door open and waltzed in, humming a beat from last night as I gathered my things.

Just as I turned around to leave, the bulk of a person caught my eye. I screamed and practically jumped out of my ever-loving skin.

"Shit!" My hands flew to my chest and my heart raced. I glanced at the ground, noticing I'd dropped my bag in the process. "What are you still doing here?" I asked, breathless.

Shaun quirked a brow. The rest of his face seemed set in stone, and his eyes would give me nightmares. The spark had gone. Even when he was biting at me, there'd been life there. Now there was nothing, just two flat pools of green and zero expression. He nursed an almost empty glass of whisky. The rest of the bottle sat at his side waiting for his next top up.

"Are you alright?"

He rubbed his eyes and squeezed his temples. "I thought you'd left."

I tried to read some meaning from those four simple words, but none made sense. Was he pissed that it looked like I'd left without saying goodbye?

Which was utterly ridiculous. Right?

"I got caught up on the way to set. Why are you here rather than on the way home with Tom?" I approached him slowly, uncertain of my welcome.

"Wasn't ready to go home."

I sat on the sofa next to him and he uncapped the bottle, pouring a generous serving into the glass. He offered me the bottle. I took it from him but placed it on the floor. I didn't need to addle my brain with alcohol right now.

"Did something happen?"

He shook his head, staring into his glass like it held the answers to his mood swings – which it probably did.

"Did someone call?"

Another shake.

Okay. Tapping my chin, I stared around the pristine space. He hadn't been drunk when he'd left me this afternoon, so he wasn't low because of the alcohol. He'd been low and the drink had come calling. What would knock him off the cheery wave I'd left him with?

"Do you want to talk about it?"

He pursed his lips. It was tiny, but my heart danced. *Progress.*

"Did something remind you of Lily?"

His gaze flicked to me briefly before he shook his head. He covered his face and groaned, sinking lower in the seat.

"Today's lines hit a little too close to home," he muttered, his voice gravelly.

I frowned, trying to recall the scenes I'd glanced over this morning. There hadn't been a romantic scene on the call sheet, just a bunch of family-focused things with his character's sister and a whacko relative.

"It's no secret that I had a shitty upbringing, but people don't really know how shitty." Shaun glanced at me, his eyes narrowing. "Are you staying or are you going? Sit properly," he snapped, referring to the fact I was sat on the edge of the seat, still unsure if he wanted me there.

I slid back into the sofa cushion, kicked off my flats and tucked my legs beneath me. He smirked when I forced a "good enough?" smile.

"My dad wasn't a nice person to be around. All he cared about was drinking." Shaun glanced at the bottle on the ground, registering the irony of his words. Here he was, repeating his father's mistakes. "He worked to drink and anything in between was just in the way – including me and my mother. He wasn't always physically abusive, but words cut deeper than a fist, anyway." Shaun shrugged, his dead eyes shifting to me and gutting me with that single look. "I only survived it because of Lily and Ryan, my mate. Ryan was a determined bastard back then – still is – who wouldn't take no for an answer."

He shook his head, and the Shaun I'd left this morning surfaced at last. He shifted in his seat until he faced me, fixing that sad mix of amusement and pain on me.

"I'd get a good mark in something and Dad would belittle me, claim it was all pointless because I'd never amount to anything. My mother worked her ass off to support us, and he just kept drinking it all away."

"I can't imagine what that must have been like." I truly couldn't. My family had always been nothing but supportive. Sure, I'd accused my parents of abandonment when they'd announced their move to Cornwall, but I'd been joking and they'd known it. This was… I had no words for the shitshow he'd grown up with.

"When I got offered my first modelling job, I thought it was a joke. When your father's yelling abuse at every little decision you make, understanding that I actually had something people wanted was…" He stared at me, his gaze unfocused as he searched for the word. "Foreign. I nearly turned it down, and then Ryan flipped out when I told him how much they were offering to pay, which dragged Lily into it. There was no turning it down with the two most stubborn people I'd ever known ganging up on me."

Again, he was smiling and his entire demeanour changed, softened. I wanted to see more of this man. The man who couldn't believe his best friends would care enough to stop him making bad life decisions, who appreciated them for their support.

"Without the pair of them, who knows where I'd be." He lifted the glass to his lips and took a deep drink. "If he hadn't died, I probably would have skipped the country with Lily. It was easier to pursue my dreams without facing his scorn every day."

Shaun's haunted eyes searched mine. They begged for comfort. I clenched my fists in my lap until the pain of my nails digging into my palms reminded me why that would be a bad idea.

"It's twisted, but sometimes I think I wouldn't be the person I am today without his abuse. Like, I wouldn't be as strong or something ridiculous like that." His laugh was bitter.

"Is that why you're drinking so much?" I whispered. My heart had dropped to somewhere in my stomach as I uttered those words without thought.

Really, Mona? Did you have to go and ruin the mood?

His head fell back against the sofa and he shut his eyes. For a moment, I thought he wasn't going to answer, and relief became a tangible thing I could taste, a mix between marshmallow and sweet cherries.

"I didn't used to," he said, his voice just a thread of sound. My gaze jumped to his, and he rolled his head towards me. His lips were set in a grim smile. "Before Lily and everything blew up, I hadn't really overindulged. Seeing your father wreck himself and anyone around him kind of puts a damper on a Friday-night binge, you know?"

I nodded but kept my mouth shut. He frowned at the half-full glass.

"I can't even remember what drove me to reach for it every time the pain got to be too much. Isn't that stupid? Can't remember what made me look at a drink as medication. There was an incident, I know there was, but I can't for the life of me remember."

Tears shimmered in his eyes when he glanced back at me and I couldn't take it anymore. Taking a breath, I reached out and grasped his hand, squeezing, trying to communicate that I wanted to help without forcing the words past the lump choking me. Shaun's face relaxed. He threaded our fingers together, holding tight.

My heart couldn't take the rollercoaster that was Shaun Martin. It pounded against my ribcage. It was a wonder Shaun couldn't hear it. He just wanted a friend, someone who wouldn't judge him for having a past.

"I need to stop," he whispered.

He considered the amber liquid in his glass with a pained expression. His hands shook as he handed the tumbler to me.

"Is that definitely what you want?" I asked, keeping my voice as casual as I could. He wasn't on the verge of committing to a life of sobriety. This was just a normal conversation people had with their bosses.

"Yes. It's turning me into my dad." He reached out, caressing my cheek. "The things I said to you, to the crew... I don't want to be that person."

I nodded, my mind racing with the things I needed to do. Find him a sponsor, sweep the trailer and the equipment room for bottles. Didn't alcoholics always have a hidden stash? Should I sweep his flat too?

"Okay. How about we get you home to bed and deal with the logistics of this in the morning?"

His head fell back against the sofa again, but he nodded.

"Shall I get Tom to stop for some food for you?" It was a perfectly normal question for an assistant to ask, but it stood out stark against his momentous decision. We should be celebrating, but from the set of Shaun's jaw, I knew that was the last thing he wanted.

Shaun agreed before launching to his feet. He stared at me, indecision eating him. I waited while he sorted his thoughts. I'd wait as long as he needed.

"I don't trust myself to throw it all out," he said, his breath hitching slightly. "Will you..." He swallowed, turning away and raking a hand through his hair.

"I'll clean out the set and trailer. I'll even have a chat with production and the producers if you want."

"No!" he shouted, his eyes widening. "No, don't tell them. I don't want anything to change."

I frowned. "You don't want them to know you were suffering from an addiction and your shitty behaviour will be a thing of the past?"

He shook his head. "It's not that. I don't want them to know I had a problem." He stared at me, his eyes imploring.

The size of the secret he was asking me to keep dawned on me. I got it: the press were already speculating; he didn't want it confirmed. I was the only one standing between him and a rabid mob of gossip rags. I nodded my understanding.

"What about Sherry?"

"Yeah, tell her."

A to-do list began forming in my head, and I was pretty sure I couldn't wait to set it in motion.

"Uh, Mona?"

I glanced at him, tilting my head with a silent "what?"

"When I said I don't trust myself to throw it all out?"

I nodded.

"Would you come home with me? Do it for me?"

"Are you going to tell me where your hidden stash is?"

His eyes widened in surprise, but his nod was swift.

"Okay." I nodded. "Let's go."

That night I cleared close to fifty bottles of hard liquor from Shaun's flat, trailer and the equipment stores. The call to Sherry was one of the hardest things I'd ever had to do, but she wasn't remotely surprised. She was, however, thankful, because Shaun had admitted his problem, but also because I was there to keep him straight.

The magnitude of the task ahead of me hadn't fully sunk

in until that moment. I was it, the barrier between him and going off the rails again. That was utterly fucking terrifying. What if I couldn't get this growing attraction under control? What happened when the show wrapped and we parted ways? If I wasn't careful, I'd get so invested the worry would eat me alive. I didn't think I could stop myself from feeling responsible for him, but I had to try. We both had to survive the next few months with our sanity intact.

CHAPTER FOURTEEN

"Are you going to stay in here every day now?" Shaun asked a couple of days later.

I sat in his trailer at the table. I'd claimed it as my office space for the moments I needed to stare a little too closely at the tablet. Trying to crosscheck his messy schedule with email confirmations gave me enough of a headache. I didn't need to add crowds of people and changeable lighting to the mix.

"I hadn't planned to." My response tapered off as I squinted at the screen, searching for a lunch meeting with Ryan Evans. Shaun's text said it should be in there for Friday, but all I could see was a full set day.

The silence stretched while I frowned at the calendar. I found him studying me with a guarded expression.

"What is it, Shaun? Did something happen?"

It had been four days since he'd admitted his faults and made a plan. He'd talked to Sherry and agreed to meet a sobriety coach. Both of them realised I couldn't be entirely responsible for keeping Shaun straight. For one, I didn't have the slightest clue when it came to addiction.

I'd cleared out every bottle I could on Thursday night, and the following days had gone pretty smoothly. And shock of all shocks, he actually left me alone on my day off, which in hind-sight might not have been a good thing. I walked in Monday morning with suspicion written all over my face. Did he drink? Would he lie about it? The answer to both was no, but c'mon, how was I meant to really trust that?

"What would happen on my set?" Shaun asked, inter-rupting my spiralling thoughts.

He looked genuinely perplexed by the question, and I relaxed. *Okay, so no one prepositioned him, and he hasn't found any bottles I missed.*

"Then why does it matter if I'm not on set with you?"

"I just noticed you weren't and I wondered why." For the first time since he'd entered the trailer, he refused to meet my gaze.

I smirked. "Did you miss me?"

"What?" he barked, his eyes jumping to my face. He tried to shrug it off with a laugh, but it sounded defensive. "Don't be ridiculous."

"You totally did."

"I just like knowing where you are."

"Whatever you say."

"Are you done?" There was an eagerness in his voice that I'd never heard before. I nodded. "Do you have plans for tonight?"

I'd been in the city for three weeks. Other than Tilly, I didn't really have friends in Cardiff yet. And she worked the same crazy hours as me. Making concrete plans with her was difficult. I just shook my head.

"Good. I'm done for the day. Do you want to do something?"

I narrowed my eyes as he bounced on the spot. "Does that something involve me running five miles?"

He smirked. "Do you want it to?"

"I'd rather go home and clean my kitchen."

"It wasn't that bad!"

"Says the man who boxes and drinks protein shakes." I gestured to his trim shape in case my meaning didn't translate. "This body is made for Pilates, not panting and labouring for breath."

His focus dropped to my lips and a heated look entered his eyes. If I had less sense, I'd say he was into me.

"Where do you want to go?"

"Huh?" His dazed gaze met mine. The embers cooled but didn't fade, which left me with a whole lot of confusion.

"You said you wanted to do something. What do you want to do?"

"It's a surprise."

My eyebrows rose at that. He hadn't struck me as a surprise type of guy. Although showing up at my door at 7AM maybe should have given me a different perspective.

"Do you trust me?"

I laughed. "Not even a little."

"That hurts, Mona." He held his hands to his heart like I'd shot him. *What a dork.* "Come on, when have I led you astray?"

"I've known you for three weeks!"

"The answer you're looking for is never," he countered, his smile stretching teasingly wide as he pulled me from my seat and collected my things.

"This is not what I expected." My voice was hushed as I gazed in awe at a short woman expertly twining herself around a purple silk.

"Pretty cool, isn't it?"

Shaun left me to my gawking. I mean, there was silence, so I assumed he'd wandered off. Tearing my eyes away from the aerial performance was too difficult. Inexplicable jealousy tightened my gut. I was flexible and years of lifting my own body weight for Pilates should make me perfect for aerial arts.

Yet despite the shoulds, I wasn't so certain.

I'd dreamed about trying aerial silks for far too long. *What if I can't even lift myself?*

I gasped as the woman overhead released the silk. The rope around her waist unravelled. My heart raced as she rolled maybe ten feet before the silk caught her in an upside-down split.

How freaking epic was that!

A tap on my shoulder dragged my gaze from the performer. Shaun wore an arrogant but dangerous smile. I didn't want to think about my dopey grin and saucer-wide brown eyes. I was too bloody excited to care.

"We've got a two-hour session, so you'd better not develop a fear of heights," he joked before leading me to a waiting instructor.

She looked about fifty with her greying black hair, but her tight workout clothes revealed a strong, toned body. She wore a patient smile, and any jitter of nerves I felt from watching the performer rocket towards the hard floor earlier eased. The extra-thick mat laid out beneath the waiting strips of silk likely helped too.

Still, my smile fell slightly as I eyed the silks. They stretched at least thirty feet in the arched space. I'd never been that high up. I had no issue with flying or standing on tall buildings. However, that was different from dangling in the air with nothing but fabric and a mat to break your fall.

"How did you know I would go for this?"

His smile faltered slightly. "Sherry might have asked your sister."

I flashed back to my phone call with Isla last week. I'd barely had time to sleep and we kept missing each other, managing not much more than a brief "Sorry, I'll call you back." It seemed she'd assumed I'd be terrible at making friends – past experience said she was right – so she'd brought one to me. I didn't think she'd condone me spending any time with Shaun outside of work after our conversation, but it seemed she could still shock me. What she failed to realise was that this was nothing more than Shaun's attempt to butter me up and play nice to ensure I'd be a good little PA.

"Penny for your thoughts?" His breath tickled the shell of my ear as he leaned into me.

My heart stalled and I jumped. His eyes laughed at me as he danced out of reach. *He's lucky I've never been the violent type.*

Before I could tell him off for invading my personal space yet again, the instructor called for our undivided attention as she ran through a safety briefing. It was for the best. For some stupid reason, I liked him being close and I didn't need him to realise it. That would lead to all sorts of inappropriate questions I didn't want to field.

We threw ourselves into the session and, thankfully, any sly and teasing looks stopped. He didn't really have a choice. If he hadn't given the silks all his attention, he would have hit the mat faster than I could say "Golden Globes."

For once in my life, my height worked to my advantage. Because I was so short, I had a much easier time than Shaun, whose six-foot-three inches of lean muscle slowed him down. Plus, the online Pilates classes I followed had improved my flexibility enough that I could hold some kind of a shape, however brief.

"You lied to me." Shaun's face tightened with displeasure. "Somebody lied to me."

"What are you talking about?" My voice sounded strangled from my upside-down position. *Note to self: don't talk while upside down. It's uncomfortable.*

"I thought you'd never done this before." He frowned at me.

I released my hold on the silk and slid down until my feet hit the ground with a satisfying thump.

"I haven't." I wiped my hands on my leggings and stepped off the mat.

Shaun stood, arms crossed, scowling at me. My answer hadn't helped. It irked Mr Hotshot Know-It-All that he might not have all the facts. Amusement teased my mouth, but I bit my lip to hold back a smug smile.

"Honestly. I did a bit of gymnastics when I was very young and now I do a lot of Pilates. I've always wanted to try this." My voice rose with excitement. I let the stupid grin I'd been trying to suppress take over my face.

I laughed at the look of horror scrunching up his features. "Are you jealous?"

"What a ridiculous question." He refused to meet my gaze. Instead, his eyes roamed the room, studying the performers practising their skills. None of them paid him any attention, too focused on perfecting their routines to care about the celebrity in their space.

"It's not ridiculous if it's true."

He grunted and turned back to the silks. He concentrated on securing his grip and started to climb.

"Thank you, by the way," I called up to him.

He froze and glanced at me with narrowed eyes. "Are you trying to make me fall?"

"Of course not. I just appreciate you trying to help me adjust to a new city."

"You couldn't have said this while I was on the ground?"

"And miss out on watching you sweat? No chance."

Shaun shook his head and continued to climb. I took a seat on the ground and leaned back to watch him manoeuvre his bulky frame into different holds. It was slow going, but my god, the man was a sight to see – hanging in the air held up by nothing but the power of his upper body. He barely shook. I'd joked that he was jealous, but truly, I was the envious one.

I quickly lost track of time, completely absorbed in the exhilaration that came with pushing my body to its limits and learning a new skill. The windows in the converted church were all blacked out and there wasn't a clock in sight.

We'd started out low to the ground, but as my confidence grew, I'd climbed ten feet or so to force myself to be braver. The more I tried, the more my body shook. When my hold slipped during the last exercise, I wasn't surprised. I shut my eyes and prepared for the impact of the mat.

I'm proud to say I didn't scream.

Rather than the soft but painful slap of the mat, I slammed into a hard chest. Shaun grunted as he caught me in his arms and my eyes flew open.

The sounds of the active hall faded as I caught my breath and tried to slow the pounding of my heart. Shaun's concerned gaze roamed my face and my heart began to race for an entirely new reason. The smouldering look he directed at me struck a match, and something sparked to life inside me. My skin tingled beneath his hands, which flexed against my torso and thighs.

A small voice in the back of my mind reminded me that my sweaty body was plastered against my boss. I shushed it, content to drown in his green eyes. So what if it was inappropriate? He caught me. I didn't instigate anything.

His head lowered and, ignoring the tiny grain of self-control I still possessed, I licked my lips. His hot eyes dropped to my mouth and mine followed. His breath tickled my face, tempting and taunting me.

Shaun smirked. "If you wanted me to hold you, you could have just asked," he muttered, our noses almost touching.

His words jolted me from the spell his concern had woven and reality set in. My body stiffened against his hold while my mind went on the defensive. A second longer and I might have taken matters into my own hands and kissed him.

"Thank you for the save, but you can put me down now."

"Good catch, Mr Martin, but next time, I advise that you

let the mat do the work," the instructor chastised, further shattering the moment.

"I like you like this," he whispered, completely blocking out the instructor. My stomach flipped at his words, churning with excitement and disbelief. Could he mean what I—

"You're easier to deal with when you're off balance. I think I'll hold onto you for a bit." Shaun grinned like the egotistical ass he was.

The fragile bubble of excitement burst, and I embraced the sting of disappointment. Hopefully it would protect me the next time I thought about succumbing to his charm.

CHAPTER FIFTEEN

*D*espite Shaun's insistence that he didn't miss me on set, he kept popping in for random things throughout each day. It was rather unfortunate that Brian tasked a runner with shepherding him back to set. At least Adrian would have stood up to Shaun. The panic in the runner's eyes grew every day as the AD team bombarded the radio with calls for Shaun. Shaun didn't even have to say anything to the poor kid these days; his disappearing acts generated the stress with little to no input from him. The guilt set in quickly.

It was just easier to focus in the trailer, without the buzz of people rushing around. Plus, if he did decide to sneak off for a drink, I had warning systems in place. Leanne had no idea why she was texting me every time Shaun so much as twitched towards the equipment room, and Tom just thought it was all in the norm for a PA to demand updates every time her boss got in his car. Despite how much time I spent there, I couldn't always watch his trailer. If he decided to come here and found a stash I'd missed…

Okay, I was avoiding him too.

What else was I supposed to do? My boss had nearly kissed me. Or at least I thought he was going to kiss me.

And I'd wanted him to.

I'd wanted his lips on mine, and the fact it might have been nothing but a ploy to throw me off balance made me want to claw his eyes out. An odd mix of relief, anger and disappointment plagued my thoughts, and I did not want to be around Shaun with that volatile cocktail. One moment I'd convince myself that it was all in my head – the interest or the deviousness, I'm not sure which – and the next, he'd deliver lunch with a huge smile and sit chatting about anything but work. If someone could have a personality transplant, Shaun had done it.

Even so, I begrudgingly conceded that my avoidance had become a distraction. And distractions meant the production fell behind chasing Shaun all over the studio. So, like the good little assistant I was meant to be, I made a point of hanging out on the sidelines again with his coffee ready.

The elated smile on his face wiped the slate clean, but today I had one regret: Why hadn't I checked the schedule before I returned to set?

Mystery Lines wasn't a very violent show, but there were still some scenes in the script that got up close and personal. And Shaun had decided to do his own stunts.

I watched the stuntman take a swing at him, and I flinched. Never mind the fact there was no impact, it looked real from where I sat. My eyes prickled and my stomach hurt. After the third hit, I put the coffee down – clutching a cup of hot liquid while he scuffled on the soundstage was not a good idea.

I gripped the edges of my adopted flight case and forced the emotions back.

When Gary called for a break, my face ached from holding a smile in place and my back muscles screamed from the lack of movement. Dragging air into my chest became a priority. And getting out of the studio.

Deep breaths, Baines. It was staged. He doesn't have a scratch on him… But why the hell do I care?

"How did it look?" Shaun asked, a cheerful lilt peppering his Welsh accent.

"Fine," I muttered, more focused on surreptitiously working out the kinks in my muscles.

"Just fine?" His voice rose with alarm. "It can't be just *fine*, Mona. I have to do it again if it was just *fine!*"

Oh, please don't.

"It was great." I injected as much pep into my voice as possible. He didn't look convinced by my bright smile. "Do you want coffee? I'll, em, I'll go get it."

I jumped down from my box and marched over to the mercifully empty Crafty table. I dumped the cup of lukewarm coffee in the bin and started preparing two more – not that I needed one; I was far too wired as it was.

What the hell is wrong with me? Panicking that he'd injure himself in a stunt he'd practised for weeks, seriously?

"Are you alright there?" Shaun appeared at my side, startling me to the point that I missed the cup and spilt almond milk all over the table.

Swearing, I crouched down and frantically searched the boxes beneath for a towel of some kind. With two clean tea towels in hand, I set to work mopping up the spill and ignoring Shaun's bewildered stare.

"I'm perfectly fine, thank you."

His lifted brows told me he didn't believe me. Oh well, I didn't either.

I blocked him out and focused on finishing his coffee. When I glanced up to hand it over, he stood frozen with a cookie inches from his mouth. His eyes were wide and fixed on me like he'd been caught doing something he shouldn't, which he had. His personal trainer had been rather specific about cutting sugar from Shaun's diet.

I couldn't see anything wrong with a treat now and again. It wasn't like Shaun tore through junk food on the regular. Plus, he'd drop some serious calories now that he was off the drink. Still, it was a comical scene and I intended to enjoy it. I put the cup down, crossed my arms and welcomed stern Mona into the building.

Shaun lowered the cookie, indecision consuming his features.

He couldn't win either way. If he ate it, he'd expect me to pipe up with a threat to tell his trainer. If he put it back, it would be disgusting and I'd have to say so. But if he binned it… oh boy, would he open a can of worms he'd regret. There was nothing I hated more than waste, and I'd seen a lot of it on this set.

He met my gaze with an assessing light. He looked like a toddler caught with his hand in a cookie jar. An adorable one with a dimple, a mop of dark brown hair and sad but sly green eyes.

And Shaun Martin as a toddler was not an image I wanted in my head! *Gah! How do I get it out?*

"Turn around," Shaun ordered, wiggling his fingers at me.

"What?"

"Turn around!"

"Why?"

"Because I told you to."

It was my turn to cock a brow. He should have known getting surly with me would gain him nothing.

Shaun sighed. "Mona, please would you turn around so I can eat this cookie before they pull me back on set for another round of gruellingly choreographed stunts?"

"If your blood sugar is low, you should probably eat an apple or have some juice." I struggled not to crack a smile at his wide-eyed desperation.

The panic slipped and a hard edge entered his gaze. "I really don't like people telling me what to do." He frowned, and I broke. I laughed. It started out thready, but as his consternation grew, I laughed harder. Silence fell around us as the crew nearby stopped moving.

After the stress of the last few days and tiptoeing around him, it felt good to banter with him like there wasn't this big "what if" hanging over our heads.

Shaun turned to the runner he'd made a habit of petrifying. "Here, have a cookie." He placed it in the kid's hands and turned his back on his bewildered expression.

Invading my personal space, Shaun forced me to straighten up and pulled me close to his body. The look of concern on his face sobered me slightly.

"Get it together, Mona," Shaun whispered, leaning so close that his breath tickled my ear and his nose grazed my hair. I shivered. "I know moving down here was hard, but if you're going to cry on set, maybe you should stay in my trailer."

His words had the same effect as a dip in the River Forth on New Year's Day. I tore my arm from his and stepped back.

"Eat the damn cookie, Shaun. No one cares," I snapped before picking up my coffee and rushing away.

He was making so much progress. I should have known it wasn't only the damn drink fuelling his bite.

"Wow! Easy there," a stranger said as I almost ran into him. I narrowly avoided tipping my coffee over him. Maybe Shaun was right: being outside the trailer was dangerous for me.

"I'm so sorry. Did I—" I froze, my eyes and brain finally communicating the fact that the very attractive dirty-blond-haired man I'd nearly knocked over was none other than the front man of Rhiannon. Ryan Evans. "Uh, I'm so sorry, Mr Evans."

"Call me Ryan. From the hair and the accent, I'm

assuming you're Mona?" He gestured to my pastel-pink shoulder length hair. I nodded, shaking off the shock.

"I need to know your secrets, Ryan. I've been trying to get her to stop talking for weeks!" Shaun clapped Ryan on the back, his eyes shining at my star-stunned expression. "Why does he have this effect on you but I don't?"

I bristled at that praise. *Help him and he makes jokes at your expense. Great.*

"I don't have to see him at four AM almost every morning six days in a row."

The high-pitched sound of a child crying swallowed whatever Shaun planned to say in retort. Surprisingly, the set didn't quiet. In fact, barely anyone reacted to the noise.

The crew were in the middle of a reset on the soundstage, preparing for another run of scenes without Shaun. I'd managed to convince Brian to rejig plans and free Shaun for the afternoon so he could spend more time with Ryan. I figured he'd need more one-to-one time with a friendly, sympathetic face. An hour wouldn't be enough. It had taken me days to convince Brian, and what did I get for the effort?

Argh, men!

Anyway, a little girl stood off to the side. She looked about five years old with her blond ringlets and blue dress. It would have been a pretty image for the camera, if her face wasn't raw red and stained with tears. The hairstylist and wardrobe mistress watched with horror as she pulled at her hair and dress, caught in the middle of a tantrum.

No one moved to soothe her. They were either too focused on their own jobs or too busy laughing at the kid. *Where is her chaperone?*

"Can someone shut that child up?" Gary shouted. Irritation reddened his round face. There wasn't an ounce of sympathy in his voice.

A lump formed in my throat and my stomach knotted. If they wouldn't help her, I bloody would. I shook off Shaun's grip on my arm. The question in his gaze quickly cleared as he read my intentions. Concern flooded his features, but he was helpless to do anything. Some of the tension seeped from him as he nodded and stepped aside for me to interfere. Someone in his position couldn't step in unless he wanted the entire production's chins wagging.

Just as I moved forward, Alys rushed to the kid's side. She knelt down in front of her, wearing a careful smile. From this distance, I couldn't hear a word she said, but the girl stopped choking on her tears.

"Who is that?" Ryan asked. Something about his voice pulled my focus. He stared at Alys with fascination.

"Do you mean Alys?" I pointed to the red-haired woman holding the girl's hands. Ryan nodded without so much as a glance my way.

"She's a coordinator. I think she's Welsh," Shaun supplied with a frown. "I've worked with her on a couple of things. I should know more than that."

"It's alright," I said. "No one here expects you to actually remember their names." It was meant to be reassuring, but his frown deepened.

Before Shaun could comment, Alys started yelling at the crew. I didn't blame her one bit. Their laughter had gone on long enough.

"Listen up, you callous idiots!" Alys shouted. She held the little girl to her side. Her hands covered her ears. "Next time a child starts crying on your set, instead of ignoring her, you might want to ask why!"

She directed her ire at the crew-at-large. *My kind of woman.*

"She's five! She shouldn't have to deal with an insensitive bunch of twats who don't understand the meaning of child performance laws. Do you want to delay production, is that it? Neglecting the well-being of a minor is a great way to do it." Those words Alys directed to Gary. She met his gaze with a fiery determination and a clear threat: *Don't do it again or I'll fucking report you.*

"Laughing at her doesn't get you home any sooner," she continued. "She has to go back through hair, make-up and wardrobe. So, when you're all still here at ten PM tonight and you're looking for someone to blame, make sure you look in the bloody mirror for the culprits." Ruffling the girl's hair, Alys led her outside, the make-up and wardrobe mistress following close behind. Neither looked particularly amused at the destruction of their work, but then, neither had stepped in to help either.

The silence on the set deepened as people glanced at each other, unsure if it was safe to move. Gary had the sense to look sheepish as he stared after Alys.

"Do you know her?" Ryan asked, dragging my attention back to him and Shaun. He stared at me with a gleam in his eyes.

"Uh, not well. Why?"

"Is she single?"

Shaun laughed. "Butt, you live in Glasgow."

Ryan punched Shaun lightly, smirking at his comment. That gleam went nowhere, however.

"I don't know if she's single." I shrugged. "We haven't talked about anything but work."

"But she lives here?" he asked, his expression turning thoughtful.

"As far as I'm aware, yes."

"Does she like music?"

"Mona said she doesn't know her well. Will you chill out?" Shaun clapped him on the back, squeezing his shoulder in one of those man hugs. Shaun's concern had faded, but his expression remained pensive, as if caught in the past. I frowned and his gaze traced the motion. He forced his expression to smooth into something more laid-back.

"I'm starving. Are you coming, Sparky?" Shaun asked,

releasing Ryan and turning his back on the shell-shocked crew.

"Sparky?" I squeaked. "What kind of a name is that meant to be?"

"A nickname." His lips twitched as he took in my outrage.

"Why Sparky?"

He tilted his head, his eyes laughing at me. "I don't think it needs explaining."

I growled and he outright chuckled.

"Are you coming to lunch?"

"That's not necessary," I bit out. "I'm sure you've got lots of catching up to do. I can grab lunch here and get some of these tweaks in."

"Are you actually going to eat?"

"I said I would, didn't I?"

Shaun's scepticism was etched plain across his face.

"What are you going to have?" He crossed his arms, widened his stance and fixed me with a hard stare.

"I don't know. I didn't check the catering menu today." I knew he was going out for lunch so I hadn't needed to arm myself with that information. "Besides, we're done for the day, aren't we? I figured I'd go home and eat."

Delight brightened Shaun's face, but I wasn't naive enough to ease my guard. "Ha! You're coming with us, Sparky," Shaun declared.

"No 'ha'. Aren't you listening, Hotshot? I'm not coming into town with you."

Ryan's eyes bounced between us, as if following a ping-pong match. *What must we look like, bickering over lunch?*

"You're full of shit. No arguing. You're coming to lunch." I opened my mouth to protest, but Shaun held up his hand, a wicked glint entering his eyes. "One more excuse and I'll carry you out of here."

"You wouldn't dare." I crossed my arms and stepped back, eying him like he'd lost his damn mind, which he had.

"Close enough," he grumbled. I screeched as he leaned down without warning and pressed his shoulder against my stomach.

He threw me over him fireman-style without pausing to check if I was okay. The pressure of his shoulder against my gut was not pleasant. My stomach might as well have detached itself and jumped into my throat. My hands scrambled for a hold, landing on his back pockets before my brain could catch up with the body part beneath my hands.

My face grew hot, and I buried it in his shirt. A couple people chuckled at us. *Great, just what I need to destroy my badass image on set.*

Shaun's biceps tightened against my thighs, and my traitorous body liked it. Need gripped my centre and I squirmed on his shoulder, trying to escape the sensation. A hand landed on my butt, holding me firmly in place and intensifying the ache.

"Stop moving. I promise I won't drop you." Unlike me, he seemed entirely unaffected by his hold.

A beguiling voice dared me to move mine to see what he would do. I banged my head against his back until it stopped.

CHAPTER SIXTEEN

"Do you remember that time you tried to steal the frogs before biology class?" Amusement shone in Ryan's eyes.

Shaun shifted in his seat, avoiding my intrigued gaze. Bet he regretted asking me to join them now. Or at least wished he'd eaten his meal faster. Both Ryan and I had finished a while ago. Shaun had been too busy talking Ryan's ear off.

"You were convinced that the teacher was only trying to freak us out and we wouldn't actually dissect them, so they must have still been alive." Laughter overtook Ryan then, and I happily sipped my lemonade until he gathered himself. Meanwhile, Shaun studiously cut up a piece of broccoli.

"He screamed when he opened the fridge to find fifteen dead frogs." Ryan sputtered with laughter again, and I joined him.

For the first time in five minutes, Shaun met my gaze. More like glared at me. My sides and cheeks hurt from laughing so much.

"You never did tell the teacher what you planned to do with them." Ryan sobered with that, sitting back in his chair and considering Shaun with something like remorse.

Shaun cleared his throat and placed his cutlery on the table. "It was for the best, anyway. I landed my first modelling job the next week and I would have been plastered in bruises if that scheme had worked."

Shaun and Ryan shared a meaningful look, the type that communicated messages. I swear I wasn't jealous. I just couldn't pull silent communication off with anyone, not even my siblings. *Must be nice to know someone that well.*

Shaun reluctantly met my curious gaze. "I was going to let them loose in my father's clothes. The asshole could never be bothered to hang them up." Disgust deepened his voice.

Understanding widened my eyes. It hadn't even been a week since he'd confided in me. For some reason, I'd assumed his father hadn't beaten him, but thinking back on it, I'd misunderstood. My heart twinged at the thought of Shaun being attacked by the one man who was supposed to teach him how to grow up right.

"I'm sorry I didn't try to stop you. Assumed Lily would put a nail in that plan before you got anywhere near the biology lab."

"I'm pretty sure she was in LA by then." Shaun muttered the words, but they lacked the hurt I'd come to expect whenever he talked about Lily.

"Oh yeah, lucky sod. You know, James still won't let that go." Ryan's amusement dimmed slightly.

Shaun frowned. "He always did have an inflated ego for a guitarist."

Ryan tilted his head. "I mean, I kind of get it. Your little cousin signs a major record deal and you can't even keep a band together. It would have stung me too, I'm sure."

"I really doubt that. You always had a clear head, unlike James Tyler. I loved her, but I wasn't even remotely jealous."

Ryan laughed, a head-thrown-back-and-sliding-low-in-your-seat kind of chuckle. "She hooked you up with the right people. Of course you weren't bloody jealous."

My ears perked up at that. I'd heard the rumours, of course, but hearing rumours and having it confirmed were two different things. Shaun considered me from the corner of his eye. Ryan pressed his lips together, his eyes widening slightly, as if he'd spilled a state secret.

"I can't exactly judge. I'm only here because my sister knew your agent, remember." I liked to think it was because I was the best person for the job, but facts were facts, after all. Whether I was a match for Shaun Martin or not, my connections got me here.

Shaun smiled and I watched as the tension drained from his face. When he looked at me like that – like he didn't have a worry in the world and it was all because of me – our unsteady start faded away. He was too handsome for one man, too handsome to be my boss. It was hardly fair.

"If the gossip rags ever confirm that story, you can blame that waiter." I pointed to a woman with white-blond hair who had spent a good part of the last hour walking past our table at a snail's pace. "I signed an NDA, but there's nothing stopping her from selling 'Shaun Martin, Frog Thief' the moment we leave."

Shaun and Ryan glanced at the woman. Clearly, I was in the presence of two pros when it came to surreptitious looks. She didn't have a clue that two of Wales's hottest creative talents were considering her like she was a threat to their freedom.

Maybe I should stop it, actually. Could I stop it?

Before I could give it too much thought, I stood and made my way towards the bar where the manager stood, his head bowed over a book. He wore a tailored suit and had his dark hair swept back. With his head bowed, I couldn't place his age, but I assumed at least forty.

"Mona, you don't have to. I'll get Sherry to handle it," Shaun said, trying to call me back to the table. I held up my hand and continued.

"Excuse me," I said, not giving myself time to pause and think.

The manager's head snapped up, and his glasses slipped down his nose. He righted them with a quick hand then gave me a cautious smile before his gaze flicked towards Shaun. "How can I help?"

"Your waitress has been watching us a little too closely. My boss and his friend are having a private catch-up and I'm concerned she might have overheard some things they'd really rather remain private. Do your staff sign NDAs?"

The man swallowed, his gaze moving between Shaun and Ryan, who I'm sure were watching our interaction closely.

"I'm so sorry. Our guests' privacy is of the utmost importance and we have strict guidelines for our staff to follow." He pressed his lips together, his eyes catching the waitress's. He tilted his head towards a door at the side of the bar. "I'll pull her aside for a chat now and make sure we get this all straightened out."

"Thank you. I appreciate it."

With a firm nod, he turned away and marched down the bar where he met the ashen-faced woman. He led her into an office as I wandered back to our table, chewing on my lip. Had I done the right thing? What if she got fired because of me?

I walked back to my chair, catching snippets of Shaun and Ryan's conversation, but not really paying attention. Something about Shaun's Hollywood friends being tapped for a big film franchise.

"Are you okay, Sparky?" Shaun asked, catching my hand as I almost walked past them. I shook my head, trying to shake off the guilt. "Do you need me to do something? I can make quite the scene when I need to." He grinned, wiggling his eyebrows at his stupid joke. *Of course he can make a scene.*

Ryan laughed at him. "Glad fame hasn't stopped you from being weird."

Before I could reply, the manager approached, wearing a pained but apologetic smile. The waitress had been reprimanded, our meals were on the house and a bottle of champagne had been popped for the inconveniences.

Before anyone could protest, the bottle of champagne arrived on the table. Shaun tensed.

"Do you want me to get rid of it?" I whispered, trying to be discreet even though Ryan was far too close for him not to overhear.

Shaun glanced between me and Ryan, his brows furrowed as he tried not to look at the bottle.

He swallowed hard. "You can have a drink. I'm okay with my water."

Drinking in front of an alcoholic felt like a very bad idea.

"I'm not thirsty." I sat back, placing my hands in my lap.

Shaun's gaze roamed my face. Something like relief swept across his features, and he nodded, gratitude shining in his eyes.

"I'm good too," Ryan said, reading the situation with ease.

Shaun rolled his eyes. He leaned forward, whispering, "Just because I can't handle a drink doesn't mean you two have to go cold turkey too."

Ryan and I shared a look, and I'm proud to say I understood it: Shaun was absolutely an idiot.

"I bet you didn't think shit like this could ever happen to you when we were just two idiot teens building dens and planning our escapes," Ryan said, trying to move the conversation along.

Shaun smirked at him but nodded. "Until my career took off, I didn't believe any of those mad schemes of ours would work. Thought I'd be hiding out in the woods for the rest of my life." Shaun chuckled, shaking his head at his younger self.

Ryan studied Shaun. "Your dad did you a huge favour."

"By dying, you mean?"

Ryan glanced away. It didn't seem to be a topic he liked discussing. I couldn't blame him. It turned me sick too.

Shaun shrugged. "Only because I don't have to deal with him blubbering to the press. I'd bet your Les Paul guitar that he would have sold his story to as many tabloids as he could."

"That's a given. No need to threaten my favourite guitar," Ryan grumbled, eliciting a reluctant chuckle from Shaun.

We finished our waters and paid the bill soon after. The open bottle of champagne remained in the middle of the table, untouched and ignored. Shaun didn't so much as peek at it, and I was incredibly proud of him. It was a tiny step, but recovery meant hundreds of tiny steps stacked together until you reached the end and found you'd climbed a mountain.

CHAPTER SEVENTEEN

I lost most, if not all, of the next day in the production office trying to source a replacement executive car service. One of the supporting actors had gotten a little too drunk and shown the driver his lunch and dinner. Funnily enough, I didn't blame the company for refusing to drive them anymore.

By the time 4PM rolled around, I'd handed two car options to Alys, learnt how to pull and format sides and triple-checked all of the cast and crew call times for the next day. When the call came over the radio that they were ten minutes from wrapping Shaun, I started packing up.

A slightly less-frazzled Alys approached me before I could hot-foot it to his trailer. I didn't want him to react like he had the last time I wasn't there waiting for him.

"You're a godsend, have I told you that yet?" Alys asked, her gratitude evidenced by the gleam in her eye and the smile on her face.

I chuckled. "About five times, I think. But I appreciate you saying it."

She glanced around. There was no one but us, Heather and Cassie in the production office. Everyone else had fled to set, either for snacks or because they had a genuine need to be there.

As her eyes settled on me, she stepped closer and lowered her voice to a whisper. "Are you happy with Shaun?"

I frowned. *What a weird question to ask.*

"I'm asking because I think you've got a knack for this, and if you'd ever consider a change, we'd hire you in a heartbeat." She gestured to Heather, but her attention remained focused on me.

A week ago, I might have jumped at that offer. Now? Not so much. The thought of leaving Shaun to fend for himself right now didn't sit well with me. He needed someone on his side who knew what he was going through.

"Thank you, Alys. It means a lot that you'd offer. I've been thinking about my next move after I finish working for Shaun, so it's nice to know you guys think I'm capable of doing the job full time." I put some serious emphasis on the *after*.

Alys bit her lip as she nodded. "Of course. If you need any help, let me know. I'm sure between us we could find you some work." She smiled, but it didn't reach her eyes. Still, her words sounded genuine. "In fact, let me add you to the drama production chat. That's where all the jobs get posted all over the country."

She took my number, and within seconds I had a notification saying I'd been added to this group. *Could it really be that easy to find a job?*

With that done, she pocketed her phone and fixed me with a concerned look. "But seriously, if you decide for any reason that you need a change, come see me."

I swallowed the denials that sprang to the tip of my tongue and just nodded. I couldn't predict the future, and she was doing me a favour. No need to turn her down flat.

❄

J'd just collapsed on my bed when my phone pinged next to me. Sighing, I picked it up, bracing myself for some wild request from Shaun. He'd been surprisingly upbeat lately and I had yet to figure out why.

The message came from my sister, and as soon as I read it, my phone rang. Her smiling face flashed across the screen.

"Hello, stranger. I was starting to worry I'd sent you to an axe murderer," Isla joked, her voice opening a pang in my chest.

I hadn't really had time to focus on the fact that I was away from home – well, the home I'd grown up with, anyway. I'd gotten over the distance from my parents and brother, but Isla had been a daily staple in my life, even though she lived over an hour away. I missed her.

"Funny. At the start I would have groaned at you predicting my future."

A pause stretched between us as she digested my words. I shut my eyes tight. Why had I said that? Everything was fine now. I didn't need to worry her with problems that had passed.

"Is he as much of a nightmare as I've heard?"

I sat bolt upright, staring at my phone with growing horror.

"You knew?"

Silence.

"Isla Mairi Baines. Answer me."

She cleared her throat. "I might have heard some rumours."

"Before you offered me up to Sherry?"

Her silence spoke volumes, and I fell back against the pillows, my incredulous gaze stuck on the ceiling.

"I think I need to reassess our relationship."

"Yeah, I would too, but fill me in first."

I rolled my eyes at the excitement in her voice. Somehow,

we'd switched roles; I used to be the one living vicariously through her.

"I'm not sure I can," I said, hesitating more because I didn't want to admit everything and I knew that once she got me started, there would be no shutting my mouth.

"Your NDA doesn't apply to sisters in the biz."

I chuckled. "I highly doubt that was an exemption clause."

"Yeah, yeah. Read it later, spill now."

The need to talk became too much. I hadn't so much as spoken vaguely to Alys or Tilly. Now, Isla's insistence invited me to break the dam. "It was hell at first. Shaun was every bit the ass the tabloids painted him: he was shouting at the crew. He purposely tried to hit me with a door—"

"HE WHAT?"

"I'm not sure he would have actually done it, but it was apparently a ploy he'd used to scare off many assistants, something neither you nor Sherry told me. Thanks for the warning there, sis," I said, forcing the words between my clenched jaw.

I proceeded to fill her in on more of Shaun's antics, charting the full rollercoaster ride of life working with him.

"I had no idea he was pulling shit like that. Sherry assured me he wasn't dangerous. Last time I offer her my help," Isla bit out, indignation rolling down the phone.

"One minute he's being an inconsiderate twat, and the next he's all apology and charm. Honestly, Is, it's a jarring sight. I tried to quit pretty fast. That obviously went nowhere."

"Eh, that went nowhere because you didn't want to quit. Don't lie to me."

Caught off guard, I fell silent, my brow furrowed as I considered her words. Had I really sabotaged myself? I'd never let a "no" stop me from doing something I wanted before. Maybe she was right. If I'd really wanted out, I would have just left, agreement from above or not.

"Now that I've set that light bulb off, why don't you tell me what's *really* going on, because this is superficial crap and I want the goods."

My answering chuckle was half hearted. I couldn't give her "the goods". Shaun trusted me with his addiction, and sharing that with my sister wasn't on the cards.

"Mona, for god's sake, you're hot for the man."

I spluttered. "How the hell do you know that?"

"There's not as much hate in your voice as you think. You're soft on him, so either he's made a complete one-eighty or you're crushing."

My brain stalled on that, and the quick denial died unspoken on my lips. I'd never been good at lying to Isla. Why did I think I could fool her for the first time in my life?

"I wouldn't say crushing…"

"In lust, then. Same difference," she huffed, amusement hardening the Scottish undercurrents in her voice. "Is he interested?"

"Isla, he's my boss," I hissed.

"So? Do you honestly think actors don't hook up with their assistants?" I let my silence speak for me. "This industry isn't very above board in most places. I can guarantee you that half the people working on that set is fucking someone else on the production. It's just a fact with these high-stress, isolated situations."

"That doesn't mean I want to join them."

Isla laughed. "Try it again with a little more conviction."

"He's my boss," I bit out, clinging to that fact with both hands.

"And other than him being your *boss*—" the quotation marks were almost audible "—are there any other reasons you wouldn't jump him if he looked at you the right way?"

My answering laugh sounded thready, uneasy. My mind raced, searching for a plausible reason. I couldn't hold his asshole moments against him anymore. I genuinely thought he was trying to do better. He'd started smiling at people on set, took the time to learn people's names, and even brought me food whenever things got crazy busy.

"I look nothing like Lily Tyler."

Isla snorted. "Lily Tyler doesn't look like Lily Tyler if you remove all the photoshop, but I'll humour you. What does that have to do with anything?"

"He clearly has a type. I'm the opposite of that type."

Lily Tyler was a five-foot-eight glamazon. She had stunning blond hair that flowed down her back and a face that would stop you in your tracks if you met her in the street. I wasn't exactly tiny next to her, but I definitely didn't have the same effect on men.

"Do you seriously think the man knew what his type was at sixteen? She was his first and only girlfriend. I'd say nothing is set in stone with him just yet."

"Can you stop stripping away my defences? I need to work with him. It's hard enough to do that when he's inviting himself out with me and touching me at the most unexpected moments."

Isla shrieked. "There's been *touching*? You didn't tell me that!"

"Honestly, what am I going to do with you? Prioritise. The. Facts." If I could have clapped and held the phone, I would have. "He's *my boss*. It's not okay to lust after your boss."

"If he wasn't your boss, would you be holding off?" Isla asked, her voice subdued and serious.

"No," I whispered, needing to say the words but also wishing I could keep lying to myself. "I've never had someone make me shiver with just the brush of a hand."

Isla whistled. "Now I'm hot and I've not even got a man. Jeez, Mona, you need to do something about this." I opened my mouth to argue, but she cut me off before I could so much as huff. "I don't mean with him – although I still say there's nothing wrong with following industry norms. If your lusting after him has nothing to do with him, then find someone else and scratch the itch."

I covered my eyes and groaned. "Finding someone else" meant having a life, and having a life meant not working for Shaun. Because one, my hours weren't sociable, and two, even if I did manage to "find someone else", there was no way in hell I could go out without Shaun giving me grief about it, or worse, tagging along. He seemed to have a sixth sense for my making after-work plans. And what if I was drunk and Shaun fell off the wagon? I couldn't exactly help him course correct if I was also drunk.

"Fastest way to get to the root of it all," Isla said, her voice matter-of-fact, as if she knew the thoughts warring inside my head.

Why did she have to make sleeping with Shaun seem like such a good idea? Now it would be all I could think about.

I hung up more frustrated than when I'd answered. Actually, when I'd answered, I'd been living in blissful ignorance land. But that was no longer an option.

Damn meddling sisters.

CHAPTER EIGHTEEN

We had a rare late call time, and I'd intended to make the most of it – catching up on lost sleep. Thanks to Isla, it ended up being more about making up for lost hours tossing and turning, caught too deeply in thoughts about Shaun and whether this thing I felt was real.

In a lust sense, of course.

I had zero interest in starting something with an actor who had been off the rails not even a month ago.

Unfortunately, a late call time did not mean the day went smoother. If anything, this well-oiled machine had frayed at the edges. The entire day had lagged behind, and now the sun was going down. Worse, the set was still ablaze, the cameras continuing to roll.

I didn't really understand what had gone wrong, but whatever it was had landed me in a trailer with Shaun as the sun set. It wasn't a sight I thought I needed to see, but now that I was seeing it, it would haunt me.

The soft orange light played through the window, caressing his face and highlighting angles I'd never noticed before… and put some particular emphasis on his lips. (But that might have just been my overstimulated imagination at work.) Either way, I could have done without noticing them.

Shaun banged his head against the back of the sofa, growling, "Can you find out how long they're going to be? I'm bored out of my freaking mind." His gaze focused on the ceiling, and I was grateful to it for distracting him.

Do you see what Isla's done to you, Mona? Grateful to the ceiling!

I picked up the radio and called in Shaun's request for an update. The answer made neither of us happy.

"What the hell are we going to do for an hour?" Shaun grumbled.

He'd been in a mood all day. As far as I could tell, it had nothing to do with the delays. I crossed my arms and assessed him. Had he fallen off the wagon and this was him lashing out because he'd failed?

He met my critical gaze with a quirked brow. "You alright there, Sparky?"

"Pretty sure I should be asking you that question."

He studied me, and for a second, I actually thought he would share. Instead, he shook his head and averted his gaze. Frustrated, I stomped over to him, sinking into the sofa cushion next to him with my legs folded under me.

"What is it? If you've had a drink, it'll be okay. We'll start again."

A small smile graced his lips. "I haven't had a drink, but thanks for worrying about me."

I frowned. "You're in a mood. If it's not that, then why?"

He scanned my face with an intensity that made me squirm. Then his eyes dropped to my mouth, hovering there for what felt like hours. They darkened as I bit my bottom lip.

He leant towards me and my body responded as if pulled by a magnetic force. His fingers danced along my cheek, scattering tingles down my body. Something clenched tight and low in my stomach. A flighty thought screamed at me to pull away, that this was a mistake, but it was faint and I could barely focus on anything but the desire in his eyes.

"I can't hold back anymore, Mona. I can't stop thinking about how your lips would taste after you've told me off," he whispered, smirking as his eyes dared me to react.

That was right about the moment my head started spinning. He wanted me? It was like my brain was trying to merge two contrasting realities. My smile was slow to grow, but I couldn't stop it when all the facts aligned. All the brooding looks, the biting comments, the touching, the almost-kiss at aerial silks. I'd refused to believe my instincts. But they were right all along.

With slow, measured movements, he tilted my face up and lowered his. Unbearable seconds ticked by as he gave me ample time to pull away. His lips hovered inches from mine. Then impatience got the better of me.

My hands slid behind his neck and pulled his face towards mine. I claimed his lips, my movements urgent and hungry, stoking the embers of desire in us both.

One of Shaun's hands dropped to my side, gripping my hip, pulling me forward until I fell against his hard chest. His hands moved up my torso and around my back, pressing us together until there wasn't an inch of separation.

Then, his lips parted from mine. We both panted for breath, staring at each other with equal measures of yearning and surprise.

"What do you want, Mona?"

My brow furrowed. Why was he asking me questions? Now that I knew he felt this draw too, I didn't want to think. I wanted this need to go away and maybe, just maybe, if we gave in, it would free me from this odd fascination.

"You. I want you."

He smiled, his lips reaching for another kiss, and I leaned into him without hesitation. My tongue danced with his, tangling in a long, drugging kiss that clouded out all other thoughts.

Shaun released my lips, pressing soft kisses along my jaw before pulling back to consider me. "I've wanted you since the first day."

I smirked. "So you tried to run me off?"

"Yes," he groaned. "I'm so glad it didn't work."

Placing his strong hands on my hips again, he lifted me into his lap until I straddled him. Our mouths fused together again, caressing, licking, nipping. My hands slid into his hair and my nails dragged across his scalp, making him shiver. Titling my head to the side, I deepened the kiss and revelled in how good it felt to be pressed against him. Feeling the bulge in his jeans scattered the rest of my common sense.

With me in his arms, Shaun stood without so much as a grunt of effort and lifted me onto the table. He kissed me again, as a hand brushed along my body. Another slipped into my hair, pulling my head back and deepening the kiss. I moaned against his mouth, urging him on.

Our clothes weren't coming off fast enough. My hands caught at his t-shirt and began to pull. I wanted it off, but Shaun seemed too focused on devouring my mouth. I tugged hard at the material – there might have been a growl when he didn't react the way I wanted.

Chuckling, Shaun leant back and brought the t-shirt up over his head. He dropped it on the floor then reached for me again, smirking. Neither of us wasted any time. His lips returned to mine, eager and full. My hands smoothed across his hard muscles, mapping out his hot skin.

He tugged my thin cami top free from my skirt before his hands skimmed my torso, bunching the material there and sending goose bumps skipping across my skin. I shivered as he brought the top over my head and his feverish eyes roamed my body.

Shaun's restless hands palmed my breasts through my bra,

while his lips reclaimed my mouth. His fingers teased my nipples through the lace, sending shocks to my core. He swallowed my moans as frustration got the better of him. He growled, and my bra went flying across the trailer.

The sound shocked me out of the frenzy, and we both paused, staring at each other, breathless. *He actually growled.*

I laughed. "In a bit of a rush there?"

"I'm impatient. It's not newsworthy." Shaun grinned.

He swallowed my renewed laughter, invading my mouth with his tongue. His fingers sent tingles up my thighs as he bunched up my skirt. He dragged it up to my waist, pulling me closer and closer to the edge of the table until he had to force my legs to wrap around his waist for balance.

He trailed kisses along my jaw and down my neck. I let my head fall back and enjoyed the sweet sensations. With my eyes shut, I was entirely unprepared for his next move. His tongue flicked my nipple and I jumped. I felt Shaun grin as he kissed my skin. My hands slipped into his hair again, holding him to my breast. His tongue returned to teasing the delicate skin, circling it until all I could do was moan.

"Something you want to tell me?" The words vibrated against my sensitised skin.

Did I tell him I hadn't had sex in more than a year? I didn't know if that was important information. I wasn't the girl who had casual sex; yet there was always a first.

My fingers tightened in his hair. He straightened up and pressed his forehead to mine. I couldn't escape the concern in his eyes. "Mona?"

"It's been a while."

His face relaxed, and what I thought might be relief slithered across his face. "Define 'a while'."

"A year at least."

He nodded. "Okay." He lowered his head and sucked my nipple into his mouth, rolling it with his tongue.

I groaned but stiffened at the same time. Why was this so damn confusing? "That's it?"

He released my flesh and leaned back again, sighing. "What were you expecting?"

"I don't know." It came out a little high and squeaky. I cleared my throat and tried again. "But more than a nonchalant 'okay'. You don't think it's weird?"

Shaun stood up, his one hand slipped into my hair to massage my scalp, and the other smoothed along my jaw. There was an open and honest quality to him – not that he hadn't been honest before, but it just felt raw, unedited.

"I don't really want to think about another man touching you, so I'm pretty happy with your year-long dry spell."

His eyes widened as his own words sank in. They bothered him for some reason. He stepped back, his cheeks turning red.

"That sounded bad."

A huge smile overtook my face. "All I heard was 'I want you all to myself'. Which is good, 'cause the feeling's mutual."

Right now. It is mutual right now. Damn it, Mona, think before you speak.

He studied me with narrowed eyes. "You're sure?"

"Might need you to elaborate."

"You still want this."

I nodded.

"Need words here."

"Yes. I still want you to fuck me."

It was like a spark catching dry wood. He slammed his lips back to mine, kissing me frantically while our hands explored each other. His fingers returned to my leg, lightly easing up my inner thigh, heating up every nerve ending. They toyed with the edge of my underwear, teasing me with their lack of action.

He pushed the material aside and slid a finger into the moisture pooling there. I jolted at that first contact, his touch electric.

"Easy there." Shaun's arm wrapped around my waist, holding me still on the table.

He grinned down at me while he continued to tease me. He worked me higher and higher until my head fell back, lost in the sensations created by his clever fingers. When the pressure broke, I collapsed back onto the table, uncaring of my office supplies or the fact I felt boneless from one orgasm.

Shaun chuckled as he leaned over me. "You still alive there?"

"Yes," I grunted.

His fingers grazed the skin at my hips, hooking into my underwear. "Do you want to keep going?"

I nodded. I was probably wearing a dopey smile, but I didn't care.

Shaun dragged my underwear down my legs and I sat up quickly, shuffling back to the edge of the table. Shaun's smirk stayed firmly in place. That self-satisfied gleam shone in his eyes and I let him keep it. He deserved it.

I hooked a finger into his belt and pulled him back between my legs. Both his belt and jeans were decorating the floor in no time. I was wearing my skirt like a belt, but taking it off seemed more effort than it was worth. I was too busy watching as Shaun searched for a condom. I'd known he was toned and in great shape, but there was something decidedly hot about being able to touch all that delicious muscle.

He caught me checking him out but made no comment as he returned to me with a knowing grin. He kissed me as he pushed my thighs further apart and positioned himself between them. I felt the teasing glide of his cock against my opening and groaned into his mouth. It was just a flutter, but oh boy.

His grin grew as he nipped my lips and pressed into me. He slid in a couple of inches with ease, but it had been a long time since my body had experienced this and he wasn't your average man. I stiffened against my will and he stilled.

"Are you okay?" Shaun whispered, his fingers caressed the skin of my hips, trying to soothe away the discomfort.

"I will be in a second."

He pushed me back onto the table until I lay flat on my back. He followed me down, catching my nipple in his mouth, teasing me until I squirmed beneath him. The pressure eased and he took advantage, slowly nudging deeper until he bottomed out.

We were both shaking and moaning, but he didn't move. I wrapped my legs around him and lifted my hips, trying to urge him on.

He leaned back and met my impatient gaze. Amusement played on his face, but his eyes seemed concerned. "Is the pain gone?"

"Why don't you move and find out?"

He frowned. "I'm not a fan of that plan."

"Shaun," I groaned, letting my head fall back against the table.

I was expecting him to keep resisting. Thankfully, he surprised me, retreating until just the tip remained. My eyes just about crossed with that friction, but then he slid back in and my back bowed.

"I'll take that to mean you're good?"

I bit my lip as he pulled out again. "Oh yeah, I'm good."

Shaun stood up straight then lifted my legs and pulled my lower half off the table, shifting me forward until I was completely in his control. In and out, he pumped, picking up speed as the pleasure grew, ratcheting the tension up until I couldn't do much else but moan his name. It was a good thing he'd taken over. I'm not sure I could have kept up.

The sounds of my moans and his grunts, the slap of flesh against flesh, filled the trailer. The walls weren't that thick, and I threw my hand over my mouth, trying and failing to muffle my sounds.

My back bowed again as I came, and again I cried out.

Shaun collapsed on top of me as his release hit. He buried his face in my neck and pressed himself deeper.

When the sweat began to cool on our skin, Shaun lifted his head and met my sleepy eyes. "I did not expect you to be a screamer."

I stiffened beneath him. "I'm not."

"Oh, so the ringing in my ears is just me?"

I slapped his arm lightly. "That's not funny."

I'd never been loud during sex, but I'd never had great sex before. My body still shook with sparks; I wasn't surprised I couldn't keep my mouth shut.

He chuckled. "Alright, it wasn't that loud." He kissed me again, and his hand slipped beneath my head to help me hold it up. All of my energy had slipped away with that orgasm. He dragged his mouth along my jaw, pressing soft kisses to my skin. "I think making you scream my name is going to be my new favourite activity."

My face fell as his words sunk in, and he pulled back, stepping away from me with a frown. He disposed of the condom, returning to find me chewing on my lip.

We should have talked first, but how the hell was I meant to predict he'd want more than one night? My eyes widened. How was I meant to know I would?

Fuck, fuck, fuck.

This was not what I'd had in mind when I'd just let go. We were meant to put an end to it, scratch an itch and move on. In my head, at least.

"We're not doing that again, Shaun."

We couldn't. Isla may claim it was the industry norm, but that didn't mean I wanted to join them. I could not sleep with my boss. Again.

"Like hell we're not." Determination hardened his features. "That was just the start."

"I'm your assistant. Think about how it would look if someone found out?"

He ground his teeth. "Then we'll make sure no one finds out."

"We just had sex in your trailer where anyone could have heard or walked in. Someone will find out."

He ran his hands through his hair. In any other moment, I'd find the sight of him naked distracting, but this wasn't that moment. Why couldn't he understand how much of a bad idea it was?

"We'll be careful."

"For what?" I snapped, pushing off the table. "So we can have sex and part ways after six months?"

"I don't know," he snapped, pulling at his hair. "I haven't thought that far ahead."

Wearing a bittersweet smile, I approached him, removed his hands from his head, and tried to convince him that there was no way this could work. He stared down at me, his face darkening as my resolve hardened.

"We're not reinventing a wheel here, Mona. It's been done before."

"I'm not willing to risk my future in this industry. If the press found out, it would blow up on us. If someone on site found out…" I shook my head. "They'd never look at me the same again. All I've achieved, all the respect I've earned, they'd think the only reason you bent to me was because you were into me. Getting you back on track would be meaningless."

No, I had to think about more than what my hormones wanted. Falling into bed with him would be easy. It's the falling out that would take me down.

CHAPTER NINETEEN

The next day was awkward as all hell. The universe must have whispered to the person setting the schedule because it was a short but busy day for Shaun on set, which meant that by 1PM he was done and I was free. I kept myself locked in the trailer – an uncomfortable experience, let me tell you – while he cemented himself to the set. We said hello in the morning, bye in the afternoon, and each time I ignored the burn of his stormy gaze on my face. Then we went home, alone.

The following day was Sunday, which meant a break in the schedule. I don't think I've ever been happier for a day off. We'd have a day apart, he'd realise I was right and on Monday morning, it would all go back to normal.

Minus the lust.

If I could make myself forget the lust.

That part of the impromptu plan hadn't gone right either. If I'd tossed and turned with the prospect of what if, knowing that "if" was far worse. The sound of his groans played on a boomerang reel in my head.

I needed to spend the day doing things. However, I had no idea what those things were. Maybe I'd brave cleaning the kitchen. Maybe I'd go white-water rafting. Maybe I'd drive to Cornwall for the day and visit my parents. There had to be something that would distract me enough to bury any thoughts of Shaun.

Answering my door to said man at 8AM had not been a part of the slowly forming plan.

"What are you doing here?" My tone sounded less than welcoming. I hadn't even showered, my hair probably stood on end and, yet again, all I wore was pyjama shorts and a tank top.

Silence reigned as his eyes devoured all my exposed skin. It made me want to both strip off and cover myself. I frowned instead. When his focus returned to my face, he cracked a grin like nothing had changed and breezed past me into the flat.

"Honestly, I'm hurt!" He held his hand to his heart. "I thought you'd be happy to see me."

I crossed my arms over my chest and waited.

"Fine. I brought you these." He held out a bundle of papers he'd wound into a tight baton. I stared at it, perplexed. *He brought me paper?* "Take them. They won't bite."

Bewildered, I accepted the baton. It unwound in my hands to reveal flat listings, most of them in the Bay area and studios – and a few circled. The prices also turned me kind of sick. I mean, I could afford it. He was paying me well, so that wasn't the issue. But for the price of a studio in Cardiff Bay, I'd been able to rent a two-bedroom flat with a living room while studying in Edinburgh. Why the hell would I pay more for a studio than a flat in a historical building?

"Why did you bring me listings?"

"Why the fuck are you living in this dump?"

"Why does it matter?"

"It looks bad."

"Bad for who, exactly?" I said, my words measured. "Me or you? And why do people involved with you need to know where your assistant lives?"

"They don't, but if anyone found out, they'd think I wasn't paying you properly."

"And that's my problem because…?" I asked, my hands falling to my hips.

If the cutting look he threw my way was anything to go by, he didn't appreciate my sarcasm.

"Why are you arguing? You hate this place." He gestured to the papers. "I arranged a few viewings already." Before I could groan in protest, he continued. "Just look at them. That's all I ask." He tried to placate me, but I wasn't fooled. The man was a master at getting his way. *Damn actors.*

"Maybe another day. I have plans."

He froze, now a standard reaction for him. Caught doing something he shouldn't? Freeze. Doesn't like an answer? Freeze.

"I thought you didn't know anyone in Cardiff yet?"

"I know the crew." And he'd been out with me and Tilly, how quickly men forget.

"Did one of them ask you out?"

My eyebrows lifted at that. "And what if one of them did?"

"I just don't think you should get involved with the people you work with." He frowned, shaking his head. "I mean, in terms of the crew." The intimate way his eyes trailed over me tried to make a point, tried to tell me we were perfectly fine and exempt. "It could get awkward."

"Like this conversation," I muttered before stomping into my bedroom to find clothes and a towel. He wasn't going anywhere. The man was stubborn, and if I wanted any time to myself, I'd see the flats and ditch him later.

I paused, clutching a top to my chest. I could do this. I could pretend everything was perfectly normal and nothing had happened. My ability to do my job depended on it.

With my arms full of fabric, I turned to find Shaun lurking in the doorway. His eyes bounced between my unmade bed and me with a dazed deer-in-headlights sheen. His fists clenched at his sides, and the memory of his fingers digging into my hips as he drove into me surged to the surface.

"Give me a good reason why you choose to live here and I'll leave it," he promised, his eyes fixed on a point beyond my shoulder.

"There are so many things I could do with that money. Paying extortionate rent isn't one of them."

He frowned. "What else would you do with it?"

"I don't know. Save to buy a house? Start a business? Anything but squander it on rent in a temporary city." I walked towards him, and his eyes met mine. Lust clouded them briefly before he locked it down and started studying the ceiling.

"That's very sensible of you."

"Surprised?"

He nodded. "I shouldn't be." His Adam's apple bobbed as I approached, and I couldn't tear my gaze away. "What business would you start?"

"I have no idea. I still haven't figured out what I want to do with my life." Although my conviction that production would make a nice interim career was growing.

"Well, let's start with fixing your living situation and I'll see what I can do about your life-goals issues later."

I didn't detect an ounce of teasing in his expression. He seriously believed he could fix my problems. Most men ran a mile the moment they sniffed out so much as an ounce of work. The fact he cared enough to want to help warmed my heart. It shouldn't have – I didn't need or want the help – but that didn't mean I couldn't appreciate it for a moment before snuffing it out. It was such a rarity. Had I given up a unicorn?

He backed away from the doorway with a sweet, knowing smile, and some insane part of me melted.

"I'll see the flats, but I'm warning you now: It's a waste of time. I've got something lined up."

"Do I want to ask for details, or is it going to piss me off?"

Holding the towel and clothes close to my chest, I crossed the living room, trying my hardest to ignore his presence. My fingers itched to pull him into the bathroom, but I bit my tongue before I could offer up my shower. *You said no repeats. Don't be a tease.*

"Tilly offered me her spare room."

Shaun's brows puckered. He had no idea who Tilly was. Sometimes he was a blank slate, but he was becoming easier to read by the day.

"She's the wardrobe assistant. She came to Axel's with us." I'd meant it when I said the crew didn't expect him to know their names. Hadn't thought he was actually beating himself up with it, though.

"You'd rather share a space with a stranger than have your own flat?" he said, his words slow and measured as he tried to decipher my logic.

"She's not a stranger anymore, and I mean, she forgave me for nearly throwing coffee over her costumes." I shrugged. Shaun's eyebrows shot up. "It's not an interesting story. She seems nice, nicer than this lot." I gestured to the four closed doors surrounding the central living space.

I'd fully vet all housemates before agreeing to rent a room in future – lesson learned. Nothing I could do about it now except move out. I'd only been in the city for four weeks, but, oh boy, did they make a month feel like a lifetime. None of them worked, from what I could tell, but then, they didn't speak to me, so I couldn't be sure.

Given they spent most weeknights out on the town and noisily crashed in the front door as I left for early call times, I couldn't imagine any of them had jobs. Can you fathom the sleep deprivation? No thank you.

"View the flats and we'll talk," Shaun said, his face set in serious lines that would have dissuaded the average person from arguing. He should have realised by now that I was not the average person.

I left him in the living room to stew while I showered. I did not suggest he join me, although I really wanted to.

What the hell was wrong with me? I'd said no. Me. Not him. I was the one stopping us from having sweaty fun, and my reasons were sound. I needed to stop thinking about it, to consider what it might feel like to ignore all the risks.

CHAPTER TWENTY

$\mathcal{F}$our flat viewings later, I was reconsidering my agreement to this farce. Shaun stood in the centre of a stunning kitchen/lounge while an agent rattled off a list of features. Most of it I didn't need. What twenty-five-year-old actually needed smart lighting?

"You're not listening to me, Shaun," I repeated for the fourth time. There might have been a tinge of exasperation in my tone. Alright, a lot. But I was tired and wasting my day off being dragged around flats I had no intention of renting.

"Of course I am. You said you hate your housemates, so we're looking for a studio or a one-bed. This is perfect, don't you think?" He flashed me that winning smile that charmed other people.

I had to admit, this place was beautiful, and if all I wanted to do with my life was pay rent and work at a job that gave me no joy, it would make a lovely home. But I wanted more. I might not have known what "more" was, but I knew it didn't include a flat with a 180-degree view of the water and a flash smart-home system.

"It's not right. I don't even want to know what the monthly cost is."

"Come on, Mona. It's safe!"

"And my current place isn't?"

"No! Have you seen the men loitering on the corner? There's going to be a drug bust on your street any day now."

"And I'll ask again: Why do you care?"

"You work for me." He stepped closer, his gaze flicking to the estate agent staring out the window. Dropping his voice, he said, "I care about you. Your safety is important!"

I ignored the meaningful hitch in his voice and focused on my indignation. "Sherry works for you. Did you inspect her living arrangements?"

"I didn't have to."

"No, you didn't do it because she'd have paid you back by signing you on for some reality TV show."

Shaun shuddered. "Don't even joke about shit like that!" He scowled at me like I was tempting the universe. "This is ridiculous. I'll give you a raise. Will that solve it?"

Horror snatched my words. My jaw worked, but I couldn't produce any sound.

The agent's head snapped back and forth between the two of us. "I've got a listing a couple streets over that might work?" he suggested, his tone kind but his eyes wide. I hoped Shaun had him sign an NDA. The chances of this guy selling all our secrets to the press increased by the minute.

"Does it have a bay view?" Shaun asked. The agent shook his head, his shoulders slumping. "Then definitely not."

"Does it have any unnecessary appliances or features?" I asked, ignoring Shaun.

"No. It's fitted to modern standards but not tech fitted."

That piqued my interest. "Where does it sit on cost?"

"Mona, we're not viewing it." Shaun's voice was clipped and his jaw clenched.

I ignored him and pressed the agent for an answer. When he quoted a figure at the top of my range, I almost kissed him.

"*I*t's perfect."

"It's not even remotely on that scale."

It was a basic but lovely studio flat with a small kitchenette, an en-suite shower and a washing machine tucked into an airing cupboard. I'd need to rework the layout, but for a studio, it was a good size. It came furnished with a double bed, a loveseat, TV stand and coffee table. There were even lamps. I wouldn't have to pay out for any furniture, which was a huge bonus for such a short let. And best of all, it had parking.

"When could I move in?" I asked the agent, ignoring the scowl on Shaun's face.

Shaun scoffed. "You can't be serious. The building is old."

"It's called character."

"It's called thin walls."

"Like new builds or trailers are actually any better?"

He busied himself opening cupboards rather than finding a way to counter my point.

"When could I move in?" I asked again.

The agent smiled. "It's currently available, so we would just need to do the checks and file paperwork. A week at most."

Shaun sighed. "If I signed on as her guarantor, any chance you could make that tomorrow?"

"He doesn't mean that. Ignore him." I shoved Shaun towards the door. "Why don't you wait outside while the adults talk!"

He dug in his heels and resisted with ease.

"A generous offer, but I'm afraid we would still need to run references," my new favourite agent said.

Grinning, I stopped pushing Shaun towards the door. He stumbled at the sudden loss of my hands, but with all that muscle, he recovered fast. *Finally, someone Shaun couldn't bribe with his celebrity status.*

"I'll think about it and let you know."

"Why do you need to think about it?" Shaun asked.

"I've still got the room with Tilly as an option."

Shaun frowned and crossed his arms. "If I can't get you in a flat with security, then this is at least better than sharing a room in someone else's house."

It was my turn to cross my arms and growl. What was this man doing to me? "And I already said if I can save money, I will. Besides don't you think it would be lonely for me living here alone and maybe I'd like someone to talk to?"

Whatever protest he had prepared stalled on his tongue. He stared at the double bed with heated eyes. I didn't want to dissect the meaning behind that look.

"I'll let you know," I promised the agent and skipped out the door.

Freedom was in reach. I'd done as promised, I'd seen the flat, and now I'd have the rest of the day to myself.

"*W*hy are you frowning at me?" Shaun asked, holding a spoonful of mint ice cream out to me. "It's just a spoonful. If you don't like it, you don't have to eat any more."

My escape hadn't gone according to plan. In my haste to get away, I'd failed to notice Shaun's waiting car on the street. The moment I'd stepped out the door, he'd ushered me into the car under the guise of a mob of fans. There were three. Two of them were under the age of five. He posed for selfies while I cursed his name to the soundtrack of Tom's laughter. At least his driver listened.

Don't get me wrong. Lunch was amazing. He'd scored a table at a super-exclusive rooftop restaurant overlooking the city. The food was delicious, and people left him alone, which was a nice perk. The servers were even discreet, which was even nicer.

"You shouldn't eat that," I said without my usual force. I'd been wined and dined, and the only thing missing was a nap in the sun.

"Are you going to tell on me?" Shaun pouted, but his eyes laughed at me, ruining his concerned facade.

He had yet to realise that I'd never grassed him up to his trainer. I hoped he never realised, or he'd start breaking his own rules just to test me.

Shaun finished his ice cream, the spoon scraping against the side of the glass.

"I think you got it all."

He smiled, that easy twinkle in his eye setting butterflies loose in my stomach. While I stared, transfixed by his lips, he stood and held out his hand. "Shall we sit on the terrace and finish our drinks in the sun?"

Was he a mind reader now?

I nodded and gathered my bag and soft drink. Shaun led the way to a plush pair of loveseats at the edge of the glass balcony. He took a seat next to me, spreading his arms along the back of the loveseat. I became hyper aware of his fingers, rubbing at the fabric directly behind my shoulders.

"So, you moved down pretty fast." Shaun leaned towards me with an expectant look on his face. "Most people would have to give notice."

Was he asking if I'd skipped out on a job? That was an obvious yes. Not that my boss had really cared. All that talk of blacklisting was meaningless. For one, I'd be glad to never see another marketing company for as long as I lived. Even with adequate notice, I couldn't believe he would have given me a good reference.

Shaun tugged on a flyaway lock of hair, drawing my attention back to him. And the finger twirling the strands, tying us together.

"Bad breakup?" He watched me from beneath his lashes. "You said it had been a year."

My ex's mean but handsome face flashed through my mind. Shaun meant was I running from a recent breakup, or I assumed he did.

"I was kind of shocked. Looking at you, it's hard to believe."

I frowned at him.

"C'mon, Mona, you're beautiful. I can't believe any Scot would be stupid enough to pass you by."

A sharp pain stabbed at my chest, as if Shaun had stuck me with a dagger and turned the blade.

"Meaning that if I was – am – single, it's my fault?" I asked, stiffening in my seat.

If I confided in him about my previous relationship, would he blame me for his bullshit need to control every inch of my life?

Shaun's eyes widened. He released my hair and his nimble fingers cradled my chin, turning my head until I could only see him. Mission achieved, he leaned in, the tips of his fingers dancing across my neck, firing off dangerous sparks that I shouldn't have been allowed to feel.

"All I meant was that any man who can walk away from you must be blind." He swallowed, his eyes skimming my face. "Because I don't think I can."

And with that whispered declaration echoing around inside my head, Shaun closed the gap between us.

CHAPTER TWENTY-ONE

The gentle press of Shaun's lips quickly overrode logic. I kissed him back, forgetting that we weren't meant to do this and meeting his tongue thrust for thrust in a dance for dominance. I was losing, but I didn't care. A hand slid into my hair, cupping the base of my head and holding me firmly in place. Not one to be beat, I ignored his attempt to hold me still. I twisted until I could lean into his hard body, embracing the flames he unleashed.

His kiss left me weak and confused. I was supposed to be fighting this. Instead, excitement rippled in my lower belly and my fingers dove into his hair. My nails scraped at his scalp, eliciting a moan from him, the sound vibrating against my lips.

A shadow fell across us and Shaun lazily raised his head. He stared back at me with fire in his eyes and a smug smile gracing his wet lips. I couldn't raise the required sarcastic response, so I just let my head fall back against the loveseat and watched him. It felt like a fog had descended, dazing me and blocking out all other thoughts.

A man cleared his throat. Our eyes jumped to a server

holding a bottle of champagne and waiting patiently for our attention. He spoke, but I couldn't focus on the words.

Free of Shaun's intense stare, my mind turned inward as my fingers stroked my sensitised lips. He was the only one who'd ever kissed me like that, thorough and with purpose. With my ex and every other guy I'd kissed growing up, it had been a fumbling mess that I'd wished would end quickly. Almost like it was an obligation I had to fulfil.

But kissing Shaun was off-the-charts amazing. Addictive.

I could spend days kissing him and never be satisfied… Something I definitely shouldn't be thinking about doing to my boss. I stiffened as the realisation settled in.

The server left us, thankfully taking the bottle of champagne with him. When it was just the two of us again, Shaun settled into the cushions, lounging against me, his body stretched out, taking up most of the room. "Now, where were we?" Lust deepened his voice.

He leaned towards me and I sank lower on the seat. His brows creased as I avoided his lips so they skimmed my forehead. Straightening up, he gestured for me to explain the sudden shift in my mood.

"I said we couldn't do this, and I meant it." I gestured towards his lips, my voice embarrassingly breathy. "That was a lapse in judgement. I should have stopped it. I'm sorry."

"I disagree. I think I need to spend the rest of the day with my mouth on you." He leaned towards me again and I pushed him away. "You liked it," he muttered, his confusion ringing loud and clear.

"I did, but we've been through the reasons why this can't happen." Under any other circumstance, his blank stare would have made me laugh. "You pay me, and that makes it weird."

His determination faded until I was left staring at his downturned smile. "I don't know how to make this end differently."

I did. I knew exactly how to remove the only obstacle. All I had to do was accept Alys's offer. Was it worth it, though? I didn't care about the money I'd lose, but who gave up a high-paying job for a man, for a fling? Because this couldn't be anything else. He might be home right now, but the day would come when he'd be caught in Hollywood's clutches again.

"Think about your image," I said, my voice weak.

"Right now, I couldn't care less. I want you."

Fuck. When he fixed his heated, tortured eyes on me like that – like I was the only person who captivated him – reinstating a professional line got exponentially harder.

"The feeling's mutual, but I was hired to keep you on track and stop your downward trajectory." My gaze flickered around the thankfully empty terrace. "Making out with your assistant in public, where anyone could snap pictures, is not going to help fix your problems. Sherry would murder us both if we caused you a scandal."

The colour drained from his face as my words sank in. His hands slipped from my body and he slumped back in the chair.

"Fuck!" He scowled out at the darkening city.

The sun was setting. I'd lost the entire day to him, but I couldn't say that surprised me. At some point, spending time with Shaun had become easy, even when I had to correct his fuck-ups or deal with him pulling my leg.

He chuckled, the sound bitter. "For some reason I thought getting here would solve everything. That I'd finally be able to be true to myself. Do and say whatever I want. But it's all pointless. I thought fame was what I wanted, that it would make me happy. I have all this money. Businesses give me free shit." He tipped his head towards the glass door the server had vanished through earlier. "Women fall at my feet and studios salivate at the thought of working with me. I proved my dad wrong years ago. And yet the one thing I truly want, I can't have. How fucking ironic is that?"

"You must love something about it. Why put up with the hours otherwise?"

"Habit, mostly. After Lily left me, it was a comfort. Everything is always the same. The faces, locations and material change, but the systems never do. I could walk onto a set in LA and it would look and feel exactly as it does here."

"It's reliable."

He nodded, relief flickering in his eyes.

"Why are you telling me this, Shaun?"

"Honestly?" An appreciative light shone in his eyes. "I don't know. I feel like I can trust you, and other than my boys, I've never really felt like this with a woman. Like I could tell you anything, do anything, and it would always stay between us."

"Surely you had that with Lily?"

He was shaking his head before her name left my mouth. "Never. I can't remember a time when I wasn't on edge with her, waiting for the walls to start crumbling. She was always this bright star. Even before The Brightside took off, she was the flame that powered them, drew people in like moths. With my shitty home life, I felt grateful, like she'd done me a huge favour by offering me her friendship. We were never on equal footing. But with you—"

"We aren't equal either, *boss*." The more I said the word, the more I hated it.

Shaun studied me, and soon a light bulb went off and a sweet smile curled the edges of his lips. I bit my cheek to stop an answering one from forming on my face.

"We could wait until after the show wraps," Shaun said, "then you won't be my assistant and absolutely no one could butt their noses in where they didn't belong."

"You'd want to wait that long for a fling?" I asked, my tone measured. If he said yes but he'd sleep with other people in the meantime, I might brain him with a glass.

Which was not the reaction of a person who wanted a fling. *Oh my god. Why are feelings so confusing?*

"Yes." He nodded firmly. "You're like a drug I can't get out of my system."

I rolled my eyes. "What a lovely description. No wonder you're gasping for sex."

"You know what I mean. I can wait. We'll get through the production and then fuck it out of our systems before the next job starts."

My core clenched at the way he said fuck. I was a goner. This was a terrible idea. I'd never last the entire production.

"When does the next job start?" Distraction, that's what I needed. Normal conversation.

He shrugged. "No idea. They're all waiting to see what happens with the show." He grinned, catching my hand and raising my fingers to his lips. "But there'll be plenty of time to enjoy this spark."

He nibbled on my fingers, the scrape of his teeth against the soft tips raising goose bumps along my arm. I couldn't tear my eyes away from his mouth, couldn't bring myself to take my hand back.

This is never going to work.

CHAPTER TWENTY-TWO

I was seriously sleep deprived when I unlocked his trailer the next morning. It was the only excuse I had for missing the fact that his table had been taken over by a desktop setup. In fact, it took me making coffee to notice the shiny new iMac.

Shaun walked in moments later to find me stood in the middle of the room eying the thing like it was a bar of Vego white chocolate. He laughed, taking the rapidly cooling coffee from my hands. He sipped it, and I didn't even care. Right then I only had eyes for the pretty, shiny new thing.

"Can't have you straining your eyes for me," he said, tugging the end of my ponytail.

He led me to the table, pulled the chair out and guided me into it. While I powered up the machine, he made more coffee, placing it and a plate stacked with a cooked breakfast on the table at a safe distance from my new keyboard.

I couldn't stop petting it. He spent an hour regaling me with tales of his early action days with his best friends Jackson Levi, Nathan Logan and Finn McCarthy, and through it all, my hand stayed clenched around the mouse. You'd think I'd never been given a gift before. The fact he'd noticed I was struggling with only the tablet softened the ache in my chest.

His eyes kept dipping to my lips, reminding me of his tongue brushing mine and his fingers twirling my hair as the sun set. Every now and again, he'd drag his bottom lip between his teeth and a knowing smile would light up his face when I tracked the gesture.

When the runner turned up to take him to make-up, I almost cheered. I needed to get a grip if I actually planned to last the five months until production wrapped.

Lunch came and went and I achieved zilch. Every time I tried to update his social media, the words blurred together, replaced with a replay of his lips on my skin. I composed multiple emails, but I forgot how to string a sentence together.

A runner appeared with a veggie burger, fries and salad. The fact things were so weird and he was crazy busy on set but still thinking about me did funny things to my heart.

And then Sherry sent me a message and guilt stabbed at me yet again. She knew nothing, but it lingered. And the more I sat with it, the bigger the crack grew until I could barely stop myself from pacing the trailer.

I didn't know what was causing my restlessness. Guilt or impatience?

If it was guilt, well, no one knew and we were both consenting adults. If Sherry found out, the damage was minimal because she'd hopefully keep it to herself. If it was impatience, then I'd better settle the fuck in because the next five months were going to be a hell of a bumpy, frustrating road.

Alys's offer popped into my head, but I brushed it away. I would not be the girl who gave up a job for sex. And even if I did quit, how would it look? All it took was one reporter finding out and the headline would still be that he couldn't keep his hands off the staff.

*D*uring a short break in his day, Shaun sat with a chair pulled up close, invading my personal space and begging me to read lines. The fact he picked the only mushy love scene in the entire show did not help. And then he kept bumping my leg with his knee, as if I could forget his presence.

He used this chance as the perfect opportunity to show me what I could have.

"I need you in my life," Shaun whispered, his voice hoarse with emotion as he read his line.

He stared at me like I had the answers to all his problems. Like the character did. I swallowed, my eyes falling to the piece of paper in front of me.

"Your sister won't like it," I read, clutching the sheet. "I can't lose my best friend."

"We'll talk to her. She'll understand." He caught my hand, pulling my focus from scanning the next line. His green eyes settled on me, and I forgot what I was doing. "How do you expect me to go on, knowing how your lips feel against mine? Knowing how my heart races when I think of you?"

My mouth went dry, hearing those words fall off his lips. They weren't directed at me, but I could imagine they were, wish they were.

The deep timbre of his voice did strange things to my body. The soft look in his eyes as he focused on me and only me made my chest tighten. Under the guise of practising, he stroked my cheek, the gesture so reverent it made my eyes burn with tears.

"I couldn't have gotten through the last year without you, and I'm not willing to go another day without you by my side," he whispered, his eyes shining and his voice hoarse. "There's no one else for me. I love you, Liv."

And when he leaned towards me, speaking his last line so close I could feel his breath on my lips. I didn't pull away. He transfixed me. Safe in his trailer, locked away from prying eyes, I had no defence against his sneak attacks.

"How was that?" he asked, resting his forehead against mine.

But for the rasp of his breath, silence stretched around us, creating a bubble that sheltered us from the outside world. Inside the bubble there was no press, no noisy crew members and no agent who would skin me alive.

Tingles spread down my neck where Shaun stroked my jaw, and my hands shook in my lap. Not trusting my voice, I nodded.

He searched my face, hunting for something. The obliteration of my resistance, perhaps. A triumphant gleam entered his eyes when he found it, snatching my breath and making my head spin.

I don't know who reached for who first, but suddenly, our lips slammed together and desire clouded our minds. Each of our frustrations added pressure to the glide of our tongues. Shaun's hands grasped my hips, pulling me to the edge of my chair. He slipped onto his knees, using his body to force my legs apart and make room for him. He pressed us together until we were plastered against each other, lost, found, groaning.

There is a reason we aren't meant to be doing this yet.

Nip.

We—I said it was a bad idea.

Lick.

Sigh. *Why did I say something that felt this good was bad?*

Caress.

We are waiting. There is a good reason for it.

Frowning against Shaun's lips, my mind chased that reason until Shaun sucked my bottom lip into his mouth, scattering my thoughts.

A bang on the trailer door jolted us apart. We were both panting, wide-eyed and dishevelled. Shaun's hair stood on end, and his shirt twisted at odd angles around his body. I probably looked like I'd been thoroughly kissed too.

The bang came again and the horror set in.

What if the person out there had been new and opened the trailer door without permission? What if it was one of the producers?

No one could see me like this – lips swollen, cheeks reddened and eyes dazed. I rushed to the bathroom, catching Shaun's concerned eye before I locked the door. Through the plastic barrier, my heart in my throat, I listened as he spoke to someone in a low voice. The door shut seconds later and Shaun wandered over, knocking softly.

"Mona, are you okay?" he called, his words level and clear. He'd recovered already, while I still stood there panting, my heart racing like a fool.

Because getting caught would do nothing to him. But it would destroy me.

I sighed. How many times did I have to toy with the fire before it burned me and I learnt my lesson? I didn't want to learn too late.

"I'm fine." I swallowed hard, forcing a calm I didn't feel. "Do they need you on set?"

"Yeah. The runner's waiting." Regret dripped from his words, and they sounded really close, like he was resting his forehead against the door. "Are you coming out before I go?"

Not likely. I needed a new plan. Ours wasn't logical. I was all for trying impossible things, but when the stakes were so high, I'd take a pass.

"No, I need a minute."

"Okay. We'll talk about this later?"

"Sure," I whispered with absolutely no conviction.

I pulled out my phone, clicking on Alys's number. I was crying as I typed out a frantic message. Was I making a mistake? Who knew? But it was better than sitting back and letting the mistakes happen to me.

CHAPTER TWENTY-THREE

"*M*ona, what a surprise. Is everything okay?" Sherry asked, curiosity dripping from her cheerful voice.

I sucked in a deep breath. It was now or never, and never wasn't an option.

"I need you to let me out of my contract."

The silence on the other end of the phone could deafen the dead. In fact, I think she might have stopped breathing.

"Sherry?"

She laughed, but a tremor belied her confidence. "I'm sorry. I thought you said you wanted me to let you out of your contract."

"I do."

"And I must have heard you wrong because I thought things were going extremely well," she said, steamrolling over my confirmation. "Shaun hasn't tried to chase you off in a while, and he's actually been rather nice to deal with for a change. So, what's the problem?"

"I'm extremely grateful for the opportunity you've offered me, but I can't do this anymore. I have to quit, Sherry."

There was no way she wouldn't read more into my words.

I didn't know how else to force her to acknowledge that anything but a "yes, of course" wasn't going to fly. There would be no bribes, no tickets to awards dinners, no pay rises. I was done.

She sighed. "I can't talk you out of this, can I?"

"No. It wasn't an easy decision to make, but it's the right one."

I couldn't keep toeing this line with Shaun. Even though Sherry employed me, he still acted as my boss. No matter what he or my sister might claim, we were different to everyone else on set.

He might have been their leading man, but he couldn't stop the crew, and the world for that matter, from dragging me over the coals. These things always turned back on the women. The press would say I'd ensnared him, call me devious, paint me with motives I couldn't fathom. I wasn't delusional enough to believe they would treat me any differently.

"Does Shaun know?" She almost whispered the words, and had I not understood why, I might have laughed. He wasn't going to be happy. I knew that. It's exactly why I wanted to have this conversation with Sherry first.

"No. He's on set right now." My eyes jumped to the closed trailer door. I swallowed, the reality of what I was doing sitting heavy on my chest. "I can't finish the day."

"What happened, Mona? The last I heard, everything was fine. Is he being a dick again?" Concern softened her words. "Or did he start drinking again?"

"No, he's been great, and as far as I can tell, he's making huge strides without the alcohol. The sponsor you hired must really be helping."

"I don't think it's the sponsor, sweetheart."

I closed my eyes against that thought.

"If that's the case, I'll still be on set if he needs a friend to talk to. I just can't work for him anymore."

Her silence spoke volumes. I could almost hear the ah-ha blaring in her head.

"Fine. I can't tell you how much of an asset you've been. I doubt I'll ever find someone as good as you at handling that man." There was a reluctant finality to the words. She might as well have reached into my chest and ripped out my heart. "If you ever decide to follow in your sister's footsteps, give me a call."

We hung up and I sank onto the sofa. A mix of emotions swirled around inside my mind, fighting for supremacy until they converged. Sadness, relief, regret.

Shell shock.

I'd experienced so much in this tiny space in the last month, I was reluctant to leave it. But I had to. I had to move before Shaun came back. Telling Sherry first wouldn't matter if I lingered long enough for him to confront me. One look at those sad eyes and I'd buckle.

Tilly agreed to my moving in the following weekend. After turning in my resignation, there was no way I could consider the flat I'd viewed with Shaun. I wouldn't have that kind of money anymore. Tilly was a far better option. If she noticed any change in my demeanour, she didn't comment. Alys gave me the day to get my shit together, and given that I'd burst into tears the moment the car door shut, that was probably for the best. Just because it was the right thing to do didn't mean it was easy.

A couple hours later, someone began hammering on my door. I lay there, buried under a duvet, seriously debating ignoring them. But that would have been a dick move. It wasn't his fault we couldn't trust ourselves around each other.

"You quit?" he said by way of greeting when I opened the door, his face set like thunder.

I stepped out of the way and gestured him in. He brushed past me, storming straight into my bedroom without another word. I braced myself for the onslaught the moment I closed the door. He paced my small room like a caged, angry tiger. I leant back against the wood and watched him.

Urgh, why does he have to look so good even when he's angry?

"What happened to talking later? Pretty sure quitting falls under the list of things we needed to discuss with each other."

"You would have argued."

"Of course I would have argued," he roared, pausing in his tenth lap of my room. "It's a stupid fucking idea. I can keep my hands to myself. We would have been fine."

I snorted. "You call this afternoon keeping your hands to yourself?" He had the good sense to look sheepish. "Shaun, we're as bad as each other. I can't resist you. If we keep working that closely, we'll be a timebomb waiting to blow. My way, we get distance."

"I don't want fucking distance."

"Tough shit. You're getting it."

His hands shook at his side, and I had the belated realisation that this could tip him over the edge and back into a bottle. I'd consoled myself with the fact that this was the right move for us both, and I'd still be nearby to talk whenever he had a weak moment, but what if I was the thing that pushed him over?

Before I could reassure him that I wasn't actually leaving him, realisation wiped the anger off his face.

"You don't work for me anymore," he whispered, wonder and disbelief merging in the lilt of his accent.

A light went on in his eyes and he stepped towards me. I held out my hand to ward him off.

"No, I don't."

"So, there's no reason we can't explore this now."

"I didn't say that."

"Mona," Shaun growled, frustration marring his beautiful face.

"I'm starting another new and foreign job tomorrow. I want time to enjoy that without getting lost in this."

"You won't get lost."

"You don't know that." I crossed my arms, fixing him with a determined look. "I also won't be the source of any unsavoury gossip headlines."

Shaun's shoulders fell before he collapsed onto my bed with his head in his hands. I joined him, keeping a small distance between us.

"It doesn't mean I don't want to be friends, hang out and listen to you vent," I said, my tone gentle, easing him into the idea.

He dropped his hands and turned towards me with a sad smile. "Same goes for you. I don't want to go five months without hearing you shout at me out of frustration."

I chuckled. "Pretty sure you'll find a way to annoy me even when I'm locked in the production office cleaning up someone else's mess."

"You can count on it."

The weight pressing down on my chest eased as he smiled at me, finally getting it. There was something potent brewing between us. I was excited to explore it when the time came, without fear of our lives imploding.

"So, our plan to wait until after production wraps still stands?" I asked, biting my lip. I thought that's what we'd just quietly agreed, but I needed the words. If I could persuade him to chisel it in concrete, I would.

"Yes, the day we wrap, I'm whisking you away from here, and we're going to enjoy every fucking moment together." His voice turned gravelly with lust.

"Maybe we should talk about it once we wrap?" I said, trying to buy more time to figure out what he wanted. To figure out what I wanted, even!

"Once we wrap."

He held out his hand to shake. I laughed at the gesture until he quirked his brow and refused to drop his hand.

Okay, so we're shaking on it.

I slid my hand into his and he closed his smooth fingers around mine. Such a simple touch and yet it had me itching to move closer, to crawl into his lap and wrap my legs around him again.

"Deal," he said as we shook, a small smirk forming as he considered my flushed face.

Oh yes. Distance is definitely needed.

CHAPTER TWENTY-FOUR

*D*ay one on the job, Shaun appeared in the production office with my tablet. Heather's eyebrows flew up when she saw him. Principle cast didn't just wander into the production office. Ever. They stayed in their trailers, away from the chaos, where they could be managed. Shaun messed with all of their norms by just being present, let alone hand-delivering me something.

"What can we do for you, Shaun?" I asked, acutely aware of Heather, Alys and Cassie observing this little scene.

He held up the device. "You forgot this in my trailer."

My brows drew together as I glanced from him to the tablet. I stood, guiding Shaun out of the production office.

"It's not mine."

He shrugged. "I thought you could use it here."

"Not that I'm not grateful for you thinking of me—"

"But it's weird for me to bring you things?"

I nodded, relieved that he got it.

"They'll get used to it." He leant in until his mouth almost brushed my ear. "You look gorgeous today, by the way, Sparky."

Heat engulfed my face as he swept a finger across my

cheek. A soft smile graced his lips. "I like it even more when you blush like that."

With that, he turned on his heel and walked away, leaving me reeling. *Please tell me this isn't going to be the next five months. I'll combust.*

"Mona, do you have a second?" Shaun called through the open production office door the next day.

He leaned against the doorframe directing a charming smile at Heather. His t-shirt stretched tight across his chest, barely containing his biceps. I was in heaven, and Heather, well, she didn't stand a chance. It disarmed her enough that she forgot to be shocked by his presence.

I pushed my chair back and rushed out of the office before he caused a scene.

"What are you trying to do?" I hissed as I caught his arm and pulled him away from the team.

He grinned. "Why? Flustered?"

No. Yes. Argh, men.

The devilish gleam in his eyes told me he knew exactly what that tight shirt did to me. In fact, it was the sole reason he wore it.

"You're not playing fair."

"We said nothing about playing fair when we made our deal."

My eyes widened. He planned to torture me for five months until I caved. *The sneaky bastard.*

"Was there a reason for your visit, or did you just come to drive me mad?"

He chuckled. "I have a question for you, but seeing that rosy colour on your face again was a nice bonus."

I sighed. I couldn't even shout at him for that. I loved his short visits. Maybe a little too much. It made me feel stupidly warm and fuzzy inside that he seemed drawn to me.

"What's the question?"

"Come to the refugee charity dinner with me in two weeks."

His words snuffed out the warm feeling. I immediately shook my head.

"No."

Good for him following through with his commitments. Still a hard pass for me.

I started walking back to the office. But I wasn't fast enough. He caught my hand, pulling me to a stop and spinning me around until I had to tip my head back to see his serious expression.

"Hear me out," he said, his eyes imploring me.

I nodded.

"I need a date. I don't want to take anyone else, but if I turn up with some random actress on my arm, the press are going to start blathering on about whether it's fake or real and giving us nicknames. I don't want that kind of attention right now."

I shut my eyes. Of course he didn't. Catch their attention on one thing and they'd start digging into him again. How long before they'd have his addiction plastered all over the front pages?

"You would be an unknown to them, they'll look you up, find that you're just a member of the crew and get bored," he said, his words rushed. "It's the perfect media distraction."

My eyes widened at his flawed logic. "Or they'll catch you looking at me the wrong way and fixate on me. Shaun, it's not a good idea."

Panic filtered into his expression. "Please, Mona. I can't deal with the cameras without you."

"So skip the receiving line."

"I can't. Sherry will flip out."

I shook my head, leaning fully into denial. "There has to be another way."

"There isn't. If I go alone, they'll roll out the same slew of articles claiming I'm still pining for Lily. That hurts my image just as much as the violent headlines." His voice edged into begging territory. "Please, Mona."

When he looked at me like that, like I could solve all his problems, I couldn't deny him anything.

"Fine," I sighed, my head falling back as I gave in. "I'll go but you need to be on your best behaviour. No lusty looks, no inappropriate touching," I said, pointing at him, hard determination settling over my features.

He nodded vigorously. "All above board, I promise."

I rubbed my hand across my eyes. This was going to be a shitshow. I'd never walked a red carpet before. Doing it with him was going to be next-level terrifying. Yet despite knowing that, I couldn't say no to that vulnerable side of him. He needed me, and as twisted as it was, I enjoyed being wanted.

"I don't have anything to wear."

"Don't worry about it."

❄

I don't know why I expected to get through Thursday without a visit from Shaun. When he knocked on the production office doorframe, I almost snorted. Yet despite his sudden appearance, the sight of him made me smile.

He caught me watching him, then tilted his head towards the outside. I nodded, somehow containing the eager smile I could feel brewing beneath the surface. Shaun backed away from the door, disappearing from sight.

"Is everything alright?" Alys asked with a knowing smile. Meanwhile, Heather and Cassie stared at each other, each wearing puzzled expressions.

I shrugged them off and chased after Shaun.

"You're going to have the entire crew talking about us if you keep this up," I said when I stopped in front of him.

He wore another skin-tight t-shirt, and my eyes devoured the defined ridges of his chest without permission. "Sorry," he lied. "I keep thinking of things I want to tell you."

"Then text me!"

"But then I won't get to see your face."

The flutters in my stomach stole any reply I might have made. I couldn't stay annoyed with him when he said things like that. "What did you want to tell me?" I asked, crossing my arms.

He pulled a book from his back pocket. "I wanted to give you this, actually."

I accepted the paperback copy of *Frankenstein*, my brows climbing. His smile dimmed at my questioning look.

"I know you like to read – not that I gave you much time to do it before." He tapped the book. "This is my favourite book. I, uh…" His gaze dropped to the grass beneath our feet, his brow furrowing. "I thought you might like to read it. But thinking about it now… it was a stupid idea."

He tried to take the book back, but I pressed it to my chest before he could.

"I've read it. We had to study it for English. I'll gladly read it again."

Shaun sighed. "I should have realised you would have read it. We had to do it in school too."

I smiled reassuringly. "Why did you want to share this with me?"

"It's always struck me as a story about the importance of human connection and life." He shrugged, meeting my gaze despite the vulnerable edge in his voice. "With my dad, it taught me to appreciate kindness and look for the truth in the actions of those around me."

"So, it was important to you growing up."

He nodded, relaxing before my eyes. "Exactly. I just had

this urge to share it with you. I don't know why." His hands slipped into his pockets and he rocked back on his heels. I grinned, drawing an answering smile from him. "What?"

"I've never seen you so nervous, Shaun."

He fixed his green gaze on me, unwavering. "I don't want to wear a perfect veneer with you."

Warmth spread through my chest as his words sank in. I wasn't sure if he understood just how much he was baring himself to me. Did everyone else get the polished version of him, cheerfully flat? He'd never been like that with me. Had he made the choice to show me the real him from the start? I'd underestimated him for so long. There were so many unexpected dimensions to this man; I was constantly unearthing new facets. Was that part of the reason he fascinated me, maybe?

I reached for his hand, squeezing as tears burned my eyes. "Thank you."

"You're thanking me for being me? That's a first." He chuckled, but it sounded half-hearted.

"For trusting me enough to be yourself. It means a lot, considering our start."

He grinned. "Well, I did put you through the ringer. How else was I meant to be sure you'd stick around?"

I slapped his arm weakly. "You joke now. What if Sherry had let me quit weeks ago?"

"I'd have convinced you to stay," he said, and from the intense gleam in his eyes, I believed him.

We said our goodbyes and he left me, slightly shaken in the deserted corridor between offices and cast trailers. Something had shifted. I didn't fully understand it, but I couldn't ignore the fact I was staring after him, on the verge of calling him back so I could hug him or kiss him or something.

"So, there's something going on with you and Shaun," Alys said behind me, dragging my attention from Shaun's retreating figure.

I felt the colour drain from my face. I knew it was only a matter of time before other people caught on, and Shaun wasn't helping. Neither was I, staring after him longingly where anyone could see.

"Of course not."

Alys tilted her head, her eyes telling me she wasn't convinced. Still, her smile was kind as she said, "I get why you don't want to tell me, but if you ever need to talk to someone and you need a sounding board, I'm here. Your secrets are safe with me."

Her intent hadn't been to shock, but it surprised me all the same. I didn't think people would be understanding. The genuine look on her face made me wonder if I was wrong. And if I was wrong and no one on the crew would care or bat an eyelid, was I wasting time holding Shaun at a distance?

CHAPTER TWENTY-FIVE

SHAUN

Wat are U doing?

MONA

Just reading. Are you okay?

Seconds stretched into minutes while I waited for Shaun's reply, unease growing.

MONA

Shaun?

SHAUN

Can U come over?

I sat up, alarmed. The book I'd been devouring fell to the duvet, forgotten.

MONA

Yes, but are you okay?

SHAUN

Feel weird.

MONA

What does that mean?

SHAUN

Just come over.

SHAUN

Please?

I ordered a taxi and rushed out the door, not bothering to change out of my yoga leggings. He'd barely said anything in his messages, but my stomach turned itself inside out all the same. And it wasn't because of the one glass of wine I'd had.

The taxi pulled onto the road and I chewed my lip. Was this his way of telling me he was on the edge? It was a Sunday, there was no filming and he'd been fine when he'd stopped by the production office to say good night yesterday. If he was struggling, it had nothing to do with work.

Dropped me off outside his building, I rushed through the lobby, waving to the receptionist, who thankfully recognised me. He called the lift for the penthouse from his desk, and I raced towards it.

As I tapped my foot, impatiently waiting for the doors to close, thoughts of Shaun sped through my mind. *What is the problem?*

I arrived to find his door off the lock. I pushed it open, hesitant to just invite myself in.

"Shaun?"

"Come in, Mona," he called back from somewhere out of sight.

I found him scowling at a bottle of whisky on his dining room table. He sat in a chair in front of it, a battle raging across his face.

"Where did that come from?"

Shaun scrubbed a hand over his cheek, his jaw tensing.

"Where did it come from?" I repeated with a harder edge.

"I don't know. It was waiting for me in reception," he said, his voice strained.

"Was there a note?" I snatched it off the table, but he caught my wrist before I could take it away. He continued staring at the bottle with painful indecision in his eyes. "You don't want this, Shaun. You're doing a lot better on your own."

He nodded, but his gaze didn't shift. I unwrapped his fingers from my wrist gently, never taking my eyes from his. When I stepped away, he covered his face and rested his elbows on the table, hanging his head.

I poured the entire bottle down the drain. Next, I fired off a quick text to Sherry with a request for her to handle the producers. *Who else would deliver expensive whisky to Shaun?*

Easing into a chair, I took his hand, pulling it away from his face. His grip tightened, clinging to me. Guilt sat heavy on my tongue. Even though he hadn't wanted anyone to know he was suffering from an addiction, I could have found a way to tell the producers, could have dropped hints for them to keep the alcohol away.

"I shouldn't have quit."

Shaun's head snapped up, his tortured eyes widening.

"This isn't your fault."

I shook my head, averting my eyes. "If I'd stayed, that wouldn't have happened. You wouldn't have had to text me, pleading for me to come over. It just flat out wouldn't have gotten this far."

He squeezed my hand, tugging until I glanced at him. There wasn't an ounce of blame on his face. That didn't mean I wasn't wrong.

"If you hadn't quit, we'd both still be struggling to keep our hands to ourselves. You are not to blame for my lack of self-control."

My eyes dropped to the table where the bottle had sat, the seal intact.

"If that wasn't the perfect example, I don't want to know what you class as self-control," I muttered, meeting his gaze again, my admiration plain to see. "You didn't open the bottle. You didn't have a drink. Yes, you may have thought about it, but you didn't. You texted me instead." He stared at me, his uncertainty plain to see. "It could have gone so many other ways, but you chose not to go there. That took some serious strength, Shaun."

The realisation slowly sank in, and the tension faded from his features as he started to believe me.

"Thank you for coming."

"I said we'd still be friends. Of course I came."

I'd always known it was possible he'd fall. Assistant, friend, lover. No matter what word he used, I wouldn't have done anything else.

He rubbed at his face before focusing wholly on me with an apologetic smile. "I'm sorry I interrupted your weekend. Was it a good book, at least?"

My lips curled, recalling the scene I'd been in the middle of reading. The guy had just realised his sweet co-worker was pranking him. "Pretty good, yeah."

"I'll let you get back to it." He released my fingers, pulling his hand back.

I studied him, searching for cracks. There had to be one I couldn't see if he'd been tempted by that bottle.

"I'm pretty hungry. Want to order in some food and watch TV?" I asked, mentally crossing my fingers that he'd agree.

His smile crept over his lips, but when it blossomed, oh boy. Maybe I should have gone home. It screamed "let me eat you instead" and honestly after that book, I was already on edge.

I mentally shook myself. Biting hard on my cheek, I pushed any such thoughts out of my head and focused on the elephant in the room instead. What was pushing Shaun to the bottle?

We ordered food and settled down on his far-too-pristine sofa. Honestly, the fact we were eating Indian food on it gave me anxiety. An action film droned on in the background. Shaun did a quick scroll through the channels and picked it when I had nothing good or bad to say about the choice.

"Why do you have a white sofa? It's so impractical."

Shaun's lips twitched, his eyes shining with mirth. "You've given this a lot of thought, haven't you?"

I pressed mine together, sinking deeper into the sofa. "Maybe."

"I didn't choose it. I just let some designer redo the place after Lily dumped me." He swallowed, his gaze flicking to the TV and staying there. "I didn't want anything left behind to remind me of her."

"Do you still feel like that?" I asked, straightening.

His focus snapped back to me. "Of course not. They're just things. She'd done all the decorating when I first bought the place, and it always looked too feminine to me." He bit his lips, considering how far he wanted to go, no doubt. "Redecorating helped close the book on her a little as well."

I nodded. "Erased the ghost."

"Exactly. It helped stop me expecting her to walk through the door at any moment."

"I did the same thing with my ex. For a different reason, but the goal was still the same: exorcise them from your space."

He seemed fine now. He'd settled into idle chatter so easily, the average person would have a job figuring out there was something wrong. But there was definitely something wrong. Despite his relaxed exterior, lines creased around his eyes from tension and his smile dimmed. He wasn't fully here.

"But she still affects you?" I asked.

"Not in the romantic, pining sense."

"But in the 'this is what my life should be' sense?"

He eyed me. "Maybe."

"Did you see or read something about her today?"

He glanced away, and I contained my internal screams of "ah-ha" like a pro.

"You know you can't compare the story told by the tabloids or even her social media to your reality, right?"

He nodded, refusing to meet my patient gaze.

"Good, because you're presenting perfect to the world too. So you know better than anyone that perfect on social media doesn't mean things are perfect for Lily either."

Surprised eyes clashed with mine. His expression softened, turning thoughtful as my words sank in. "I hadn't thought of it like that."

"So let me ask again… did you see something that pushed you the wrong way?"

He nodded.

Progress. If I could get him to admit it, maybe it wouldn't hurt him the next time. "What was it?"

"Her band won a Grammy," he said quietly.

"That's huge."

"I know. For a second, I was proud of her, and then I remembered I had no business feeling that way."

I frowned. "Why not?"

He shrugged. "She's not mine anymore?"

"But you were friends once, weren't you?" I waited for his confirmation, ploughing ahead when he gave it. "And you grew up together, started your careers together. At one point, you both loved each other. Just because you don't anymore doesn't mean that you have to throw out all the good moments and stop being proud of the people who meant something to you."

Only I had. They were all lies, so holding onto them would have been pointless. I didn't like the person I'd spent four years with. But I didn't think that was the case for Shaun; otherwise, why would he propose?

For the first time since I set foot in his flat, he smiled properly. It lit up his eyes and eased the tension overshadowing him. He put his food down on the coffee table and reached for my hand, pulling me towards him. I held my takeaway box out before it painted the white sofa yellow.

His arms wrapped around me, his head rested on the top of mine and he hugged me. It felt so right that I had to close my eyes to get a grip. *He's just grateful. No need to get all mushy on the man.*

"I think I needed to hear that," he whispered into my hair. "I've spent the last year hating myself for not being able to forget how important she was in making me who I am. At times I thought the press were right – I was failing to move on – but you've helped me see it differently."

I pushed off his chest and placed the takeaway box on the table. Settling back into his arms, I was hyper aware of his fingers toying with the edge of my t-shirt.

"You make it sound like you're living in her shadow."

He groaned. "Come on, Mona. You know that's not what I meant."

"How do I know that?" I asked, shifting so that I could see his face. "You don't talk about it."

He tilted his head, conceding that I was right.

"I'm just grateful for the way my life turned out, and I'm man enough to admit that I couldn't have done it without help." His eyes fixed on me, unwavering as he said, "And I've been ready to move on with the next chapter of my life for a while. I just didn't know what it was."

"And you do now?"

"Can we stop with the twenty questions, please?"

"I'm just trying to make sure you're okay," I said, my voice sounding shriller than I'd like.

"I am."

"Okay, but—"

His mouth covered mine, cutting me off. For a second, I stiffened against him, hyper aware that we'd agreed to wait, but then his tongue flicked against mine and I was lost. My hand smoothed up his chest, grasping onto his shirt as he worked his lips across mine.

Within moments, pressure started to build between my legs and I needed more. More of what, I didn't know, but *more*. I shifted until my breasts plastered to his chest, trying to get closer. But that wasn't good enough for him. He placed his hands on my hips and tugged me into his lap until I straddled him. I groaned at the feel of his hard-on pressing against my core. With little thought, I rubbed back and forth, driving us both crazy with nothing but my thin yoga leggings and his joggers between us.

So much for waiting.

I broke the kiss, panting for air. His lips were red from my kisses, his hair stood on end and his eyes were at half-mast. *I did that. I put that dazed look on his face.*

"I don't think I can wait until the production wraps," I whispered.

He smiled, but the cautious edge remained. He brushed a featherlight kiss over my lips.

"What about our employment issues?" Shaun whispered. He sucked my bottom lip into his mouth, distracting me.

"I'm not your assistant anymore."

"And plenty of people work with their partners." He trailed kisses along my jaw.

"Exactly," I sighed against him, latching onto that tidbit with both hands.

"And the press issue?"

I groaned. "Shaun, stop stalling."

He chuckled, the vibrations delicious against my skin. "I just want to make sure you're in."

"We'll be careful," I said, breathless. "Keep it quiet."

He smiled, reaching for another kiss, and I leaned into him without hesitation. My tongue danced with his, tangling in a long kiss that clouded out all other thoughts.

Shaun pulled back to consider me. "So, we're fuck buddies until we say otherwise?"

"Until we say otherwise, but we keep it between us. The crew can't know." I searched his eyes, desperate for him to agree without argument so we could get to the good stuff.

He nodded. "Fine, but not just sex. We're friends. I get to see you regularly out of hours?"

"I'd like that." We smiled at each other like a pair of fools.

"And you won't shout at me if I turn up at your door at six AM on a down day?"

I almost nodded. The bugger was trying to take advantage of my dazed state. "Not a chance. Find another running buddy."

"But my current one looks incredible in leggings." He pouted like I'd stolen his favourite toy. After a hard stare, he buckled. "Alright. No more early morning running dates.

He captured my mouth again, but rather than the frantic mashing of our lips like our first kiss, this one was slow, measured. His hands worked their way under my t-shirt and around to my bra. My nipples peaked with the first pass of his fingers across the thin fabric, and I moaned.

My t-shirt came off and his followed. When we'd had sex in the trailer, it had been hot and fast. I didn't get a chance to just revel in him. Now, my fingers danced across his chest, tracing every line.

He dusted kisses down my neck and across my shoulders. My bra fell away and his fingers circled my nipples. Groaning,

I started grinding on him again, and then he was the one unable to keep his noises to himself.

"I need you out of these fucking leggings now," he growled, his fingers dropping to my waistband.

I caught his hands before he could tug them down. "We are not having sex on this sofa."

"Mona." His head fell back and a pained look crossed his face.

"No."

"Fine," he muttered.

In a rush, he stood, and I squeaked, wrapping my legs and arms around him before he dropped me. He chuckled, shaking me as he made his way through the flat and up the stairs.

Placing me on the bed, he hooked his fingers into my leggings and underwear, dragged them down my legs and threw them across the room. He raked his gaze down my naked body.

"Fuck, you're beautiful," he said, his eyes smouldering as he took me in. "I was a bit distracted to tell you last time."

I let my eyes roam his bare torso, coming to rest pointedly on his joggers. "Fair's fair."

Grinning, he tore his trousers off but kept his black boxers in place as he advanced on me. My eyes lit with pleasure, wandering his toned thighs, the ridges of his abs. All of it testament to the hours he'd spent dodging his opponents on the tips of his toes.

"Uh, that's not my idea of fair." I held him off with an outstretched hand. "Boxers on the floor. Now."

"You're a hard woman to please." He said it like he'd relish the challenge, and I just about melted into the bed.

He climbed onto the duvet, straddling me. His fingers immediately reached for my skin, caressing up my sides, making me shiver. I reached for him, desperate for another kiss. Shifting until he lay next to me, his fingers continued to explore the hollows of my body until I squirmed against him.

He captured a nipple between his teeth as his talented fingers delved into me, curling and pressing softly against a bundle of nerves I'd never felt before. My eyes rolled back as he concentrated solely on that spot. He sucked hard on my nipple, the contrast making me moan.

"Please, Shaun."

"Please what?" he asked, raising his head with a lazy smile.

"Let me come."

Grinning, he slid down the bed, feathering kisses as he went. I jumped when his tongue flicked my clit, adding to the flood of sensations coursing through me. I came fast and hard, crying his name.

CHAPTER TWENTY-SIX

Glaring sunlight woke me early the next morning. I squinted at the strange bedroom with its wall of uncovered windows. Who wanted to torture themselves like that every morning? The fog cleared and a smile curved my lips as the memory of last night resurfaced in glorious technicolour.

I didn't want to look at the time. I just needed to enjoy the peace and quiet in our own world for a little longer. We were due on set at 8AM, and with the sun rising, we probably didn't have long.

Giddy with happiness, I rolled over to find Shaun's side of the bed empty, the sheets cold to the touch. Frowning, I sat up, holding the duvet to my naked chest, self-conscious in the cold light of day.

"Shaun?" My voice echoed in the big room.

The bedroom door stood open and our clothes lay scattered across the floor. The flat was eerily silent. There wasn't even a ticking clock to break it.

Scrambling from the bed, I grabbed my leggings and tugged them on, then padded on silent feet into the bathroom. Empty. *Maybe he's downstairs.* I headed to the main level and the kitchen, collecting the rest of my clothes while the time glared back at me in block blue numbers above the oven. It was well past 8AM. I'd slept late and Shaun had left me.

My phone sat on the counter with a sheet of white paper wedged beneath it.

Meet me on set. Shaun, it read in surprisingly crisp handwriting. I don't know why I'd expected him to write in pidgin scratch.

I frowned at the brief message. No kisses. His texts had been more expressive than this. I couldn't read his mood from those five words.

Oh god, what if he's changed his mind and decided the sex wasn't good enough so we should be friends and nothing more? I wasn't a professional at masking my feelings, unlike him. If we entered the "only friends zone", I wouldn't have to deal with him as much, but I'd still run into him.

One week on the production team and I was going to be late. *What a way to prove my worth!* I fired off a quick text to Alys, thankful that we'd finally started to shift into later call times.

In a mad dash, I showered, dressed and hot-footed it out of Shaun's lush penthouse, taking extra care to avoid looking at the rumpled bed. I needed my head in the game, not flashes of last night blindsiding me.

Exiting the building, I took a deep breath and forced my shoulders to relax. I could handle any shit he threw at me.

"Ms Baines," a familiar voice called, haunting my determined stride towards the nearest bus stop.

Except that.

I spun to find Tom leaning against his SUV with a borderline gleeful smirk on his lips. Well, the cat was out of the bag. Chances of Tom keeping his mouth shut were slim. He'd been my only source of set gossip for the last month.

"Tom, what are you doing here?" I asked, my voice squeaking from surprise and disuse.

"Mr Martin sent me to fetch you. I'm to take you to your

flat and then to the set." The delight shone in his eyes as he spoke. He might as well have been rubbing his hands together. It would have been less obvious.

I nodded, forced a polite smile to my lips and got in the car. Tom spent most of the drive watching me through the rearview mirror. It's a wonder we arrived in one piece.

"There you are," Shaun shouted as I stepped into the costume trailer. His cheerful tone raised my eyebrows, but his eyes stayed focused on the wardrobe mistress working at his feet. I'd met the woman three times now but still couldn't recall her name.

"Feeling better?" he asked, as if he hadn't stripped my clothes off last night.

I stopped in the doorway, my bullshit radar at the ready.

The wardrobe mistress continued placing pins in the pair of trousers he wore. She muttered to herself every couple of seconds.

"Yes?" I said, my voice tripping over the word while my brain tried to dissect every aspect of his appearance. What did that even mean?

"You don't remember slapping me this morning?" he guessed, meeting my confused gaze. Amusement shone in his eyes and my guard slipped a few inches. "I was trying to wake you up to get ready for work, but you mumbled something and when I tried to take the covers, you slapped me. It stung." He laughed, touching his face like he could still feel the burn.

My eyes widened, flicking between him and the wardrobe mistress, who had frozen with a pin hanging from her slender fingers. First Tom and now her. If Shaun was trying to broadcast the very new shift in our relationship to the world, he'd gotten off to a great start. Thankfully, I'd seen Tilly on her way to set. I tried to communicate with my eyes that he should shut up, but I guess Shaun felt chatty.

"What do you think of this suit? It's for the charity dinner you're making me attend."

"It looks great, and I'm not making you do anything. You committed yourself to that event."

He nodded. "And it's a very good thing you agreed to go with me. It's black tie. Moira here will find me a bow tie to match your dress."

Moira didn't move an inch. Her eyes were fixed on Shaun's leg, and if I were him, I'd be worried his wardrobe mistress might stab him in the thigh. *Why is she so still?*

His easy smile fell as the silence stretched, and his eyes hardened as he assessed me. "Did you change your mind?"

"Maybe we should talk when you're done," I suggested, shuffling towards the door.

"No, we're discussing it now. Have you decided that last night was a mistake?"

"Shaun, we have company."

"I don't care." He took a step forwards, wincing when a pin caught him. "Did you?"

"Did you?" I countered, my voice rising. He didn't care if the entire set found out? We were supposed to keep the fact we were fuck buddies low-key until we wrapped.

"Of course not!"

"Well, your oh-so-brief note didn't tell me that," I snapped. The rise in volume seemed to snap Moira out of her haze. She sat back on her heels, her intrigued eyes finding mine. Oh yeah, we didn't have a hope in hell of keeping this a secret.

Understanding flickered across his face and he smiled at Moira with the dazzling grin known to cut women off at the knees all over the world. I had to give it to Shaun; he knew how to command attention.

"Moira, love. Would you give us the room, please?"

"Of course, Mr Martin," she mumbled. After tucking the loose pin into his trousers, she left us without so much as a backwards glance.

When the door closed, Shaun crossed his arms and considered me. He raised a brow and waited.

"I don't know why you're giving me that look," I muttered, mirroring his stern stance, more to maintain some level of self-control than to be indifferent. "You're the one that snuck out, left an emotionless note and then told the biggest gossip on the crew where to find me."

Did I mention that he was shirtless? Yes, that was a problem since my heart was telling me to jump him.

"Tom wouldn't tell anyone."

I laughed. "Get your head out of your ass. It's not a hat! Tom is the source of all crew gossip. And Moira." I pointed towards the door. "That woman had money signs in her eyes. She's on the phone to some tabloid paper as we speak."

He chuckled, approaching me at an offensive pace. He made me feel like a wild animal, ready to attack or run away. Maybe I was offended because he wasn't far off the mark. I was not ready for paparazzi clamouring outside my front door for unflattering pictures.

"She's not selling our secrets, and Tom won't tell anyone," Shaun assured me, a gentle smile curving his lips. He rubbed his hands up and down my bare arms, soothing me despite my resistance to being soothed.

"How can you be so certain?"

"They signed NDAs before they started. If they tell a soul anything about my private life, I'll sue them." His tone was deadly serious, and honestly, for a second, I was a little afraid. Shaun Martin could be a piranha when he wanted. Who knew!

"It'll be fine. No one will know unless we're obvious or we tell them."

"So, you still want to do this?"

Shaun smirked, and the heat in his eyes made my pulse accelerate. He fitted me against his chest, tilted my head back and stroked his talented fingers along my lips. The proximity was enough to rekindle the fire he'd built last night.

"You need to tell Tilly you're not moving in with her."

I frowned at the unexpected twist to our conversation. "Why?"

"How would you explain me in your bed and shower? Or your constant absence?"

My eyes widened with the realisation at the same time disappointment filled me. I'd been looking forward to having a nice flatmate for a change. But I couldn't argue with his logic.

"We could just tell her."

He quirked a brow. "You just freaked out because you thought I was running my mouth in front of witnesses and you want to add another?"

"She could sign an NDA too. A production secretary doesn't make as much as your assistant. I can't afford to squander money on a studio flat just so you can have all the booty calls you want."

Shaun groaned. "Why did you have to quit again?" I opened my mouth to answer, but he cut me off. "It was rhetorical. I understand why."

"So, we'll tell her?" A smile tugged at my lips for the first time since I'd woken up.

He nodded. "I'll get the paperwork sorted."

Then his head descended and his lips reached for mine. I leant away, and he groaned again. "What now?"

"What about Sherry?"

"What about my agent?" He frowned.

"She's going to figure it out."

"So let her. There's no HR issue here. You don't work for me; you work for the production. We're now co-workers, and the last I checked, there was absolutely no rule against co-workers fucking." His thumb smoothed across my lower lip as though that would calm me down instantly. It almost did. "And if she tries to say otherwise, I'll point out that half the AD team are currently involved with the art department."

My eyes widened. "Are they?"

I'd spent hours in that production office. Cassie hadn't breathed a word.

He shrugged, chuckling at my expression. "Hell if I know, but she definitely wouldn't have a clue."

I relaxed into him, satisfied that other than my face getting plastered across the tabloids and gossip blogs, he no longer posed a threat to my career.

"We're in this until we say otherwise," he whispered, his voice husky with desire.

"And if I say 'otherwise'?"

"Then I'll make it my job to convince you to stay."

With that heart-stopping statement, he caressed his lips against mine and I sank into him. Focusing on the soft and hard dance of our mouths was much more fun than worrying about the world outside, anyway.

CHAPTER TWENTY-SEVEN

Shaun laid off his production office visits for the next week and I'd never tell him this, but I missed his excuses to see me. I had still planned to move in with Tilly at the end of the week, yet the most I'd done at my flat was change my clothes – no packing whatsoever. It would all have to wait until tomorrow now. The crew had embraced me anew, inviting me to their weekly Saturday night out on the town.

I'd seen a lot of Shaun in the last week. It felt like we were making up for lost time in bed. I kind of hoped he'd wanted to do something else with our day off. Could I even say that to him? We were meant to be all about the sex, and I defi-nitely loved that part, but I couldn't stop myself from wanting more. Maybe this was why I'd never tried casual sex before. It was an emotional minefield that I didn't know how to navigate.

SHAUN

Wat crew thing?

MONA

The guys get together at Jackson's every Saturday to celebrate surviving the week.

SHAUN

Cute.

SHAUN

So I won't C U 2nite? :(

MONA

I need to pack my stuff too. Moving to Tilly's tomorrow morning.

SHAUN

K :(Have fun.

No Sunday plans? What the hell, Shaun?

I started to demand a plan but then thought better and deleted it. This was meant to be casual. Demanding plans to hang out did not equal casual. *Chill the fuck out.*

I placed my phone on the table and turned it over. For the rest of the day, I focused on my job and not the fact that I might actually want more from Shaun. It was just all the sex confusing me. I probably didn't want a relationship with him, and a day apart would help me see that.

"So, Mona, are you going back to Scotland after wrap?" Aidan asked.

We had crowded into a large booth at the back of Jackson's. The place was heaving, but Brian knew the owner and scored us access to a roped-off section he'd dubbed "the VIP section". Really, it was just a platform that lined the side of the room with black leather booths – nothing anywhere near as fancy as "VIP" made it sound. But we were separate from the crowded main floor and afforded a pretty nice view of the band on stage.

"Probably." I shrugged. "My sister lives in Glasgow."

"Sweet. Do you have your next gig lined up? Scotland's almost as busy as the South West."

I shook my head. "I've not thought that far ahead yet. Just trying to confirm I like the job."

He pulled a sympathetic face. "I get you. The hours make it pretty hard to have a life, and on a Scotland-based production, I can imagine you'd find yourself all over the country."

"If you know that, why do you keep coming back?" I asked. The job exhilarated me at times, but mostly I was exhausted – and I'd only been doing this for a few weeks, not years like some of these people had.

"You get used to it," Tilly said. She sat on my other side nursing a bottle of beer, her eyes watching the band on stage. It was a rather subdued sight compared to the gig I went to with her, but then, her favourite band wasn't on tonight's line-up.

"Plus, don't you feel the rush of making something all your friends and family will be raving about in a year's time?" Aidan grinned, his eyes shining with glee. "I get so many questions for spoilers at behind-the-scenes stuff, and I get to be the asshole that smiles and says nothing. I freaking love it."

The entire table laughed.

"No, Aid, you're just an asshole plain as," Brian called across the table, his eyes smiling. Then his focus shifted to me. "I've been doing this for more than twenty years now." He pointed at Aidan. "Make one crack about my age, I dare you."

Aidan pressed his lips together, barely containing a grin.

"Some days are harder than others," Brian went on, "but it gets into your blood. I couldn't imagine doing anything else with my life. Yeah, some parts of the job are pretty fucking serious, but how many jobs do you know pick up the bar tab and let you see some beautiful parts of the world?"

I shook my head. *Certainly not my old job, that's for sure.* However, I didn't have enough experience in the entertainment industry to know if the answer was none.

"It used to be most of them, but times are changing. Budgets are tightening. But even if they stopped paying for the drinks tomorrow, I'd still do it." Brian tapped the table, his face serious in the way of someone who'd had three drinks and would probably sway when he stood up. "The experiences fuel me through the painful call times and the slow days."

"Plus, how many hours would we have to work at a desk to get paid half of what we do to dick about on set?" Aidan asked to a chorus of "I don't want to fucking knows". "A lot. My brother's a teacher, and I compared his hourly to mine. He deals with screaming kids every day, works overtime to get his classroom prepped and he makes half what I do in a day."

Cassie shook her head. "That's no comparison. He's not being paid for the extra hours. You are." Her clear gaze caught mine. "Don't listen to his comparison bullshit. He doesn't know what he's talking about. He gets overtime; you don't. Ask Alys about it if you need to, but for some backwards reason, production don't get paid for the extra hours," she said, her annoyance clear. "Here's my advice: Never underestimate your worth and always push for more than they're offering, because by the time the production wraps, you'll have racked up unpaid overtime in the double digits."

"Aw, come on, Cass. You're going to scare her off," Aidan shouted, slamming his beer on the table.

"Somebody should warn her," Cassie said, frowning at Aidan. "It's not all sunshine and fooling around. This job is hard, the hours do suck and the pay for production is even worse. She needs to know what she's getting herself into, and if she decides then that she likes the rush it gives the rest of you enough to put up with your shit, then fine."

I blinked at the force behind her words.

"Well, that definitely went places I wasn't expecting." My laugh was uneasy as Cassie and Aidan glared at each other. My eyes dropped to my empty bottle. "Can you guys let me out? I'm gonna grab another drink."

I didn't really want another, but escaping the uncomfortable atmosphere that had descended over the table became a definite must. It felt like they were about to come to blows, and I didn't want to see that. Still, the crazed look in Aidan's eyes had been pretty funny.

"Can I buy you a drink?" A familiar voice asked as I cleared the rope.

I smirked as I took in Shaun's sheepish smile. I hadn't heard from him after his final text this afternoon. We hadn't been messaging that much in the last week so I had no reason to think it odd. But judging by the amusement gleaming in his eyes, I was wrong not to question it.

"Well, this is actually a nice surprise." I smiled.

I itched to fling myself into his arms and kiss him, but my gaze flickered to the oblivious group I'd left in the booth. They sat far too close for someone not to notice. I could still hear Aidan ploughing on with the heated discussion.

Shaun's eyes narrowed. "Do you mean that, or are you being nice?"

I'd forgotten I'd told him I didn't like surprises. Our rocky start felt like a lifetime ago.

"I mean it." I tilted my head towards the bar. "But let's get drinks before they stop arguing and notice you."

Shaun glanced over at them. "What are they arguing about?"

"Whether I should work in TV after this show."

His focus snapped back to me. "Are you considering not?"

I shrugged. "Too soon to tell."

For a couple minutes, I enjoyed being pressed to his chest as he forced his way through the crowd to the bar, his hands firm on my hips, holding me to him. We ordered, and his hands slid from my hips to wrap fully around me.

Taking advantage of the crowd, he trailed kisses down my neck until I shivered.

"Are you sure you want to hang out with the crew?" I asked, my voice breathy.

He smirked against my neck. "Thought you were tired of being cooped up in my bed?"

I spun around to face him. I hadn't said anything to him. How did he know?

"You're pretty easy to read, Sparky. When I invited you over the other night, your face fell." He shrugged, his gaze moving over the bar and tracking the bartender's progress. "Thought a night out might help, even if I can't touch you like I want to in front of the crew."

"Just so we're clear: I'm not against ending the night in bed."

"That's good, because I have every intention of taking you home tonight."

The fact he'd noticed and had come here was huge. And confusing. Was he here as a friend, or was he trying to tell me he might want more too?

I considered myself a brave person, but I wasn't ready for the answer to that question. If he said friend, then the disappointment would hurt. And if he said yes?

I couldn't think about that now.

The bartender delivered our drinks and we weaved back through the crowd to the booth. Aidan spotted Shaun first. His eyes widened, and silence fell around the table as heads turned to locate the source of his shock. Mouths dropped.

I guess this was the first time Shaun had graced them with

his presence off the set. I chuckled at their uncharacteristic silence.

"Come on, guys. It's just Shaun," I said.

That broke the spell. They started shifting out of the booth to let me back in.

"Just shuffle in. I'm good on the edge."

They did as instructed and slid down the seat until there was space for both me and Shaun on the edge. I sat wedged between Shaun and Cassie. He had to rest his arm on the back of the booth to comfortably face everyone. Whether it was a ploy on Shaun's part to lean close to me, I don't know, but I enjoyed it all the same.

Silence stretched around the table until it tipped the scale into awkward. None of them knew what to say with their star sharing the table, which was just odd considering the things they'd said before.

Leanne grinned as she took in their serious, sullen faces. "I should take a picture of this moment. It'll be the only time you're sitting still and quiet."

Brian snorted. "If we could replicate this on set, we'd get a heck of a lot more done in a day."

Everyone laughed, while Aidan scowled. "I know that was a dig at me," he muttered.

"Was it?" Brian asked, his face a mask of innocence. He turned to Shaun before Aidan could respond. "It's nice to see you off the set, man. How's it going?"

"Little more disorganised now that you lot have stolen my assistant, but things are looking up." He nudged me with his leg. *As if I could miss the meaning behind that comment.*

Brian's gaze flicked to me. It was brief, but I noticed. I sank back into the seat. *He suspects something.* Other than surprise, I didn't feel all that much about it. When had I stopped caring if people figured us out? A week ago, it terrified me. Maybe it was nothing more than the endorphins from a week of great sex messing with my head.

I really needed to talk to Isla. If my perspective had shifted, she could help me figure it out.

"We haven't noticed on set. Bonuses of being a professional actor, hey?" Brian asked, raising his glass to toast Shaun.

Shaun chuckled. "It definitely comes in handy sometimes."

The lights shifted and guitar riffs echoed through the room. The crowd hushed, and everyone's focus shifted to the band on stage.

"Well, don't you all look lovely tonight," the lead singer of Lover's Knot shouted, smirking as the crowd screamed.

Tilly gasped. So much for them not playing. She didn't bother asking anyone to move. She stood up on her seat, scrambling over the table. Everyone grabbed their drinks before she could knock them over.

"Geez, Tilly, men don't like it when you're that eager," Aidan shouted after her, his voice carrying across the crowd.

Tilly, to her credit, didn't turn around. She held up her middle finger and ploughed into the crowd.

The singer didn't so much as pause, taking it all in his stride.

"That was a pretty shitty thing to do to a stranger, but your colleague? Geez, man. Don't take lessons from me," Shaun muttered, his voice cutting.

Aidan's face reddened. At least he had the good sense to shut his mouth and stew in his shame.

"I'm so surprised you got on with them," I said when we were locked in his flat a few hours later. The clock on his oven said it was after midnight. *No wonder my stomach is trying to eat itself.* "Do you have any food here?"

I was sat on the island counter, watching Shaun pour us waters.

"Are you hungry?" he asked, glancing over his shoulder with more than a little bit of lust darkening his eyes.

"For food."

Shaun nodded, a devious look taking over his features.

"I've got potato waffles, I think. I've been on set so much I haven't been shopping, and I don't have an assistant to stock the fridge." He shot me an amused look.

"Blaming me for your inability to feed me," I muttered, shaking my head. "And I thought you wanted to get laid."

He rushed me then, pushing my legs apart and sliding me closer to the edge of the counter until I was flush against his rock-hard body. I shivered as his hands slid featherlight up my back and arms, leaving tingles in their wake. In a movement as graceful as his dance moves, he lowered his head and began tracing kisses from my jaw to the edge of my lips. The counter lined us up perfectly, the bulge in his jeans pressing into me. I couldn't help the moan that left my mouth when he rubbed himself against me.

"Still thinking about withholding sex?" he whispered against my cheek.

I growled. "Gimme the potato waffles."

Chuckling, he pulled back and set to work feeding me. When my stomach had stopped grumbling, he took the plate and returned to his previous position.

"Need something?" I asked, smirking at him.

"Hmm."

His fingers wandered over my thighs, catching the edge of my dress and pushing it up until it bunched at my waist. With one hand, he pulled me to the edge of the counter again while the other dipped to the top of my underwear, toying with the lace, teasing me.

He watched me through hooded eyes while I bit my lip against the need to beg him to touch me properly. Instead, I threaded my hands in his hair and kissed him, hard. He groaned, the sound vibrating in my mouth as he tilted his head to deepen the connection.

Pushing the fabric aside, he slid two fingers into me. My hips jolted, his hand on my other thigh the only reason I didn't fall off the counter. He pushed, in and out, until all I could do was press my forehead to his shoulder and hold on for dear life as sensation folded me. He stared back at me, his gaze fiery with promise and his lips curled with the knowledge that he could do this to me.

"Lean back on your elbows," he urged, his voice thick as he removed his fingers.

I welcomed the feel of the cold marble against the heated skin of my forearms. It momentarily distracted me from watching Shaun. He dipped his head, his tongue flicking against my already sensitised flesh. My hips automatically shifted, chasing for more.

Chuckling, he held me down again, continuing to lick and tease me until holding myself up became too much. I lay back against the counter and shut my eyes, lost to the rub of his tongue lapping at me.

Soon pressure started to surge, and I gripped the edge of the counter. He added his fingers to the mix and I gave in, falling over the edge. His name echoed around the big space as I came back to myself.

"I'm never going to get tired of that," he said, his voice hoarse. He was grinning with pleasure when he pulled me up.

Me either.

Without another word, he carried me to his bed, stripped us down and continued to fuck me into the early hours of the morning. Only somewhere along the line, it stopped feeling like fucking to me. His tender touches spoke louder than that one word.

I shut my brain off and I enjoyed every single moment.

CHAPTER TWENTY-EIGHT

"Y ou have a thing about leaving me hanging, sis. I was expecting an update weeks ago," Isla said, her tone teasing but her words sparking guilt.

I used to call and text her almost daily before the move. Only, once I got here, I'd been so busy with everything that finding a quiet moment had proven difficult.

Shaun still lay in bed as the sun just crested the sky, and I'd barely slept. I couldn't shut my mind off. It was too busy trying to pinpoint when things had shifted in my head. I was getting nowhere on my own, which is why I now sat curled up on Shaun's sofa talking to my sister.

"Sorry. Time's just gotten away from me." I glanced at the rising sun, the reflection refracting off the water and surrounding glass. "I didn't wake you, did I?"

She'd always been an early riser, but I should have thought.

"No, you're good. I was just about to head out for a run," she said, her voice soft. I could imagine her tiptoeing around her flat to avoid waking the neighbours. "Put the phone on video chat. I need to see your face."

I did as told, trying for a smile to ease the tiredness. Isla frowned.

"Mona, what are you doing up? You look exhausted." Concern filled her expression and a wave of homesickness hit me.

Nothing was wrong, really. I had the man – for now. I enjoyed my job. Soon I would wave goodbye to my awful flat-mates. Things were exciting for once.

Yet seeing my sister made me want a hug.

"I've just got some things on my mind," I said, frowning as I tried to figure out where to start.

"Man things?" Isla's eyebrows rose. "As in Shaun things?" At my nod, she grinned. "How's the sex?"

"Isla."

"What? This is big news." She laughed at my pained expression. "I couldn't understand why you quit when Sherry called me, but now it makes so much sense. Well done, sis."

I chuckled at that. I hadn't quit to sleep with Shaun. I'd quit to escape him. Even so, the fact she felt proud of me for having sex seemed pretty ridiculous but so like Isla. It made me miss her more.

"So, you got the guy and you've found another job I assume?" She tilted her head in question and I nodded. "So, what's eating you?"

"You remember you said that it's normal in this industry for people to get involved?" I chewed my lip.

"With bosses and co-workers, yes. The lines are pretty blurry."

"Do you think that means they don't actually care?" I took a deep breath while her eyes narrowed, trying to decode my meaning. "If they found out about me and Shaun, would it cause me problems?'

"You're not his assistant anymore. There's nothing for them to say. They'll gossip. Everyone does in this industry, but will they burn you? No." She shook her head. "Not that I think it would have caused you any real issues if you were still working for him."

"But the press—"

"Honestly, Mona, don't believe everything you read. You could be perfectly above board and all it would take is one completely innocent look from him caught by a photographer and you'd be having a secret affair with a baby on the way." Isla snorted, her eyes shining with memory. "One day, I'll point out all the lies the tabloids made up or the real stories they missed. Once I retire, of course."

I smiled at that. She'd always been tight-lipped about her clients, no matter how much she claimed NDAs didn't apply to sisters.

"So, circling back," I muttered, "if the crew found out, it wouldn't stop me getting another job in TV?"

"Definitely not. They'd probably hire you in the hope they could talk him into cameos." Her amusement faded, and she watched me with a gentle smile. "But you don't care, anyway."

It wasn't a question, but I answered all the same. "I don't know when I stopped caring. I'd rather have him kiss me good morning than go the entire day without it. I like him bringing me lunch. I don't want him to stop because the production staff are suspicious."

"The production staff knew the moment you quit," Isla said, her incredulous gaze telling me I should have known that already. "Production know everything. It's their job to be two steps ahead of the rest of them."

Alys's knowing look popped into my head. Maybe she was right.

As terrifying as that thought was, it also gave me relief knowing that nothing I did from here on out could actually do me any damage. Yes, the press could find out and they'd print whatever they wanted, but we would know it wasn't true. Things looked a lot brighter.

*W*hen Shaun ushered me into the make-up trailer at 3PM the following Wednesday, I thought he was being a bit keen. Then Jenna, the hair and make-up assistant, forced my head over a basin. The curls I'd carefully crafted overnight melted in seconds, and I went back to square one.

Shaun was extremely lucky that he was needed on set because I might have shouted at him for the lack of warning. Instead, I got to scowl at the poor assistant, who was doing nothing but following orders. Mind you, she scowled right back at me, and I relaxed.

Or I relaxed as much as possible knowing a thousand people would stare at me tonight at the charity dinner. I'd break out in hives if I thought about the cameras and the millions around the world who would see me walk into the venue beside Shaun.

Jenna did her best to calm me, but in the end, only threatening my eyes with liquid eyeliner brushes and mascara wands controlled the agitated bounce of my foot.

Neither Alys nor Heather so much as blinked when I asked to take half the day off to attend this event with Shaun. They agreed faster than I thought they would, making me think that Isla had been on to something.

It took two hours, a bottle of pastel pink hair dye, heated curlers, many strips of hot wax, a truckload of body lotion and an ungodly amount of make-up before Jenna released me. I sighed when she finally declared, "That's you finished."

And then Moira appeared and the torture recommenced, but with shapewear and boob tape that refused to work. I said as much, but Moira disagreed and forced it on me.

As predicted, it lasted less than thirty minutes before its fight against gravity failed.

I might have crowed with delight when Moira had to ditch

her plans of putting me in a backless dress. And Moira might have worn a huge grin while she ripped the tape and a layer of skin off my torso. We silently called a truce after that.

The backless black dress returned to the rack, and Moira disappeared into the rows of clothes she'd picked out for me. When I say rows, I mean *rows*. There were at least three of them. Why did I need so many choices for a charity dinner?

Moira held up a burgundy-red dress and I shook my head. Red dress and pink hair… could I please not look like a wash gone wrong in the photos?

She shelved it without comment.

Next came an emerald-green satin gown that made my mouth water. It matched Shaun's eyes and was the epitome of a dream dress with its bunched skirt. I'd never worn anything like it. Unfortunately, or fortunately, I wasn't in lust enough with it to forget that I would look like a washed-out Christmas tree.

Maybe it's time for the pink hair to go.

"I love the statement, Mona. It looks great on you, but can you be any harder to dress?" Moira scoffed, pulling two more options off the racks.

My eyes fixed on the rose-gold dress. It was glittery and form-fitting, but in the old-school Coco Chanel style. I'd be able to breathe and eat without worrying about photos.

"Do you think that'll be too matchy-matchy?" I asked the question begrudgingly. I didn't need Moira to answer. I already knew it was.

She nodded, her mouth pulled in a sympathetic pout.

"Give me the black one." I held my hand out for it without really looking at it.

I loved my hair, but oh boy, did it restrict my choices. If this thing with Shaun was going to last, I needed to consider dyeing my hair a more normal shade.

And then I mentally slapped myself for even thinking that. *If it was going to last?* Geez, I needed to study the definition of casual. Things might feel different for me, but that didn't mean Shaun was on the same page.

Six PM rolled around, and I was decked out in the floor-length, figure-hugging lace dress. It had a huge slit up the front, and most of my chest and stomach was exposed under the black lace. Three-inch rose-gold Louboutins completed my glitzy outfit.

We'd had another argument over those. She'd tried to hand me four-inch heels. However, considering I'd nearly fallen on my ass the moment I tried to take a step, Moira conceded to limiting her expectations.

"This is an Elie Saab," I gasped while I studied myself in the mirror at the back of the trailer.

"It is," Moira confirmed, far more focused on returning designer clothes to their hangers than my wide-eyed glittery freak-out waiting to happen.

"But what if I destroy it?" My hands wrapped around my stomach, as though I could protect the dress from myself.

She shrugged. "It's insured."

Mildly comforted, I returned to studying the person in the mirror who couldn't possibly be me. My hair was perfectly curled in a 1920s wave. My lips were painted with a deep red I'd always shied away from, certain it was too bold for me. My shying days were over.

"Do you think it's too much?" I asked Moira. It was a beautiful dress. I looked incredible in it. But I showed a lot of skin and this was a charity event for refugees. *Is this normal?*

Moira didn't answer. Impatient for a reply, I spun around to demand her attention like the off-kilter little girl I was.

Shaun stood before me, his muscular body encased in a well-tailored black suit and crisp white shirt. His hair was clean but untamed, and mixed with his formal attire, it gave him a rich bad-boy vibe that was doing far too much for me. His bow tie was rose-gold, a touch that both surprised and delighted me.

His wide eyes appraised my body, and I couldn't miss the heat in them when they reached my face. He swallowed. "You look incredible." His eyes dipped lower then, fixating on the lace covering my chest.

"You don't think it's too much?"

"It's more than perfect." He smirked when he caught me watching him. "I might need to keep my arm around you all night. Can't have anyone trying to whisk you away from me and causing a fight. Sherry would not be pleased if your dress got me on the front cover, torn up and bloody defending you."

I laughed as he'd intended.

He pulled me into his arms and I went more than willingly. I settled against his chest, my hands creeping around his neck to toy with the fine hair at the base.

The laughter faded from his face as he considered me. "It's all going to be fine, Mona. You look great. We just have to take some pictures, eat dinner, have one dance, show our faces and then we can skip out while no one's looking."

"You actually think we can sneak out without anyone noticing?"

He shrugged. "I've done it before. This time will be no different." His expression darkened, the lust returned and an answering heat unfurled inside of me. "It better be no different. I need to be in control when I take this dress off you. Moira's too good with her pins to miss out on revenge."

I patted his shoulder, amusement easing the nerves holding my stomach hostage. "I'm sure you can survive a few hours, Hotshot."

"I'm glad one of us has faith in me."

CHAPTER TWENTY-NINE

As expected, a crowd of cameras waited to snap me as I took my first stumbling steps from the limo.

Can we pause on that: *A freaking limo!*

My jaw hit the floor when Shaun guided me to the set car park and the sparkly, black stretch limo waiting for us. We hadn't even gotten limos when we were kids. It had been a bit of a fad with my classmates when we were twelve. However, my parents didn't catch on to that particular trend.

The car was noticeably stripped of all alcohol, which was a relief even if I could have done with a stiff drink to quell my nerves. I'd rather be nervous than have Shaun on edge.

Soon we pulled up outside this swanky hotel, and the flashes started. I shied away from the window. I'm sure I had Bambi eyes when I glanced at Shaun. Yet his reassuring grip on my hand helped calm me a little.

"We can pull around back and skip the press line if you want."

It was sweet of him to offer, but rather stupid if he'd paused to think about the consequences. Sherry would blow a gasket if tomorrow's papers didn't all hold his clean, sober face, and that was really the whole point of my presence.

Instead of snatching the offer as I wanted to, I squeezed his hand, forced a smile to my lips and pushed back my shoulders. "You have to be seen and I have to be seen with you. I'll be okay. Just don't let me trip."

He nodded, amusement pulling at his lips. "If it gets too intense, touch your earring and I'll get us off the carpet, okay?"

Yep, they'd laid out a red carpet for a charity event.

I guess I should have expected it, considering they'd had a flood of ticket requests after Sherry confirmed that Shaun would attend. The organisers had to change the venue three times before they decided enough was enough. I felt a pang of sympathy in the pit of my stomach at the thought of how much extra work had gone into running the event. *Rather them than me.*

Without giving me any warning, Shaun threw the door open. If sound had a physical presence, I'd be flat on my back with the wall of noise that crashed into the quiet confines of our limo.

The chaos of the press line invaded, and Shaun got out. A nervous flutter settled in my throat, and I pressed my fingers to it, hoping it would stop, or at least not make me throw up. Not that that had ever happened, but it would just be my luck.

When Shaun reached back into the car for me, I didn't have it under control. My nerves had snatched away my ability to speak, which was fine. I didn't need to speak to walk on a carpet. That was Shaun's job.

His concerned gaze met mine when I didn't immediately take his hand and slide out of the car. "I can send Tom around the back with you."

I could only just make out the words.

Again, I firmed my spine and plastered on what I hoped was a serene expression. For ten minutes, I needed to pretend I was someone who did this. That's what author Neil Gaiman recommended when you were forced into new situations.

Pretend that you're someone who can do it until you believe you can.

I didn't try to answer Shaun. It would have been pointless even without the lump in my throat. Instead, I took his hand and slid towards the door. An encouraging smile morphed onto his face, and some of my nervous energy subsided.

The noise level grew as I stepped from the car, and Shaun immediately wrapped his arm around me. He guided me down the carpet at a snail's pace to an onslaught of press and questions, none of which he dignified with an answer.

After ten minutes of it, my feet started to pinch. I might have agreed to three-inches, but that didn't mean I was used to them. I tried not to shift from foot to foot to ease the pressure.

One moment we were posing for photos, and the next Shaun whisked me down the carpet, skipping at least four markers. I don't know if it was some internal timer Shaun had developed for these events or if he'd grown bored. Maybe he caught the pain in my eyes. Whatever the cause, I was grateful.

But the attention didn't stop there.

The huge ballroom was laid out with large circular tables that sat ten, maybe twelve, people surrounding a large dance floor and stage. Lights dangled from the ceiling, creating a relaxed atmosphere. Instrumental music floated through the space, the volume turned down and almost drowned out by the chatter of a thousand people.

A thousand people who now stared at me as the hosts led us to our table. My head, neck and back itched with all those eyes on me. Didn't they have anything better to do than speculate about a celebrity's date?

Shaun pulled my chair out, and I sat, my forced expression of calm still firmly in place despite the whispers surrounding me and the anxiety stirring in my mind. Shaun thanked the hosts and moved his chair closer to mine before joining me.

He leant close, his smile patient. The whispers intensified. "How are you doing?"

"This is a bit much." I tried to speak without moving my lips. Those who couldn't eavesdrop kept squinting at my mouth, trying to read my lips.

Shaun laughed. "They'll get bored soon." He placed a finger under my chin and tilted my head until I met his happy gaze. "I'm really proud of how well you held it together out there."

"Thank you. I'm still shocked I didn't throw up."

"Damn, that would have been a great way to get their attention off of me," Shaun joked, trying and failing to look serious.

"Nah, it would have backfired on you. They'd want to know what you did to make me sick."

Shaun nodded. He didn't look around the room or pay the faintest bit of attention to the women vying for his. His focus stayed on me.

The upbeat, easy light in his eyes dimmed then. "Take your shoes off for a bit if you need to."

Surprise shot through me. "How did you know?"

He stroked my hair, careful not to disturb the five layers of hairspray holding it in place.

"You know how they say the eyes are mirrors to the soul?"

I nodded, although I really didn't believe it.

"I think that's a load of bullshit, but yours are next-level expressive. I'm sorry I made you do the last two. They were major tabloids and I wouldn't have heard the end of it from Sherry if I'd skipped."

I pulled his hand into my lap beneath the table and squeezed. "Don't worry about it. I'll protect you from Sherry."

He laughed. "No one can protect me from Sherry, but I appreciate it." Then for the first time since we entered, he glanced around the room. "I need to mingle for a bit, be seen and all that. I'm loath to leave you sitting here, but I really want a dance later." His eyes dropped to my lap.

I frowned as I tried to puzzle out his meaning. Did he want the sexual kind of dance or a literal dance?

Shaun pressed a finger to my brow, smoothing the concentration out. "I figured you'd want to rest your feet so you can keep up with me on the dance floor later." He nodded towards the empty wooden slab beside us.

My eyes widened as I caught on, and Shaun laughed again. "Do I want to ask what you thought I meant?"

"Not unless you want to burn your control and this dress."

His eyes darkened as he leaned in to whisper in my ear. "Don't tempt me." Then with a knowing smirk, he left me to wander the room.

❆

It didn't take long for some woman to sidle up to him and try to attach herself. She wore a short, strapless dress, and her dyed platinum-blond hair tumbled down her back.

Despite knowing better, an ugly stab of jealousy squeezed my heart. She was taller and thinner than me. Yet I was endowed in the breast department and hers were definitely fake, so I had that pro in my column. Okay, so it was debatable whether she was actually prettier than me. But fuck buddies or not, he was still mine, and she was touching my man. I held my breath and waited for his reaction with laser focus. My toes dug into the heels I'd kicked off, ready to shove them on and power walk across the room if I had to.

He glanced down at her and stepped away, shaking her off and continuing to talk to a gentleman with salt-and-pepper hair.

My heart pounded with the relief, but it was short lived.

The vulture followed, pressing herself against him, trying to touch his neck with her raptor claws.

Sighing, I shoved my screaming feet back into my heels and forced myself to stand. Then I picked up both our glasses of sparkling water and stomped across the room.

"Excuse me." I smiled, but it probably looked more frightening than a shark baring its teeth. I used my shoulder to shove her away from Shaun and handed him his glass. She backed away, huffing and pulling a face.

"Clearly I can't leave you anywhere alone." I kept my tone light, but when I glanced at Shaun, his open grin told me I hadn't fooled him. He pulled me into his side and kissed my head. "Jealousy looks good on you," he whispered, his lips caressing my ear.

Before I could comment, he turned back to the silver fox he'd been talking to. "John, I'd like you to meet Mona Baines."

Introductions were made before they settled back into a boring conversation about union fees. I zoned out, sipped my drink and enjoyed the heat of Shaun's hand pressing possessively against my hip.

I appreciated the time inside my head, anyway. I needed to process this new development because when I'd spotted Ms Fake Platinum cosying up to Shaun, I'd felt more than jealous. In fact, I'd been braced for the floor to be torn out from under me.

If I wasn't sure of my feelings before, I sure as hell knew them now. This definitely wasn't a have-fun deal for me anymore. I'd developed an attachment to Shaun. Don't ask me when it happened, don't ask me if the L word was involved. I didn't know the answer.

I was screwed no matter what.

CHAPTER THIRTY

The staff had just cleared the last of the dessert plates when the sound system kicked in. Couples flooded the dance floor — mostly women dragging their reluctant partners. Turning to me, Shaun stood and offered his hand, his eyes daring me to say "no" so he could flip the image and drag me out there.

I hesitated. "I'm not a great dancer." As excuses went, it was probably the most overused one in the universe. Shaun shook his head, took my hand and pulled me from my seat. I guess I *was* being dragged.

"Nothing some practice won't fix. You had rhythm with aerial silks. You'll be fine."

He backed onto the floor, pulling me along. I couldn't help but smile at his ridiculous grin and shining eyes. He looked like a kid at Christmas. We stopped in the middle of the dance floor, and Shaun tugged me forward until I was flush against him. A blush crept up my neck at the press of the bulge in his trousers. It only made his grin widen.

"See? Now you have to dance with me or everyone will see and that will make the tabloid news." He shook his head, a remorseful light entering his eyes. "Think of my image, Mona."

I laughed. "Fine."

With that, he rested a hand on my lower back and gripped my right hand in the other, then whisked us around the dance floor. My cheeks hurt from laughing as he teased me.

"Shaun! I thought that was you," a tall dark-haired man said, interrupting our fun. He and his partner had paused at our side, seeming to materialise out of thin air.

Studying him, I noticed his face shape wasn't all that dissimilar to Shaun's, except his had an extra twenty-five years of wear. His eyes seemed almost the exact shade of green.

Shaun's entire body went rigid. "Uncle."

Well, that explains the similarity.

"How are you, boy? I haven't seen you in – has it been ten years?" He glanced at his partner, a redhead of a similar age and almost a foot shorter than him, for help.

"Ten," Shaun supplied, the word clipped.

He still held me against his chest, though he'd dropped the dance hold. His heart beat frantically beneath my palm.

"A shame about your dad. He was a good man."

Shaun's jolted at his words, and the thin veneer holding his emotions in check cracked. I caught a flicker of anger pass over him before he locked it down.

"If you'll excuse us, my date needs to ditch her heels." The words left Shaun's mouth in a monotonous string.

The woman's gaze dropped to my feet with a sympathetic frown. "Pretty shoes, to be sure, but they always punish the wearer."

Shaun nodded, shook his uncle's hand and frog marched us out of the room. He didn't say goodbye to the host or try to sneak out; he just stormed out the door with a singular focus. The only thing that slowed him down was the line of photographers still huddled outside the hotel's front doors.

He swore before swerving into a quiet corner. Only then

did he release me and pull out his phone. His fingers moved across the screen deftly, firing off a text between deep breaths.

"Hey, look at me," I demanded, turning his favourite trick on him and forcing his head up. The mixture of pain and anger in his eyes constricted my chest. "What can I do?"

He shook his head, his eyes travelling around the lobby. The silent message sank in as I followed their path. Despite the festivities inside, a number of people remained in the area. *Best not let them hear.*

Our limo pulled up outside and Shaun tucked me under his shoulder. We rushed to the car, ignoring the shouts and flashes around us. Tom opened the door and I slid in, with Shaun following close behind.

My shoulders slumped as the door slammed on the limo, blocking out the shouts of the press. *Free at last.* Then my gaze shifted to Shaun as he settled into the seat at the opposite end. He buckled in and buried his head in his hands.

"Shaun?"

He ignored me, which, I'll admit, stung a little. I wanted to go to him and gather him in my arms, but the distance and the fact the car was moving overwhelmed me. I didn't want to damage my twenty thousand pounds' worth of designer lace by getting it snagged on anything.

"Shaun, talk to me."

Again, he ignored me.

Giving a frustrated growl, I kicked off my torture-device heels and stood – or crouched, whatever. If I fell flat on my face and ripped the dress, it would all be on him. The forward momentum of the car made me almost fly across to him. I slammed into the leather seat with zero finesse. He jumped as I approached, and I hoped that our night wasn't ruined by the memories holding his mind captive.

With tentative pressure, I placed my hand on his forearm, testing him. When he didn't immediately pull away, I wrapped my fingers around his wrist and pulled his hand from his face.

Weaving our fingers together, I tugged on him until he looked at me.

Shaun rolled his head towards me. He smiled, but it was a frightening sight. It was like someone had sucked all the joy out of him.

I let my fingers trail across his slack-jawed face. "What's wrong?"

"After everything he did to us, they still think he was some kind of saint."

"Your uncle?"

He didn't answer me. His dead eyes fixed on me, but his mind wasn't in the car anymore.

I bit my lip, considering my limited options. I could shock him, try to crack a joke or slap him. I opted for my quickest bet: shock.

"Shaun?" I used my grip on his hand to shake him, but all I got was a disconnected "hmm" for my efforts.

I could always…

I was wrapped up tighter than a Christmas present, but that could be remedied with some work.

Without allowing myself much time to think, I parted the skirt of the dress and shuffled myself into Shaun's lap. It took my straddling him to elicit a response. His hands dropped to my thighs, stabilising me in the bumpy car. His head shot up, mild interest flashing in his eyes.

"What are you doing, Sparky?"

"The night's not ending with you miserable."

He quirked a brow. "Is that so?"

My nod was firm, but the press of my lips was even more forceful. It felt like minutes ticked by while I worked my mouth and tongue against his with no response.

In that moment, it turned personal. If I couldn't get him to respond, it was a comment on his interest in me. I point-blank refused to allow a different outcome.

I shifted my hips, grazing his semi-hard dick and changed

up the pace of my kisses. His hold on my hips tightened, pulling at me, keeping the movement going. I swallowed his groan with triumph.

His hand travelled up my back and I shivered as he traced my skin through the lace.

"Okay, you've got my attention," he said as he dragged his mouth along my jaw and down my neck. "You won't let me rip this dress off you like I want to, so you'd better have a plan if you want it to survive."

"Well, first you need to free me from the lycra. I'm sure you can figure it out from there." My tone was dry as I shifted back to my seat.

Shaun chuckled, but his hand slid up my skirt without argument. The laughter died when he reached my waist and still hadn't found the waistband.

"What the hell did Moira do to you?" he asked, despair dripping from his voice.

It was my turn to laugh. "Just keep going."

In the end, I ended up with the dress hiked to my chest. Thankfully, it wasn't skin-tight, so moving the fabric didn't hurt. Getting shapewear off was not the sexiest thing in the world. When he dragged the elastic material over my hips, he caught my underwear and divested me of them at the same time. Efficient man. After dumping the material on the floor, he didn't wait for me to straighten my dress or sit up properly. His fingers trailed up my thighs, sending off sparks as he pulled me in for a heated kiss.

His fingers slid against my clit without pause, massaging in circles that succeeded in driving me out of my head.

Shaun groaned into my mouth again. "How are you so wet already?"

Thankfully, he didn't wait for a response. My speech capabilities had skipped off with my underwear. He slipped two fingers inside me, pulsing them in and out while applying pressure with his thumb.

A minute tops and I was panting, moaning into his mouth. I'd thank the location for it. Who knew sex in the back of a limo could be so hot?

Too impatient to wait and desperate for the feel of him filling me, I pushed him away until he sat upright again. He watched me with a lazy smile, content to let me do whatever the hell I wanted. *Smart man.*

Satisfied, my hands dropped to his belt and zipper, making quick work of them. As I pressed him back against the seat, he lifted himself to release his trousers. I dragged them and his black boxers down to his knees and called it quits. Free of its confines, his hard erection jolted forward, captivating me.

Shaun fished his wallet from his pocket and removed a condom. He set to work unwrapping the rubber before helping me climb into his lap with an intense stare. "You sure you want this here?"

I nodded, not trusting my voice not to wobble.

His gaze roamed my face, assessing me. Satisfied with whatever he saw, he pressed the blunt head of his cock against my entrance and paused. He had a firm grip on my hip, and when I tried to lower myself, his fingers dug in, stilling me. He wore a teasing smirk that added to my desperation. "I want to savour this," he whispered, his voice gravelly but devious. He knew exactly what his delaying tactics were doing to me. Frustration unravelled within me at the teasing press of him inside me.

I circled my hips, taunting him in return. He groaned, pressing down on my hip until I sank down, impaling myself on his length bit by bit. Somehow, he seemed bigger in this position. It rode a fine line between pleasure and pain.

Shaun's grip on my waist tightened, stalling me again. He gritted his teeth, feeling the pressure as much as me. A hand slid behind my neck, pulling my lips to his. Our kisses were interrupted by intermittent gasps and moans as I sank lower.

When he finally bottomed out, his hands grasped my sides,

pressing me down and holding me still. All the while his lips kept working at my mouth, swallowing every noise I made and duelling with my tongue.

Without warning, he dragged my body up his length and slammed back down. The sensation skittered up my spine and jellied my brain. Again and again, he repeated the movement. I tried to keep up, but with each press of his groin against my clit, my eyelids drooped, my head lolled back, and I lost all sense of rhythm.

The sounds of our flesh slapping together filled the air, and I was certain Tom could hear. But with the pressure coiling in my core, I couldn't remember why that was a problem.

When the coil snapped, I cried out and slumped forward into Shaun's waiting arms. I buried my head in his shoulder as he continued to pound into me, wracking my body with tiny aftershocks. Shaun buried his face in my hair as he came.

Boneless, we held onto each other, oblivious to everything else. In this dark space, nothing bothered us: no family problems, no scandal-hungry media or rabid fans. It was just us.

I could get used to just us.

The car had been parked for a while, but neither of us moved. We were content holding each other, still connected. The fact Tom hadn't opened the door was a merciful surprise. We'd have to move soon, and I didn't want to. Right here, tucked into the dark of the limo, I didn't need to worry about what life after Shaun might look like.

Shaun's grip tightened around me, as if he could hear my thoughts.

"Sorry I cut you out."

I lifted my head, needing to see his expression. "Your

uncle was evidently deluded. I get why you needed to get out of there."

His head fell back against the seat, and his sad smile made my stomach drop. He hummed as he considered my words. "I always knew I wanted to act, be in films. My mother was massively supportive, but the lack of money made it harder. Even though certain members of my dad's family were rolling in it." He shrugged, his nervous gaze finally meeting mine. "I guess he blew it all on booze or drugs. Seems like something he would have done."

He bit his lip, torn.

"I'm not going anywhere," I whispered. "No matter what you say."

Shaun nodded. "I told you he was a drunk. He was hard to be around when he was sober, but when he drank, he made it his mission to make me feel worthless. Lily never met him. I didn't want him so much as breathing the same air as her."

My eyes burned and my heart hurt. Tears tracked down my face, and I made no attempt to brush them away. I didn't want to distract him.

"He died when I was sixteen, but he did a lot of damage in that time. At the funeral, all his family could do was praise him. It was like they got together and agreed on a story. They erased his entire married life, erased the monster he'd become. Until then I thought they'd help, that they'd step in. They made all the right noises. And then my uncle stood up at the funeral and spouted a stream of utter bullshit." He smoothed my tears away, his smile sad. "I might be good at playing other people, but I'm not great at trusting my eyes, okay?"

I nodded. What else could I do?

"Anyway, it all got better after he passed and we shut his family out, but I'm still dealing with it. He was always convinced that no one would love me if I followed my dreams, and then Lily left me for no real reason." He shrugged.

"And you started sabotaging yourself because it felt like everything you did was pointless?"

"I guess that about sums it up. Without Finn, Jackson and Nathan keeping my head above water in LA, I don't want to think about how much worse this all might have gone." A dim light entered his eyes. "I'm sorry I was such an asshole to you when we first met. I thought it would be easier if I kept people away." His hands framed my face, a sweet smile overtaking his features. "I'm glad you proved me wrong."

I smiled. "I am too."

"I've gotten so used to being alone with my demons, Mona. Sometimes I forget you're here to help me." His fingers traced along my face, the sadness giving way to wonder. "I was such an asshole. I was turning into him and without you," he swallowed, his eyes shining, "I think I'd be lost. What did I do to deserve you?"

A tear ran down his cheek and I swept it away.

"I don't care what you were like at the start," I said. "You're getting better, that's all that matters." I pressed my lips to his in a soft kiss. "You've got me."

He pulled back, holding my searching lips away with firm hands on my shoulders. I frowned at him, confused by the change. "What's wrong?"

His smile was sweetness itself. I wanted to bottle the flutters it set free in my stomach.

"Absolutely nothing. I just need to make sure you're in the same place as me."

"Which is?"

"This isn't some fling to fill the time between takes. I want you now, after wrap, three years from now. There's something between us. If I had sense, I'd let you go and find someone who could give you a normal life, but with you, I don't know how to be sensible. I need you."

It was my turn to get watery-eyed.

"Are you saying you want to *date* me?" I asked, the words low and scratchy with cautious hope.

"I guess we'd better start there." He wore a teasing grin, but I sensed an edge beneath it, like he'd happily pull out a ring and marry me if I let him.

"We'll be monogamous?"

His eyes narrowed. "You haven't been sleeping with other people?"

I scoffed. "When do I have time? I'm either working or in your bed."

He relaxed into the seat.

I dared another. "So, we're giving each other labels?"

"Fuck yes. I've been calling you my girlfriend in my head for weeks."

I slapped his chest playfully. "Then why didn't you say something?"

"I thought you'd be resistant." He laughed.

Alright, so maybe he had a point. I'd only made the shift in the last two weeks to not caring what other people thought about our relationship. Maybe I'd needed time to come to terms with my own wants. I was glad I'd taken it, because I could look at him and feel comfortable with my choices. He might not lead a very private life, but at least I'd had the chance to get used to that before I started falling for him.

"It's just you and me from here on out," I whispered.

CHAPTER THIRTY-ONE

Things moved full-steam ahead on the production for the next two weeks. We spent most of our evenings together, but the later in the day filming started, the less either of us could function afterwards. Falling into bed together, worn out, was about all we'd managed for the last few days. However, with a four-day break in the schedule, Shaun booked a cottage on a private estate for us to recover and actually have some time together. All I could do was count down the days until then.

Four days off, no stupid morning alarms or supporting cast asking inappropriate questions. It sounded like heaven.

We wrapped early that day and the crew decided to celebrate with impromptu drinks in town. We wanted to get on the road early in the morning, but Shaun couldn't talk himself out of putting in an appearance. By the time we escaped the bar, it was 9PM and we were both on the groggy side of tired.

We walked through the door half an hour later to a notification that a new supernatural drama had dropped. Our early night plans went out the window without much resistance.

Two episodes in to what was going to be a very long binge, Shaun's laptop started pinging.

"Shaun, your laptop is ringing."

"Answer it," he shouted from the bathroom.

"But it's Jackson?"

"Then definitely answer it."

"If you say so." I frowned, reaching for the mouse pad as if it might bite. With one swift move, I accepted the call and forced a smile to my lips.

The beautiful faces of mega-actors Nathan Logan, Jackson Levi and Finn McCarthy filled the screen in tiles. Together they formed a lethal bunch, with Finn's classic Irish dark hair, light eyes and pale skin and Nathan's dark and brooding look; Jackson was their complete opposite, with short dirty-blond hair and a tan you could only earn on a surfboard. (What? I wouldn't be a good assistant if I didn't research all of Shaun's friends.)

"Boys, we're in luck!" Finn said, his Irish accent singing through the screen.

"We were calling to get information out of Shaun, but you're exactly the person we wanted." Nathan laughed, rubbing his hands together.

"He's been impossible to reach the last few weeks. I said there was a woman!" Finn crowed, more than pleased with himself. The other two rolled their eyes.

"Where is Shaun, anyway?" Jackson interrupted, his voice husky and his serious blue eyes distracting me from the puzzle. "It must be serious if he's letting you answer his calls."

My mouth opened and closed, but no sound emerged. Three of the kings of screen grinning at me was a bit much.

"I think you're on mute, love," Finn offered in a helpful tone. They all stared back at me with expectation in their eyes.

"Well, isn't this an interesting development," Shaun said, drawing my attention away from the man candy on the screen. With his arms crossed, he leaned against the bathroom door, laughing at me.

The fog cleared and suspicion moved in. My head turned back and forth between the four of them. Amusement reigned supreme. *He set me up.*

I smirked at the men before us. "Excuse me. My boyfriend needs to learn his lesson." Their answering laughter gave me strength.

I shut the lid, sprang to my feet and stalked towards him. He held up his hands and backed into the kitchen. Once the island separated us, Shaun stopped trying to escape. Instead, he stood there with his trademark "look at me I'm gorgeous" smirk. He stared me down, and the closer I got, the more his confidence slipped.

"Why is it that they can stun you, but I can't?" he muttered, trying to hold me at arm's length.

"Is that what the call was about, you wanting to see how I'd react to three of cinema's finest talking at me?"

He nodded. "Maybe a little. You've never been affected by me."

Little did he know, I'd been lucky to get words out of my mouth the first time we'd met. "And that bothers you?"

Shaun frowned, the resistance pushing me away relaxed slightly. Again, he nodded. "I think it does. I don't know why."

I chuckled. "I do. You're used to women falling at your feet."

"Sometimes, but I wouldn't have been interested if you'd been easy."

I raised an eyebrow at that.

"I mean, if you hadn't resisted, I probably would..." He paused, frowning down at me with the realisation that his ditch kept getting deeper. "This isn't coming out right. My point is: You were different to them all, and that's why I wanted you."

"But you still want me to be affected by your fake smouldering thing?"

He spluttered. "Fake? What do you mean fake?"

"Well, it is, isn't it?"

"I don't know what you mean." He lifted his nose in a hilarious display of haughty.

I took advantage of his weakening attention to push his arms away and step into his personal space. Automatically, they wrapped around me. I beamed like the lovesick woman I was.

Using his chest as a support, I leaned up on my tiptoes and whispered into his ear, "The way you looked at me this morning was much more effective."

His eyes lit up with the memory of him pressing me against the shower wall. "So, I do affect you?" he said, his voice husky.

"Would I have agreed to this relationship if not?"

He paused, considering my words. "I don't know. We haven't known each other that long." His tone seemed deadly serious, and it took a moment for his meaning to sink in.

"Take it back, you rat!"

Shaun laughed at my indignation.

I dug my fingers into his sensitive sides in retaliation. He backed into the corner of the kitchen, trapping himself against the cabinets, and he soon apologised, his chest heaving with laughter and his eyes wet. Who knew he was that ticklish. Smiling, I wrapped my arms around his waist and rested my head on his chest.

I couldn't remember the last time I'd felt like this. Content and at ease in a relationship. With my ex, it had felt like a constant uphill battle, declarations followed by betrayals. Some had been accidental, like the time he'd forgotten to turn up at my sister's birthday party because he hadn't been listening when I'd invited him. Or when he'd ordered my brother coffee with cow's milk even though I'd told him multiple times that Cameron was intolerant. I spent a lot of time wondering which of my requests or hints he'd ignore next.

With Shaun, it was easy. And despite the short time we'd known each other, I trusted him with every aspect of my life.

"I was joking," he murmured, his lips brushing against my hair. "I love everything about you. From the top of your pink head to the tip of your toes. Your weird ability to hang upside down from a silk without getting winded. The way you can't function in the morning without coffee. The dazed look you get in your eyes when you're working on a problem."

I leant back until I could see his handsome face. "That's quite a list."

The fact he'd used the L word hadn't escaped my notice either.

"I'm not done." He grinned, tightening his hold on me. "You've made me trust that no matter what I say or do, you'll always be waiting to catch me. That's probably the best gift you could give."

By now, I was a blubbering mess and my chest hurt looking at the love shining in his eyes. And it *was* love. He might not have said "I love you," but it was there, clear as day. I don't know when I fell for him. It might have started the day he'd handed me his copy of *Frankenstein*, but it had grown slowly, hidden beneath my attempts to keep us apart.

What an absolutely idiot I was.

I couldn't imagine never waking up to his smiling face. Never experiencing another one of his carefully thought-out surprises. Never seeing that vulnerable look he got in his eyes when he shared something that made him uncomfortable. I missed him when he wasn't around, and I relished the moments we could grab alone, whether in his trailer or in a secluded corner of a restaurant. I didn't want to remember what it was like not to have him in my life.

"I love you too."

His eyes widened briefly, but then the surprise washed away, replaced by pure satisfaction. His fingers danced across my face, worshiping, cherishing. "Sherry has no idea how big a favour she did me bringing you into my life, Mona."

"Should we send her a gift?" I asked, teasing.

"I think that would be a hell of a way to break the news."

I chuckled. "You just don't want to tell her on the phone."

"You've heard her. She's all sugar until you piss her off."

"I'm afraid I've not experienced that side of her. I didn't do anything to piss her off." I pressed my lips together, suppressing my laughter at his shocked expression.

"Not even when you quit?"

I shook my head.

"Bloody hell, teach me your secrets."

I grinned. "It'll take a while, but I'll try."

He grinned, his hands stealing into my hair. "Well, fortunately, we've got plenty of time."

On my tiptoes, I met him halfway, our lips gliding against each other's. Shivers raced down my spine, and I sighed against his mouth. I never wanted to stop being this responsive to him. When we broke the kiss, he stared into my eyes with more emotion than I could fathom.

"Why don't you go get the next episode queued up and I'll grab us some drinks?"

I left him in the kitchen, smiling goofily as he pulled soft drinks from the fridge. I opened his laptop to select the next episode in the list with hesitation. What if the call hadn't ended and I had to talk to the three amigos again? After Shaun's revelation, I could handle them, I just didn't want to.

Thankfully, the screen was clear of Golden Globe winners and the risk of my having to volley questions dropped exponentially. For now.

But before I could reconnect the TV, a ping sounded and an email notification popped up in the corner of the screen.

The subject line made my heart hit the floor.

CHAPTER THIRTY-TWO

reat news. Your visa cleared. I promise you'll love LA in the winter.

I rubbed my chest, struggling to ease the pain there. Frowning at the screen, the words blurred before my burning eyes. *Is Shaun leaving?*

Then his whispered words in the kitchen echoed in my mind. He loved me. He didn't want to be without me. This didn't make sense. Why would he make those promises if he'd always intended to leave?

He hadn't talked about his next project. Maybe this was a temporary thing. Or maybe it was a job.

We hadn't discussed a plan for after wrap in any detail. I still didn't know what I wanted to do, but I did enjoy production. A number of Scotland-based jobs had been advertised on the group Alys had added me to, and there, of course, would be loads here. I'd also enjoyed managing Shaun, so I could always talk to my sister about training me at her agency.

But what did it matter if Shaun wasn't here? If he took a job in LA, we'd never see each other.

The fist squeezing my heart didn't ease its grip.

Why hadn't he asked me?

It was a simple question. We'd shared a lot. He knew I was still figuring out the future; he knew I wanted him in it.

Fuck. I just told him I loved him.

Which was flat-out terrifying since the last person I let myself love had used it against me. Shaun wasn't like that, though. He wouldn't use my feelings to manipulate me.

And then I read the rest of the email:

Your Artist Green Card will take a few days to finalize, but you'll be able to make the permanent move to the USA after Mystery Lines wraps. If you'd like, I can set up a meeting with a great LA realtor to start putting the pieces in place. I've got some studio meetings lined up next week and will report back on some potential next options that will finally get you that elusive Oscar.

My stomach dropped, and the room spun. Hot tears splashed down my cheeks, and if I hadn't been sitting down, I would have crumpled. A low, bitter laugh broke through my clenched jaw.

What use is Badass Mona if she can't recognise when someone is manipulating her?

"Sparky, did you say something?" Shaun called from the kitchen, his focus on the contents of his fridge.

I couldn't be here. I wasn't capable of pretending that everything was peachy. I'd perfected the act with my ex and I refused to do it again, refused to wait around for him to decide whether or not I was worthy of a life update, refused to fall deeper for him while he geared up to dump me.

Why the hell had he bothered saying all those lovely things if he planned to leave me?

I had no answer to that. Nothing made sense. Evidently, I couldn't trust my instincts with men. I scrubbed hard at my tear-stained cheeks and scrambled off the sofa, my shaky legs barely holding me. I picked up my purse and threw my phone inside.

"Do you want another drink?" The cheery note in his voice worsened the ache in my chest.

I couldn't answer him. He wouldn't have heard my teary croaks, anyway.

I considered the stairs to his bedroom. My small suitcase of clothes sat on his bed. I'd packed a bag ready for our long-weekend break to avoid having to go back to my flat in the morning. I didn't want to lose them, but equally, the longer I stuck around, the more painful this would get.

It would be much worse if I had to come back for my things.

I took a step towards the stairs.

"Where are you going?" The edge of hurt and disbelief in his tone gutted me.

I froze, my body tense, and a lone tear got the better of me. I scrubbed at it angrily and squashed the bubble of emotion threatening to knock me on my backside. He didn't get to make me feel like shit when he was planning big life changes without me.

Maybe it was cowardly to make my escape without talking to him. I'd wear the label proudly if it stopped the shattering of my fragile ability to trust others.

Somehow, I buried the hurt. I wasn't a good-enough actor to hide my anger, but at least he wouldn't see the wound he'd opened.

"You got an email from Sherry." I spun around, spitting the words at him.

Whatever Shaun saw on my face, it made him take a step back. Concern overtook his features as he considered me.

Maybe this was a mistake. Maybe Sherry had gone behind his back and arranged it all.

"Something's wrong. Talk to me, Mona."

I rolled my eyes. *Stating the obvious much!*

"Were you going to tell me about LA?"

He flinched at the question, and the tiny grain of hope

floated away. I wasn't imaging the guilt that slithered into his emerald eyes.

"It's not confirmed." Shaun approached me, and I backed away. His face scrunched up at the movement. "Sherry thought it would be a good move, and the guys have been nagging me to try it for years."

"Were you going to tell me?" I repeated, my tone as hard as the wall I was constructing around my heart.

He shook his head. "I didn't think it would happen."

I snorted at that. "You didn't think a Golden Globe–winning actor would get a green card?"

"I didn't think of it like that." He groaned, raking a hand down his face.

"Is it a temporary thing?"

Shaun bit his lip. "I don't know."

"When are you going?"

His eyes flicked to his open laptop. "Maybe after the show wraps. Sherry's working on lining up projects in LA."

"You didn't move when you were with Lily, so why now?" I had to force myself to say her name. Reminding myself of the usual calibre of his tastes was not something I needed front and centre.

"When things were shit, it was easier being near the guys."

His eyes begged me to understand, and unfortunately, I did. He didn't have a support network here. His best friends were in LA, and when you're hurting you need your friends. He'd made a brave choice.

Too bad he hadn't thought to talk to me about it.

"Would you still go if it came through now?" The question left my lips before I could claw it back. It was stupid, redundant and reeking of a neediness I swore I would never give anyone. His career meant the world to him; it would open far too many doors for him to turn it down.

Shaun nodded, and old Mona laughed hysterically in my head.

"Well, your green card's on its way, so I hope your new life is everything you dreamed it would be."

With a sad smile, I continued towards the stairs. Taking them two at a time, I rushed into his bedroom, and upon seeing his bed, memories of the things we'd done and said in it came racing back. They added an extra pang of loss that I could have done without. My teeth sank into my lip, the sharp sting reminding me why I was leaving. I averted my eyes, scooped up my suitcase and backed out.

He was waiting for me when I came back down.

"Let's talk about this," he pleaded.

I ignored him, my focus on the door and leaving before I started crying.

"Wait!" he shouted, his bare feet slapping against the hardwood floors. His hand landed on my shoulder before I could touch the door handle. He spun me around, his frantic eyes searching mine. "It doesn't mean we have to end."

My eyebrows rose. "You're moving to LA in five months."

"Yes, but that doesn't stop us from seeing each other."

"For how long?"

Shaun frowned. "I don't understand the question."

His hands caressed my face and arms. He wouldn't stop touching me.

My eyes started to burn again. It was too much. I really needed him to stop.

"When would we see each other, Shaun?" I pressed my hand against his chest and tried to push him away – tried being the operative word; he didn't so much as budge.

"I don't know. I haven't thought that far ahead. I could visit." His eyes glazed and his focus turned insular, scrambling for pretty words to fix the situation, no doubt.

It fit perfectly with the image I'd built in my head. I turned away from him, using his distraction to shake off his grip.

"I don't think this is going to work for me. We gave it a good shot, but I can't do it." It felt like another entity had taken over my body and was forcing me through the motions. The words fell dead from my lips, scrubbed until the emotion faded away.

"You don't mean that," he whispered, the pain in his voice making me wince.

I paused in the doorway. The thought that he would have abandoned me without notice burned, its heat slowly melting all of my progress. I needed to know the answer.

"Would you have told me you were leaving the country, or would I have woken up one morning to the tabloids reporting you'd landed?" I wasn't able to stop the hitch in my voice. I kept my back to him and waited.

I heard him swallow, but thankfully, he made no attempt to touch me again.

"I would have told you."

The lack of certainty in his voice pulled the pin on my pain. Tears trickled down my face, and I walked out of there, grateful that he couldn't see my heart breaking.

I got in the elevator and glared at the white face of a woman I'd dreaded seeing again. Her red-rimmed eyes had been an on-and-off feature of my life for four years. At least I had enough control left to hold back the dam of tears until I'd crawled into the back of a taxi.

I'd expected more. More than a shell-shocked, reluctant Shaun. A stupid part of me might have hoped he'd try to convince me to go with him. It wouldn't have been a difficult argument.

I was prepared for angry, biting Shaun. I glanced up at the streamlined glass building with a frown. I'd expected him to chase me, to fight me, to see through my shaky walls to the truth. I wanted him, I loved him, and I would have gone anywhere with him. If only he'd thought enough of me to ask.

Despite all of the shit I'd gone through, I was still the hopeful romantic who wanted to believe that people wouldn't willingly use me. I wanted to believe that when they messed up, it was truly a mistake they regretted.

Instead, I got that pathetic and unsatisfying end. The whole thing just confirmed that his words were nothing more than pretty sounds. I meant very little to him. Once again, I'd fallen for an untouchable man and I was going to pay for it.

How could I have fallen for his lies?

Choking on the tears, I slumped in my seat and buckled myself in.

"Where to, love?" The driver glanced at me over his shoulder with an impatient frown.

"What time is it?" I didn't recognise my own voice. It sounded hollow.

"Uh, one-forty. Where to?"

Last train left hours ago. I sank low in the seat and gave him my address. I'd have to drive.

CHAPTER THIRTY-THREE

Resigned to a night of bad sleep and crying, I crawled into bed and failed to block out thoughts of Shaun. For once, I was grateful for my flatmates' partying. At least no one was home to hear my painful sobs. Or answer the door when the pounding started around 4AM.

Sometime before then, I'd finally fallen asleep to fitful dreams. When the noise started, I'd jumped out of my skin, not sure where I was or what was making that awful noise. It's not a pleasant feeling going from peaceful blackout to heart-racing, frozen-in-your-bed-unsure-of-the-noise-that-woke-you fear.

Of course, when more knocking sounded, I recognised it for what it was and rolled over. He could knock until his hands bled. I wasn't opening that door.

After that, I tossed and turned for another two hours. Sleep wouldn't come, and the longer I lay there free of distraction, the more my blood started to boil.

As the sun started rising, I picked up my suitcase and considered the remaining things in my room. I hadn't brought much in the first place, but I didn't want to hang about and pack it all. I'd have to come back anyway.

With that disconcerting thought, I whisked myself out of the flat and into my car. The age-softened cushion and fruity smell of my air freshener offered a familiar comfort. It could also take me to a person who could make it all better.

"*A*re you going to let me in or just keep staring at me?" My words slurred from tiredness and crying. Have you tried driving nine hours on a motorway? There are no distractions, just a radio and your mind on repeat.

Isla stood in her doorway, blinking at me with mild shock. So maybe I should have called ahead. I'd thought about it and then decided that she'd talk me out of leaving, and I really wanted to.

I braced myself for the questions. They would come. If not now, then after dinner – they always did. I'd nicknamed Isla "Pitbull" when we were kids because she refused to let anything go. Once, she accused Cameron of stealing her crayon. She kept at him for two weeks until he threw the thing at her. She wouldn't let me escape now either.

My words finally registered and her surprise cleared, but the concern remained. She pulled me into the flat and slammed the door.

"That smile needs some work," she said, prying the bag from my tight grip.

"It's the best I could do on short notice. You'll live."

"Then stop trying. It's going to give me bloody nightmares."

I followed her into the living room and collapsed on her sofa, instantly pulling a cushion to my chest. I'd done my part: I got myself to Scotland. I'd let her take over from here.

"Who do I have to put a hit on?" Isla asked, her voice tight. Doors slammed in the kitchen and glass clinked.

My face hurt and my eyes itched with tears yet again. I'd

finally taken a step forward, and he had to go and ruin it. Couldn't he have logged his email out before giving me his laptop? That – no, I didn't want that. Then I'd be none the wiser and even worse off in the winter when he left me.

Fuck, I didn't know what I wanted.

I buried my head in the throw pillow and screamed.

"Okay, let the pillow go and talk to me." Isla tugged hard at the cushion, and I released it without a fight.

She exchanged it for a glass of red wine and a soft, patient smile. My sister was a pro at that smile when she wanted something; it's what made her a top-notch agent.

I hesitated, staring at the glass as guilt stabbed me in the gut. *I'm not with him anymore. I can get drunk if I want.* I drained the glass without pause and placed it on the coffee table.

Isla's eyes widened, and she got up to grab the bottle.

I sank into the sofa then and let the story go in a rush. The sooner I got it out, the sooner I could stop talking about it.

Isla's mask of calm slipped at multiple points until only pity and anger remained. My stomach turned at the pity. I could handle anything but pity.

"I know, alright! Mona can't pick a decent guy and needs to stop trying." I sounded bitter to my own ears.

"I wasn't going to say anything of the sort. I'm sorry it didn't turn out the way you hoped."

"But I shouldn't have gotten involved with Shaun to begin with?"

"I didn't say that and I encouraged you, remember?" Isla tilted her head, momentarily lost in thought. "Besides, you wouldn't be the first Baines to fall for an actor."

Questions exploded on my tongue, all vying for first place. What the hell did she want me to do with that?

"Yeah, I kept that one kind of quiet," she mumbled.

"Understatement of the century. When was this? *Who* was this?"

"It was years ago, my first job out of uni and I'm not sure

I should say who." She shifted in her seat, her eyes fixed resolutely on the wine swirling in her glass.

"Nuh-uh. Spill." For the first time in hours, something other than grief filled me. I practically bounced in my seat.

"Bryce Reid."

My eyes widened. "What? How could you not tell me?" I screeched, and it was a mighty sound. Her neighbour's dogs would have heard it on the ground floor.

Next to Shaun and his friends, Bryce Reid was the next level. He'd landed awards ridiculously early in his career. He'd started out as the bleeding-heart bad boy of a huge drama and transitioned into chick flicks and action films. The films could be shit, but his face alone would sell out the box office.

"It was a hot and fast fling." She brushed it away nonchalantly, but she peeked at me from beneath her lashes, giving herself away.

I crossed my arms and waited. Sighing, she continued.

"We were attracted to each other like moths to the flame. He was a client at my agency. Agent-client relationships weren't allowed – aren't allowed. If we'd gotten caught, they might have overlooked it if I was fully qualified, but as an assistant, it would have ended my career."

"You didn't get caught." It was a fact. She was still an agent, so whatever happened, she'd bailed before anyone found out.

"No. His rising star thankfully took him away before the agency noticed anything fishy. We weren't very discreet, though. I thought we were, but after years of reflection, we were incredibly fucking lucky." She shrugged, drained her glass, then topped us up.

"Anyway, he landed a pilot in Hollywood. The series got a full order and took off. He was meant to come back for me, but instead, he ghosted." Isla recounted it the same way I recounted my history with my ex, detached and emotionless.

I stared at my sister. "I can't believe you never told me. I can't believe I never noticed."

"I'm only telling you now to give you some perspective."

I frowned at her. *What does that mean?*

"I have first-hand experience of both sides. I understand why you're upset, but I also see their side of things. Most actors wait years to break out and never do. Those that do wait years to step up and never do. Moving to LA could give Shaun that."

I spluttered. "Whose side are you on?"

"Yours, of course. I'm just saying, as an agent who has given up her own Shaun, I get both sides. As a professional in this business, I knew Bryce leaving was the best thing for him. But that didn't mean I didn't scream and cry any less. I just did it with bitter resignation."

I shook my head and covered my face. "Then he should have told me. He should have been honest in the beginning and I…"

"You'd never have let your guard down." It wasn't a question. Isla knew – I knew – it was true. I would have blocked him out and never started this sham of a relationship.

"He shouldn't have lied to me."

"Maybe he genuinely didn't believe it would happen."

"Can you stop playing devil's advocate? He's leaving. It's good for him. I've got it," I snapped, springing to my feet. I paced the small living room, circling the coffee table and wearing a path in her plush cream carpet.

I frowned at the stupid fabric. I'd never understood why she bought a cream carpet. How was it practical when your drink of choice was red?

"He should have told me. He shouldn't have pursued me after I quit. He should have given me something to defend myself." My chest hurt, and I pressed my hand hard to it, trying to rub out the ache. I turned to Isla with tears in my eyes. "He shouldn't have made me love him if he was going to leave me."

Isla's face crumbled as she considered me. *How awful must I look? Swollen red-rimmed eyes, blotchy skin and wild hair.* I hadn't even bothered showering this morning, so my pink locks probably stood on end.

Isla placed her wineglass on the table and rose. She pulled me into her arms and held me tight. Not resisting, I sank into her, burying my face in her blouse. Then I let the sobs wrack my body and trusted her to keep me together.

CHAPTER THIRTY-FOUR

For the rest of the evening and most of Saturday, we lazed on the sofa with chick flicks, wine and sugary snacks that would come back to bite me. I'd worry about it another day. Isla ordered fajitas from my favourite Mexican restaurant in Glasgow and mocked the stream of bad decisions unfolding on her TV screen.

When we switched over to a broadcast channel to search for more options, Shaun's face appeared. It was the shock I needed to get me out of the house – or more, seeing him brought it all back to the surface and undid my efforts to bury him.

I almost ran out the door in pyjamas, but Isla caught on before I could leave. She dragged me into the bathroom and laid down her orders. Looking like I was in mourning for my broken heart wouldn't help me get over my broken heart. Shower. Change your clothes. Wash your hair.

I didn't fully understand it, but I did feel much better with clean hair.

An hour later, my foot tapped restlessly against the concrete landing while I waited for her to lock up the flat. If she needed three locks on her door, she should probably move.

As if I could talk.

I skipped out the ground-floor door without looking and slammed into a hard chest. Isla grunted as she caught me, saving me from hitting the floor. I apologised without looking and stepped out of the doorway.

I started down the street, expecting Isla to follow or tell me I was going the wrong way. She did neither. In fact, the tell-tale sound of her heeled boots clicking against the cobbles didn't follow me at all. Muttering, I turned back and wished I hadn't.

My sister stood in the doorway staring at the man I'd almost run down. Her arms were folded and her body rigid, hostile.

I stomped back to them, working up the heat of anger and burying the delight that fluttered in my chest.

"What are you doing here?" I channelled the Badass Mona who'd taken him to task in front of the crew. That was the only Mona he would see from now on.

"You wouldn't answer your phone," Shaun said, the words quiet and almost lost to the traffic. His pleading eyes scanned my face as he stepped towards me.

I crossed my arms, hopelessly trying to ward him off. "That usually means someone doesn't want to talk to you."

"You're not taking Sherry's calls either," he muttered, a relieved note to his words, but little did he know, Sherry got her updates elsewhere.

I still didn't understand why she'd called, but I'd caught Isla on the phone to her early this morning. Turns out we were a threesome with Hollywood-shaped baggage. She'd offered to speak to the production team to get me more time off. I refused. Avoiding work wasn't going to help me. I needed distraction – even if the distraction shared a set with Shaun. I could avoid him.

Now, out in the street, it was getting kind of awkward.

None of us spoke. Isla continued to glare, while I just watched Shaun with expectation.

He's come to say something. So bloody say it and leave.

But he was too busy drinking me in, his eyes studying me with a regretful light, missing nothing.

With a huff, I turned around and retraced my steps. If he wanted to stand about there, he could do it without me.

I heard the whack of shoes on cobbles before I heard his shout for me to stop. But I didn't listen. Instead, I kept power walking like a woman on a mission – a mission to escape a charming actor who, if given half the chance, would make her forget all her issues with him.

His hand caught my shoulder and spun me around. Off-balance, I fell into him. Our chests touched for mere seconds before I shoved him away, but that was enough to open the cabinet of memories.

My voice shook when I spoke. "What do you want, Shaun? You're leaving permanently. You didn't see fit to share that with me. I obviously didn't rank high on your list of priorities, which is fine. It was new and fast, and you don't owe me anything." The words tumbled from my mouth, tripping over each other while my voice rose. "I'll be back on Tuesday. I'll finish the show as contracted. I can be professional."

Shaun blinked at me. I didn't know what I'd expected, but confusion was not it. Then something sparked in his expression, and his big hands landed on my shoulders. He shook me hard, his fingers biting through my thin t-shirt.

"I don't want you to be fucking professional. I should have told you. I would have told you if you'd given me a chance to process any of it. Instead, you ran away." He growled my name and pulled me into him. This time, I didn't push him away. I was too shocked by the frustrated expression contorting his beautiful face.

"You're accusing me of leaving you, Mona, but you did

the same. I didn't think it would happen. Yes, that was an incredibly pessimistic outlook, but four months ago I was the angry broken-hearted drunk trashing expensive cars. I didn't think the studios would ever touch me again."

"You said the studios aren't smart," I repeated his words from a couple of months ago, my voice small compared to the angry boom of his.

"They aren't." His bruising grip eased a little. "My reputation was in tatters. Nothing should've happened. They shouldn't look at me like I'm their solution to adding more Golden Globes to their coffers." The anger in his gaze softened as he considered me. "But they are, and I owe that all to you."

I frowned. "Me?"

"You were right, Sparky. If I fuck up *Mystery Lines*, my career is over. I'll be relegated to bit parts in B-movies, or worse. I was fucking it up before you crashed into my life and stomped your foot."

"I did not stomp my foot."

Shaun chuckled. "You wanted to." His fingers crept up my neck, and my heart pounded.

I should stop him, step back, shake him off. Something. But I let him continue.

"Without you in my life, I might as well let it all go up in flames tomorrow. It means nothing." His expression turned serious. "Yes, I want to go to LA and the thought of what it could do for my career is exciting. But I'd be lost without you."

Frowning was becoming my resting expression, and if I didn't cut it out soon, I'd need to buy stock in an anti-ageing moisturiser. I'm sure I was meant to take something from that other than he'd be lost without me. He was still leaving, though, so it didn't exactly matter in the grand scheme of things.

"I don't understand."

Shaun shook his head, smiling. "Of course you don't. I'm not explaining this well." His hands dropped from my shoulders and face, and grasped my hands. "Come to LA with me."

"W-what?" I couldn't have heard him right.

"Come to LA. You can work in production there. Or be my assistant again if you want, but I love you and I'm not hiding it anymore. If the world wants to judge me for dating my assistant, they can get over it."

I hadn't heard him wrong. He'd asked me to move to Los Angeles. That was an awfully long way to go for someone to manipulate you.

Wait, he didn't manipulate me, and despite my reservations, I believed that he would have told me.

But LA?

"Somehow I thought that would sell better," Shaun muttered, eying me like a puzzle he couldn't figure out. "What do I need to do to convince you?"

"I—"

"Name it, Mona, and I'll do it!"

Silence followed his demand. I stared into his desperate eyes, searching for the answer. There was nothing he could do. The problem wasn't his to fix, though. It was mine.

"I need time."

Shaun's shoulders slumped, and he nodded.

"I'm not saying no. I just need time to think, to stop being mad at you."

Some hope returned to his expression as he studied me. He pulled me into his chest, engulfing me in the heat of his body. Playing dirty.

"I'm staying at the Clarice all weekend, room 420. Come find me when you figure it out." He rubbed his stubbly chin against my hair and tightened his hold.

"Okay, but she can't come back to you if you don't let her go," Isla said, stepping in and pulling me from his arms.

His fingers slipped from my body slowly. They brushed against the fabric of my t-shirt and down my arms until I shivered. My heart begged me not to let him go, and I shushed it. It wasn't the problem, my brain was.

CHAPTER THIRTY-FIVE

"*E*xplain it to me again," Isla said, her brow furrowed as she perched on the edge of her sofa. Wine swirled around her glass in her tell-tale sign of agitation. It mesmerised me.

It was only 2PM, but we'd cracked open a bottle of red because when making life decisions, alcohol was needed. (Said no one ever. Don't follow my lead.)

"Can you believe he wants me to move to LA with him and be his very public girlfriend?"

It seemed so simple when I laid it out like that. Yet my brain was in a tizzy over it.

"Yeah, I still don't understand the problem." Isla shuffled back into the sofa, tucking her feet beneath her and continuing to frown at me. "Why do I feel like that shit has his claws in this?"

'That shit' being my ex. It had been a while since she'd been able to say his name without looking like she was sucking on a very bitter lemon.

I kept pacing her living room. I couldn't stop, couldn't sit still without feeling this horrible itch telling me to move. My step count was going to be through the roof, at least.

"Oh, he does. What if I move all the way to LA and it turns out Shaun was manipulating me the entire time and it all just repeats?"

The look on Isla's face stopped me in my tracks. It was concerning but also incredulous. *What does that mean?*

"I've been in that man's presence for less than five minutes. I've not had a conversation with him, but I can tell you with certainty that the shit never looked at you like that," she spat with fire in her voice.

"Like what?" I whispered, the words nothing more than a reluctant puff of breath.

"Like his entire world was going to grind to a halt if you didn't go home with him."

Did Shaun really look at me like that and I'd missed it?

"Mona, he listens to you." My eyes jumped to Isla. "You're the reason he got his shit together and clued into his career again. Sherry's been bugging me for thank you gift ideas for weeks." Isla chuckled at my surprised expression. "Do you have any idea how many times I've had calls from Sherry on a fact-finding mission because Shaun Martin wanted to make sure you settled in okay? Lay that one bare, Mona. We both knew he was interested in you, and he risked us outing him just so he could find out if you'd like to try aerial silks."

With one elegant eyebrow quirked, she waited for me to jump in. When I bared my teeth instead, she sighed. "That sounds like a man who appreciates the person he's got, not one that wants to change her."

My wrist screamed as my fingers continued to pinch at the tight skin there. It was red raw, but I couldn't stop. She was right. I'd been so locked in my head and my past that I tarred him with a shadow that didn't fit.

"I know you as well as I know myself, and I'm sure the first thing you did when you read that email was figure out the reasons you *could* go with him." Isla grinned at me across her wineglass when I didn't reply. "I'm right, aren't I?"

"Yes," I growled.

"So, when you list it all out, you've got nothing standing in your way. You're using something that you got over a while ago to protect yourself. You're scared." Isla placed her glass on the table and stood. Coming to stand before me, she rested her hands on my shoulders and regarded me with sympathy. "I get it. Making huge life-changing decisions is terrifying, but I think you've picked the right one."

She was right. I was focusing on the wrong thing and hiding from my reality. It didn't help take away the pain because at the end of the day, I'd wanted to leave my dickhead ex; I didn't want to leave Shaun. He listened to me when I wasn't comfortable, and although he made himself a constant presence, he would have waited for the production to end.

And I was glad he'd kept trying. If he hadn't and we'd waited, I'd have nothing. No relationship. No memories. Nothing to prove that not all men were assholes looking for ways to tear me down.

I was terrified of getting hurt, but most of all, I was petrified of losing him.

My family were scattered all over the UK now. I didn't have a home. Now was the ideal time to uproot my life. Would I rather it be after I'd been in a relationship for a couple years? Yes. But this was the hand life dealt me, and I was not going to miss out on it.

"When you're sunning yourself in California, think of your poor sister stuck in rainy Scotland." Isla smirked, patting me on the shoulder.

It had the desired effect: I chuckled. I threw my arms around her and hugged her tight. She rocked me like she used to when we were kids, like she'd learnt from our mother, and I felt a pang for leaving her. But it wasn't strong enough to keep me either.

"Go get your man."

✳

*N*ervous energy propelled me through the lobby, into the elevator and up to Shaun's floor. It carried me as far as it could before abandoning me right when I needed it. I stood outside room 420 with my hands clasped together. I needed to knock, but I couldn't release my grip. My heart pounded, and I was sure I'd collapse soon if it didn't chill out.

But then the door flew open, startling and confusing me. *I didn't knock, so…?*

I barely registered Shaun's surprised face, too distracted by the expanse of skin on display. Of course he was shirtless. I didn't need to concentrate to get words out at all.

"You're here." The sound of his voice jump-started my brain and my anxiety returned full force. But no matter how much I'd have loved to have chased the distraction, I kept my gaze fixed on his.

He stepped back, gesturing me inside. I rushed into the room before I could change my mind and chicken out. All I had to do was admit I was wrong. Why was that freaking me out?

I was struck dumb by the space. Considering the size of his net worth, I'd expected him to be in a penthouse. Instead, he had taken a relatively small room on the fourth floor. It was nice and the double bed looked comfortable, but it was just pokey with limited walking space.

"I'm sure you didn't come just to gape at the size of my room." Shaun took a seat on the edge of the bed, amusement sparkling in his gaze.

The dark crescents beneath his eyes had darkened, and I felt a twinge of guilt. He'd clearly not been sleeping. I probably looked just as bad, but his life was stressful enough without all this. The least I could do was give him some relief.

I swallowed, trying to find the words. *Why hadn't I had Isla help me write some kind of speech? I should have prepared!*

"Okay, now I'm nervous," Shaun joked. "I wanted you speechless, but not like this." He stood and placed his strong hands on my shoulders, squeezing gently. As he stared into my eyes, his expression serious but earnest, I found my confidence.

"I want to come to LA with you," I said, the words tripping off my tongue before I could think about how maybe that wasn't the best place to start.

"You're sure?" His eyes searched my face, and the start of a smile pulled at his lips. I nodded, and he lit up before pulling me into a tight hug. He lifted me from my feet in his excitement, spinning me around.

"You won't regret this, Mona. Once we get some job options, I'll get a studio to sponsor you for a visa. You don't have to worry about anything." He allowed me to stand again but didn't release me.

Part of me was relieved it was over, that I would get to be with him. I should take that and run. But the other half, that part was concerned that it had been too easy. Why wasn't he demanding explanations?

"You're frowning. Why are you frowning?"

Was I overthinking it?

"Should we talk about it?" I whispered.

"Talk about what?" Shaun's hands slipped to find mine, pulling me to the bed. Retaining a firm grip, he forced me to sit while I puzzled out my thoughts.

"The fact you hadn't thought about what would happen if you got the green card? The fact I ran rather than gave you a chance to process it?"

Shaun's features smoothed as he relaxed. "You chose to trust me, and I didn't fully understand the significance of what you'd given me. Everything was so new I didn't consider how it would look to you if LA happened. That was my mistake, not yours. I would have left me too."

I nodded as some of the turmoil turning my stomach eased.

"This is all pretty new for us both. I love you so much. Two months ago, I couldn't have imagined I'd be capable of feeling like this. You helped me, and I want to be the person holding your hand as you figure out your next steps."

Staring into his earnest eyes, it was hard to understand how I could liken his actions to my ex. A kindred spirit held me in his arms, and I'd almost lost him.

"I want to be that for you too, Shaun."

"Good. Consider me your emotional crutch and use me all you like." His fingers toyed with the edge of my t-shirt as his smile turned cheeky. "Speaking of using me, have you ever had make-up sex?" His voice deepened, mirroring the heat darkening his eyes.

I shook my head, and his grin grew.

"How about I introduce you to it?"

Before I could form a response, Shaun's fingers slipped under my t-shirt and his head lowered. He caressed my lips with his, the gesture tentative and the pressure soft. It might have been gentle, but let me tell you, it was the best kiss I'd ever had. He worshipped me with his mouth, and any remaining apprehensions I held evaporated under his attention.

"I do have one request." Shaun said, breaking the kiss.

"What's that?" My voice sounded husky, but I got over it, watching lust skitter across his face.

He caught my hand, squeezing. "Next time I do something you disagree with or I'm not quick enough to share, go back to the beginning."

Go back to the beginning?

"Don't let me get away with it. Yell at me like you did on set if you have to, but don't let me shut you out."

Smiling, I nodded. "Only if you do the same."

"Always," he whispered before his gaze turned teasing. "But Sparky, I'm not worried."

Shaun kissed me hard. His tongue invaded my mouth, and I focused on winning his little game of wills.

Groaning, he pushed me onto the bed. "You're wearing too many clothes."

"Then fix it," I ordered.

In reply, he pressed light kisses to my neck, and I shivered.

"I shouldn't love it when you talk like that." He grinned. "But I really do. I'm going to enjoy spending my life with you."

The promise in his tone and the implication in his words should have frightened me. I waited for my heart rate to pick up, but it remained steady, calm now that I had his body next to mine.

"Not as much as me."

Shaun reared back, his eyes scanning my face. "Is this a challenge now?" At my nod, a wicked light entered his eyes. "Then prepare to lose."

He pounced on me, his fingers prodding sensitive skin and turning the tables on me. He tickled me until all I could do was giggle and gasp for mercy.

CHAPTER 36

Five months later

"Have neither of you heard of packing light?" Finn complained. He dropped the box he held on the kitchen counter and dragged his dirty hands through his dark hair. "Seriously, who moves across the ocean and ships all of their possessions?"

"Talk to Shaun. I tried." I placed my own box on the counter and tried to wipe the sweat from my face. Finn's lips twitched and I rolled my eyes, not even bothering to ask for an explanation. If my face was now streaked with dirt, it wouldn't be the first time today.

It was January and it was still unbearably hot in LA. Shaun and I had made the move just after Christmas, choosing to spend a festive few days with all my family and his mother first. We'd piled into my parents' tiny cottage in Cornwall. It was a fun send-off but a tight squeeze, and I'm certain my parents were happy to see us off in the end.

"You're honestly telling me that the majority of these boxes are Shaun's?" Disbelief dripped from Finn's words as he eyed the fifty-plus boxes piled up and littering what had felt like a spacious open-plan living room. Now it seemed dangerously crowded.

"What are you moaning about now?" Jackson asked, stumbling through the front door carrying another box. Trailing behind walked Shaun and Nathan, both loaded down with what I hoped signalled the end of the boxes.

"Shaun's fucking hoarder habit, what else!"

"I don't have a hoarder habit," Shaun argued, placing his box on a pile near the steps to the sunken lounge.

We had a sunken lounge!

I had yet to get used to the crazy opulence of this place. Shaun had bought a house in a gated community in Malibu. We had beach access and an incredible view of the water from almost every room.

"Pinky claims this is all yours." Finn hooked a finger towards me.

Nathan and Jackson's eyes widened as they fully took in the changed space. We'd spent the better part of an hour unloading boxes. No one had really stopped to see it; we just wanted the boxes and the heat to stop.

Shaun smoothed his fingers over my face. He wore an adorable smile and, even though I knew it was made of nothing but amusement at the state of me, I melted.

"They aren't all mine," Shaun argued, turning back to his friends.

Finn's eyebrows almost hit his hairline as they jumped to me. I could read the accusation in his eyes. I braced myself for the gleeful shouts I'd come to expect from him. The first time we'd met in person, we'd had to endure it for hours while he waxed poetic about the guys never doubting him again. It took a while for them to admit that it was all because they'd bet fifty thousand dollars between them on the outcome of our relationship. The figure was staggering to me, and I'd been unable to do anything but blink in shock.

"About ten of them are Mona's." Shaun started opening

boxes, ignoring the ruckus laughter that followed his admission.

Finn shook his head at Shaun. "You know I ditched everything but a suitcase when I moved, right?"

"You were a struggling acting student without a single credit to your name. Don't make yourself out as some kind of minimalist. I've seen your closet!" Nathan said, slapping Finn on the back, grinning at his friend's expense.

Finn and Nathan started sparring in the middle of the living room, surrounded by towers of boxes containing god knows what. They'd mostly all come out of storage. I'd wager Shaun didn't even know what was in half of them.

Even so, my stomach lurched as Finn lost his balance. He recovered before he could plough into a box, but oh boy, had his almost-fall sent my heart into my throat.

Jackson turned his back on his friends with a sigh. "I hope you've got insurance on this lot, Shaun." He placed a hand on my shoulder and turned me away. "They get worse with an audience."

Shaun chuckled.

"Where are these beers you bribed us with?" Jackson took a seat at the island, his expectant gaze fixed on Shaun.

Shaun had grown more confident with his ability to resist the lure of alcohol in the last few months. I no longer tensed when someone cracked open bottles around him, but I refused to drink in his presence. I wanted to support him in every way I could. He didn't need to taste the fumes on my lips.

A few weeks earlier, while we waited for our stuff to ship, we'd managed to go shopping for some pieces of furniture. Although, looking around the room now, I was glad we'd only bought a bed, bar stools and a sofa at this point. I'm not sure we'd have much manoeuvring room otherwise.

Shaun took three bottles of local craft beer from the fridge and two waters. He placed them on the counter before turning to Nathan and Finn. "Hey, assholes, if you're done trying to trash my new house…?" He held two bottles out to them, and the sparring stopped. They stumbled to the island, wearing huge grins despite their dishevelled clothing.

I picked up my water and followed the call of the ocean waves crashing on the beach outside. I'd found myself right here on the patio, lost in thought and staring at the sea, far too many times to count in the last month. It was such a calming place.

Arms wrapped around my waist, pulling me back into a well-muscled chest. Shaun kissed my bare neck and a shiver raced down my spine.

Another change. I'd lasted a week before taking scissors to my shoulder-length hair.

Joking. I went to a hairdresser, and he cut it into a bob. I'd had a fit at the price, but at least my hair no longer drove me crazy.

"Still sure you made the right choice?" Shaun's lips grazed my ear as he whispered the words.

I turned in his arms, and slid mine up his chest until they wrapped around his neck. He'd asked me variations of this question every day for the last month, and every time my answer stayed the same. "Still a resounding yes."

I tipped my head back, pushed up on my tiptoes and kissed him. I'd quickly realised that my boyfriend was a little pessimistic. It had been fun convincing him that I hadn't changed my mind, though. I smiled against his lips. In fact, I hadn't stopped smiling since we'd arrived, other than the hairdresser visit.

Next week, I started prep on my first feature film. When Shaun accepted his next role, he'd attached me as a requirement. It still seemed odd to me that something like that could be worked into a contract, but I was here, and I wouldn't change it for anything. I got to explore a job I enjoyed and share this next chapter of my life with the man I loved. Yeah, I was pretty bloody happy about how everything had turned out.

Shaun pulled back, smirking. His eyes gleamed with happiness. "What's this about?" He brushed his finger across my smile.

"For as long as I've got you in my life, my answer isn't going to change."

"So, you wouldn't be against marrying me?" From his tone, you'd assume he was talking about buying a new suit. It took a moment for his words to sink in.

A pulsing started in my throat, and I swallowed again. "Is that a 'now' or 'in the future' question?"

He turned his head towards the sea, pretending to consider the question. All the while, I could see him watching me from the corner of his eye.

"What if it's a now question?"

My heart rocketed in my chest, and I tried to reign in the excitement. "Are you going to propose or just keep being a dick about it?" Okay, so I failed in that effort.

Shaun laughed then pulled a small velvet box from his pocket. Slowly, he lowered himself to the patio on one knee.

"Mona, my saviour. Put me out of my misery and marry me?" He opened the box, revealing a pink rectangle-cut diamond surrounded by smaller white diamonds.

It was beautiful, and I got lost for a moment in the sunlight refracting from the stones.

"Mona?" Shaun prompted.

"As if I'd say no."

He sighed, and I held my hand out for him to slip it on. When he got to his feet again, he pulled me into his arms and kissed me so happily he took my breath away.

"We should get back in there before Finn finds my chocolate stash," he grumbled against my lips.

"Hey, Shaun," Finn called from the kitchen. "You don't

mind if I open the Vego, do you? Why don't they make chocolate right here?"

Shaun buried his face in my neck and pretended to cry. *It's almost like he heard us.*

The sound of the wrapper opening echoed out to us, and Shaun stilled. "He didn't?" Horror widened his eyes.

"How many boxes of it did you bring?"

He met my curious gaze. "You don't want to know."

"So, you won't miss a bar of it then?" I asked, my brows raised as I silently laughed at his pain. "Well, we need to celebrate our engagement somehow."

Smiling, Shaun raised my ring finger to his lips and pressed a soft kiss to the stone. Then he pulled me back towards the house as lust darkened his gaze, Finn's raid almost forgotten.

"Just let me kick them out." He dropped my hand, his heated eyes never leaving mine. "Two minutes tops."

I laughed at his desperate expression and followed him inside, confident that there was no reason to rush.

EPILOGUE

Three months later…

"Shaun, I'm home," I called from the marble foyer.

"In here," he called back, sounding distracted.

We were two weeks into a new film. My first Hollywood job. It was insanely exciting but also nerve-racking. Everyone knew I was connected to Shaun. How could they not? My face had been plastered all over the gossip blogs and tabloids the moment Sherry put out the announcement that we were engaged. I very quickly learned the worth of a gated property with security.

There had been photographers and cameramen roaming the road beyond the walls for a couple weeks. Thankfully, the interest had died down before filming started and Shaun had been able to show me around LA without us getting mobbed. Settling in was easy; there was a never-ending list of events to attend while we waited for the film to start just after Valentine's Day.

The wedding planning also started in earnest.

That wasn't my fault. Finn and Nathan liked to blame me for the influx of cake and appetisers, or the weekly dance classes they'd been mandated to attend. But I had nothing to do with it. I would have been happy to set a date and enjoy life for a little while. Shaun, however, was determined to get things moving.

We had set a date for December, exactly nine months from now. It was a little close for comfort, but considering who I was marrying, I shouldn't have been surprised when pieces fell into place quickly. Well, almost all the pieces. We still needed to finalise the guest list. I thought we'd nailed it multiple times, and then Sherry called with a reminder, growing the list by another twenty people. We were reaching the point of needing a new venue.

I found Shaun in our dining room area – which really just meant a section of the huge open-plan room. He sat frowning at the table. I scanned the papers laid out in front of him.

"What am I looking at?"

Shaun chewed on a pen. "Hmm?"

"What the hell is that monstrosity and why are there so many dots?"

He glanced up at me, dropping the mangled pen on the table. "It's the seating chart," he said, his words drawn out as his face scrunched up with confusion.

My heart jumped into my throat as the pieces clicked. There were hundreds of brightly coloured little circles with names scrawled on them spread out on a sheet of paper that covered at least half of our eight-foot dining-room table.

It couldn't be our seating plan.

No way.

The last time we talked we were on a hundred, which was fifty too many in my book, but this…

Unable to tear my eyes from the plan, I pulled out a chair opposite him and collapsed into it. I couldn't focus on any one name; there were too many of them.

"Mona?" Shaun asked, his voice barely audible against the roaring in my ears.

He was going to cut it down, surely. It couldn't be the final guest list. *Was there even a wedding venue big enough to fit them all in LA?*

Our families and friends had equalled forty. This thing must have had half of Hollywood's top hitters plus another couple dozen hangers-on.

Shaun's fingers grazed my chin, turning my stunned eyes to meet his. He'd lost the distracted edge. Now he kneeled at my side, smiling softly at me with concern.

"It's a lot, I know."

"I thought we were capping it at a hundred," I said, my voice croaking. I cleared it before adding, "Where did they all come from?"

He grimaced. "Sherry, the new film." His gaze skittered over the table. "I'm not really sure. I don't know how it got this out of control."

"Can we say no to them all?" I whispered, my voice hopeful. "The venue we booked won't hold them…"

"I know."

I was generally a confident person, but the thought of walking down an aisle with hundreds of people – strangers – watching me made my blood run cold.

A light entered Shaun's eyes and he straightened. "I have a suggestion."

"Go on."

"We elope," he said, the two words uttered so casually you'd think he'd suggested nothing more than a holiday.

"Elope," I repeated, my brows slowly climbing.

He nodded. "Yeah. We'll cancel all the plans, pick a resort and go on a date of our choosing."

"What would we tell my parents and our friends?"

He shrugged. "They'll understand."

I tilted my head, making a face. "You've met my father, right?"

We would not get away with eloping. I was the only one of

his three children engaged despite being the youngest. My mother wouldn't care. Dad would guilt me for the rest of his life.

"What about Sherry?"

"She'll book me on some unsavoury reality TV show." He shrugged, trying to cover the horror I could read in his eyes. "I'll live with it."

I bit my lip. That didn't sound pleasant. Plus, as this film picked up speed, our time together would get more and more restricted. I really didn't want to lose more of it to a show he didn't want to deal with.

"Can we just tell her we're capping it at a hundred and be done with it?" I leant towards him, letting my fingers dance along his cheek. "We could decide our top hundred right now and tell her it's done and locked."

He grinned. "I'm good with it, if you tell her."

"Me?" I sat back, a scowl overtaking my face. "Why me?"

Shaun chuckled. "She listens to you."

"Have you gone soft on me?" I grinned. Once upon a time, Sherry had struggled to control him.

He nodded. "I have this pretty fiancée who stole my thorns." He smoothed his hands along my arms, smiling like a lovestruck idiot. I couldn't get enough of it. "I'm much happier now."

I rolled my eyes, chuckling at him. "I'm pretty sure that was emotional manipulation."

"Does that mean you'll do it?"

I sighed. "Fine."

Couldn't exactly say no when it would solve all of my problems. And he wasn't wrong. These days Sherry readily agreed to anything I suggested. I think I'd won some brownie points saving his career.

"Yes," he hissed before capturing my lips with his.

My hands slipped around his shoulders and I edged

forwards on the seat, desperate to get closer. I tilted my head, deepening the kiss, and he groaned, shuffling closer.

I'd been on late nights with the film for a week, while he was barely needed. We'd hardly seen each other, and I was starved for his touch.

With a hand pressed to my lower back, he slid me closer to the edge until we were pressed flush together.

It wasn't enough.

I caught his t-shirt and tugged it up. He reluctantly broke the kiss to free himself from the bunched material.

My fingers roamed his naked chest as he brushed his lips along my exposed collar bone. One huge bonus for LA: hot weather. Getting undressed was much quicker than at home.

The sound of a throat clearing startled us apart. I was panting when I met Finn's amused gaze. Shaun didn't even bother turning around. His head landed on my shoulder, and he growled.

"Do we need to have words about knocking again?" Shaun muttered against my skin.

Finn smirked. "Nah, I got it the first time." He shrugged. "Not my fault if you don't answer."

I bit my lip, trying to suppress my smile. Finn McCarthy was a law unto himself.

"Uh, do you have a second, Shaun?

Shaun tensed. I could imagine the scowl blanketing his features without effort. He straightened, his hands slipping from my waist. I silently mourned their loss.

His shoulders sagged as he rose, meeting my gaze with a silent apology. Turned towards Finn, he asked, "What the fuck do you want now?"

"My agent's lost it," Finn said, racing towards Shaun. "You've got to help me." He reached for Shaun's chest, pausing at the lack of fabric, his fingers grasping nothing.

Shaun brushed his hands away. "What did you do this time?"

Finn stepped back, crossing his arms. "I resent the implications in your tone."

Shaun mirrored his stance and waited.

"There might be some unsavoury pictures hitting the blogs tomorrow." His eyes dropped to the ground. "He signed me up for *Married Blind*."

I frowned. What the hell was *Married Blind*?

Shaun sniggered. He patted Finn on the shoulder, his lips twitching. "Best of luck, butt."

Finn wasn't exactly the most sensible of men. Shaun had plastered the tabloids because he handled a breakup badly, but it went away as soon as he got his act together. Finn seemed to enjoy dragging the paps along on a game of cat and mouse. Each time he'd get caught doing something crazy – like getting snapped with his head between a woman's legs at a club – he had the look of an adrenaline junkie high on his latest fix. It was only a matter of time before his agent lost his patience.

Finn frowned. "That's it? Good luck? You're not going to help?"

He held his hands up and backed towards the kitchen. "I don't know what you want me to do. I've never pissed Sherry off enough for her to follow through."

A light bulb went off in my head. "It's a reality show?" I asked, glancing between the two. They nodded, their expressions set in unenthusiastic lines. "What is it about?"

Finn glanced at Shaun as if he'd been betrayed. "Why does your woman sound intrigued by my impending torture?"

Shaun shrugged. "Because it is entertaining?"

Finn spluttered. "You're an eejit too?"

"Surely it's not that bad." My attempt at reassurance earned me a hard stare.

"I'm not liking your definition of bad," he muttered, his tone panicked. "They're going to make me marry some stranger and you think that's going to end well?"

My brows furrowed. "Can they actually make you marry someone for a TV show?" That couldn't be legal.

Finn scoffed. "They have and they will." He fell into the chair opposite me and covered his eyes. "I'm doomed. Bloody damn well doomed."

Shaun placed three bottles of water on the table. "I'd say that about sums it up."

"You don't want to do it for me, do you?" Finn asked, his tone hopeful as he peeked at Shaun through his fingers.

I chuckled, but Shaun's face darkened.

"Out," he shouted, pointing at the door.

Finn's hands dropped to the table. He grinned. "You don't mean that."

Shaun remained silent, staring Finn down.

"What did I do?" he asked, his voice high as he glanced between us.

"Suggesting he marry someone other than me might have done it." I took Shaun's hand and squeezed, unable to contain my amusement. This was much more fun than planning a wedding. As lovely as Finn could be, I was going to enjoy watching him squirm.

Turn the page to read a bonus scene of the meet cute from Shaun's perspective. I usually reserve this for my mailing list but this is easier in print. Plus, it's just nice to have it all together, right?

If you enjoyed *Between Takes*, please consider leaving a review on your preferred platform.

Shaun

A soft knock on my trailer door jolted me from sleep. I groaned as the small sound shot through my head, sharp as a sucker punch to the face. I clutched my skull, wincing at the pain while I glanced around the bright space.

The light bounced off every surface, blinding me and making the pounding in my head exponentially worse.

Half empty bottles of whiskey and liquor cluttered the breakfast bar that cut the space in half. Just the sight of them triggered the thirst. The sun streamed through the bottles, refracting light across the walls.

When did the sun come up?

The TV droned in the background, some comedy show I'd switched on when I'd arrived on set at stupid o'clock this morning. It was meant to focus me. Instead, the swirl of alcohol in my veins had lulled me to sleep.

The runner outside knocked again. Every day we did this dance and each day they learned nothing. I dropped my head back against the sofa, groaning rather than shouting at them to leave me the fuck alone like I wanted.

Clearly I was late. Again.

Serves them fucking right for calling me at stupid times.

The 3 AM call times didn't bother me before Lily —

Don't go there asshole. You'll regret it.

Sprawled out on the leather sofa, my stomach churning as that familiar hungover sickness rose up.

I covered my face with a pillow, willing myself to fall back asleep. Unfortunately, the idiot outside refused to take a hint. Instead, they graduated from hesitant to downright violent. The trailer shook around me, the motion making my stomach twist dangerously.

In my right mind, I might have enjoyed torturing the poor sod assigned to me today. As it were, the banging made my head pound like a jackhammer, making my already volatile mood darken.

All I wanted was to crawl back into bed and take down a crate of salt and vinegar crisps. Instead I had to deal with this.

Muttering, I forced myself up and off the sofa. The room spun for a second as I staggered a few steps forward, catching myself against the bar.

Glass tinkled as the counter shook. The golden liquid sloshing around inside captured my attention and for a second, the sound of incessant knocking faded away.

My fingers itched to uncap the whiskey.

One drink won't hurt, a tiny persuasive voice in the back of my mind whispered. But it wouldn't be just one drink. I'd already had the *one* drink today and it would never be enough to drown out reality.

Then have the bottle, that voice pushed.

Only it wasn't even 10AM. If I drained the bottle, I'd be no better than my abusive, useless father.

Fuck.

I needed to stop before I completely lost myself to the booze like he did. I knew it and my liver would thank me. But if I stopped, if I put the bottle down, how would I block out the pain?

Of course, I had this argument with myself every morning. Every morning I promised myself it would end and then something set me off without fail, driving me back to the bottle.

"Like the annoying fucking knocking," I ground out, my jaw clenched and my temper fraying with each pulse of pain in my head.

New plan. Remind the runners who's boss and then drain the pissing bottle and be done with it.

I stormed across the space, my feet slamming against the hardwood floor and shaking the trailer as much as the knocking. I flung open the door, my face screwed up in a scowl, ready to roar at whoever dared disturb me.

I slammed the door open and a pink haired woman scrambled back. A sick satisfaction unfurled inside of me at her shocked expression.

I nearly hit her and I'm amused? What the fuck is wrong with me?

"What?" I shouted, glaring at the bubble gum haired runner.

But then her brown eyes met mine and suddenly I forgot why I was so angry. Nothing could have prepared me for the vision before me. Her plump lips pressed firmly together, sending my mind spinning into the gutter.

She was petite, more than a head shorter than me, with curves in all the right places. The sundress she wore hinted at her delicious figure beneath and my mouth was suddenly dry.

My gaze drifted to her white blonde roots peeking through her bubble gum hair and I felt my cock twitch.

She was beautiful—and I had a feeling that if she stuck around, we'd be trouble...

She pushed her shoulders back, cleared her throat before offering her hand. "Mr Martin, I'm Mona Baines. It's nice to meet you," she said, her Scottish accent catching me by surprise.

My first impulse was to take her hand, to feel the warmth

of her skin against mine. But I held back the urge. Instead, I forced myself to glare.

"May I come in?" she asked, smiling like she had every right to make my head split open.

Her smile hit me like a blow, my breath catching as arousal slammed through me. I stared down at that coy curve of lips and vivid images filled my mind, desire coiling hot and tight in my gut. Those plump, pink lips wrapped around my aching cock, stretched wide as I thrust between them. The urge to crush my mouth to hers was a physical ache, to swallow her whimpers of pleasure like the finest wine.

I hardened at the thought, heat and need pouring off me in waves I had to fight not to act on. It took every ounce of restraint not to grab her, to back her into the damn trailer and show her what that tempting smile did to me. My hands itched to grip her hips, to lift that flimsy excuse for a dress and lose myself in her.

The pounding in my head was nothing to the pounding desire now raging in my blood. I couldn't tear my gaze away from that smile, feeling my control slipping with each passing second. How dared she? How dared this gorgeous woman walk in here and undo me with no more than the curve of her mouth?

I fought to regain a measure of composure, to shake off the images crowding my mind and remember why she was here.

Silence stretched between us as I stared her down, grasping for the remnants of anger like a lifeline. She would not best me.

I scowled at the thought. It had been months since I'd slept with a woman, since I'd felt so much as a glimmer of attraction, not since Lily... Not since Lily dumped me like I hadn't been her rock for more than ten years. She convinced me that we were each other's end game, that we would always be together no matter the distance or the job. And like a pissing idiot, I'd let her.

Staring at Mona's pretty face, my anger solidified again, but not towards the woman in front of me. Lily had taken so much from me already, why did my first thought have to be about her? I hadn't been able to look at a woman with anything but suspicion in months and now she'd ruined this too.

So instead of kissing her and relishing the scandalised shock like I wanted to, I crossed my arms and blocked the doorway.

But neither my glare nor my tough guy act fazed her. She thrust a coffee at me, the smell turning my stomach. Prattling on about Sherry and my order. When did Sherry start telling runners my coffee order?

"Why is my agent telling you my coffee order?" I rasped, my throat dry. Every word hurt.

She blinked up at me, confusion written on her face. "She didn't tell you?"

My eyes narrowed. What the hell had she done now?

Mona's confident mask cracked and her smile wilted. "I'm your new assistant."

New assistant? I didn't bloody ask for another assistant. Anger sparked in my chest, burning through the desire still lingering from her smile. Would they never stop thinking they knew best how to 'handle' me?

I glared at her, resentment rising swift and bitter. Another of Sherry's bright ideas to puppet my life, forcing attachments I didn't ask for. As if I couldn't function without a minder, as if I needed my every step shadowed.

"Not a chance," I muttered before slamming the door shut and immediately regretted the loud noise.

I'd barely taken two steps when my phone rang. My traitor agent's name flashed across the screen.

"She had better be lying," I snapped as soon as I answered the call, my tone sharp and biting.

"Good morning to you too, Shaun. I'm great, thank you for asking," Sherry chirped, her regular cheery voice like nails on a chalkboard. I held the phone away from my ear with a wince of pain and annoyance.

"Don't fuck with me right now, Sher. Tell me she's lying." The last thing I needed was an assistant. Especially now. Everything set me off, emotions raw and close to the surface.

"Why would she be lying, honey? You need an assistant."

"I really don't." My foul mood deepened by the second. I slammed a fist against the side of the trailer, rattling the thin metal walls.

"Sure, sure," she said, almost sing-song. I grimaced at her patronising tone. "Whatever you need to tell yourself right now to accept the truth."

"There's nothing to accept." I growled. Couldn't she leave me in peace? Her grating voice made me want to hurl the phone through a window.

"Considering I hired her and she is your assistant, I'd say there's lots for you to accept."

"You did what!" I bellowed, agony ripping through my head at the volume. But my anger burned hotter, always close to erupting.

"Really, Shaun?" Sherry tutted. "How about we save the theatrics for the sound stage?"

"I don't want an assistant," I said, ignoring her admonishment. "I'll just fire this one too."

"Oh no, you won't." All the cheer drained from her voice. "I don't care what you think. You need her."

"No, I bloody don't."

And I'm getting rid of her right now.

I dropped the phone from my ear and rushed back to the door, just knowing she'd still be out there, waiting to smoke me out.

The door slammed against the side of the trailer as I threw it open again. I fixed the pink pixie with angry eyes and she froze on the spot.

"You!" I shouted, pointing at her. "Just to be clear: I did not hire you. I don't need you."

Sherry's shrill voice exploded from the phone. Begrudgingly, I lifted it back to my ear, holding it slightly away in the misguided hope that the sound wouldn't gut through me.

"Don't you dare speak to her that way, do you hear me?" Sherry shrieked. "Do you have any idea how much trouble you're in already? How many directors and crew refuse to work with you because of your behaviour?"

"It was one time." I insisted, scowling. Why was she determined to make everything into a drama? "They can't get their knickers in a twist over one late start."

"One time?" Sherry shrieked. "You were late three times just last week! You disrupted filming for hours just yesterday after throwing a tantrum over wardrobe. I don't care if you like it. Mona *is* your assistant, whether you think you need one or not. She will make sure you arrive to set on schedule and you will get your act together."

"I don't need a babysitter. I'm handling it." I dragged a hand through my hair, tugging at it until a satisfying pinch at the roots calmed the simmer of anger in my blood.

"Clearly you can't handle it yourself!" Sherry snapped. "And she's not a babysitter, she's an assistant, and you will find the last shreds of kindness left in that damaged heart of yours and treat her well. This is non-negotiable, Shaun. The showrunner wants to replace you and if you screw up one more time, he'll get his wish!"

"That's ridiculous," I muttered. "I'm the star! They wouldn't."

Silence greeted me on the other end of the line. I could almost see Sherry's look of disappointment and frustration.

After a long moment she sighed, a heavy, defeated sound that mirrored my own internal exhaustion.

"You just don't get it, do you?" Sherry said at last, sadness leaching into her voice. "You're off the rails, honey. I know you're hurting but people will only turn a blind eye for so long. I'm afraid you're reaching the end of the line. The showrunner won't keep making allowances."

I started to argue but she cut me off sharply. "Stop. Just listen for once. You need to accept Mona's help. She can fix this train wreck if you let her but you have to meet us halfway."

I clenched my jaw, resentment burning in my chest as I waited for the inevitable 'I told you so'. But it never came.

"Please Shaun," Sherry said softly. "Do this so we can get through this show together without another catastrophe. Your talent is too important to throw away over a broken heart." Her tone took on a pleading note. "Let Mona help minimise distractions so you can focus on your work. Give her a chance; you might find she's the lifeline you didn't know you needed."

The fight slowly drained out of me, leaving behind weary acceptance as her heartfelt words hit their mark. As much as the idea rankled, she was right. If I wanted any hope of survival, I needed to accept the help offered before I self-destructed completely.

"Fine," I muttered into the phone. "But it's a trial run. When I say it's done, it's done. Are we clear?"

"No, actually we're not," Sherry said. "Mona stays until the end of filming. And before you get any ideas, I've hired her on behalf of the agency so you can't fire her."

I froze as fury bubbled up inside me. How dare she go behind my back! I'd never given permission for an assistant, let alone a babysitter.

"Are you fucking serious?" I exploded. "Pretty sure I employ you, Sherry. Are you enjoying the beach house my fee earned you?"

There was a heavy silence on the other end of the line. I knew I'd hit my mark; Sherry lived well off the exorbitant fees I commanded that afforded her no small amount of comfort.

When she spoke again, her voice was tight. "There's no need for that. I'm trying to help you, if you'd stop fighting me at every turn!" Sherry said, her voice annoyingly calm. "We've worked too hard to get you here, Shaun. I'm not going to let you destroy your career over a woman. I won't apologise for not running this past you."

Sherry's words cut deeper than I'd ever admit. To be reminded how close I was to losing everything stung, another slap to still-raw scars. I never used to need handling or threats to get the job done. Just another failure to add to the list.

"You forget I know you." She laughed, the sound strained. "You're determined to drive yourself into the ground and I can't figure out why — yes, I know Lily broke your heart but you love acting — I'm not going to just sit back and watch you implode."

Shame burned through me at this weakness, what I'd tried so hard to escape in the roles I poured myself into. I'd worked to the bone to claw my way here, chasing a dream they always said would never be mine. Now all their doubts and disdain were proven true. If this wasn't ironic justice, what was?

Lily. How her name alone could still stop me in my tracks, I couldn't say. It almost acted as a reminder of what might have been if I were someone worthy of keeping. She took everything when she left, all the strength I'd found escaping my father and the purpose I'd built this dream on.

But I'd have to be an idiot to fall for Sherry's idealistic schemes. With the way Mona stared at me, her emotions plain to read in her brown eyes, it left little doubt in my mind. A soft-hearted woman couldn't save me from my demons.

Only if I told Sherry that, she'd argue her case for the rest of the day.

"I'm telling you this won't work, but whatever."

I'd let her think I'd do as she asked. It wouldn't stop me finding a way to make Mona quit. Given the way she flinched each time I opened the trailer door, it wouldn't take much. The woman was clearly skittish around me and I was nothing if not persistent when it suited me.

"I'm just asking you to try," Sherry said.

She wanted a heck of a lot more than that but I didn't call her on it. Getting her off the phone was all that mattered. I made pleasant sounds that she bought enough to end the call.

I walked down the metal steps, pocketing my phone as I approached her with a deliberate slowness. She tensed, eying me like I might bite her if I got too close. My gaze tracked down her curvy body at the thought. *If only.*

"What did you say your name was?" I asked as I took the coffee cup from her.

Of course, I remembered her name. The woman worryingly captured my fascination with ease. By the time she left tonight, I might have memorised every inch of her I could see. But she didn't need to know any of that.

"Mona."

"Fine, Mona. It looks like you're my PA." I sipped the coffee, pulling a face when the lukewarm liquid hit my stomach.

I lowered the cup, breathing deeply while I willed my stomach not to revolt.

"Ground rules," I said, my voice cutting through the silence like a whip. "Stay out of my way and we'll be fine. Take my calls. Your number one job is to keep the producers and my agent away from me. Clear?"

I turned to head back to my trailer, done with this conversation. Mona's next words stopped me in my tracks.

"No dice. I'll do my job. I'll keep you on track and that includes keeping you out of a bottle and attending creative meetings with the producers who took a massive gamble on your falling star."

Falling star? The cheek of this woman!

"Now, wait—"

She raised her hand, cutting me off. "You may not like me. Or the situation, but I'm what you've got. It's me or a huge fee when you fail to complete this show and maybe the end of your career as you know it. You have no choices left."

When she finally finished her tirade, I glared at her, waiting for her to cower. But she didn't bend.

"Fine. It's you. Now do your job and leave me the fuck alone." I stomped off to my trailer, slamming the door to get away from her.

Seconds later, fists pounded at my door. I threw it open. "What!"

"You're in make-up in five minutes."

"Then I'll go in five."

"No. It'll take you five to walk there. You leave now."

The hard look in her eyes told me she wasn't going to budge. I ran a hand through my hair and sighed. Looked like the little firecracker meant business.

"You're a hard-ass. Anyone ever tell you that?" I muttered.

Mona just smiled and waited. No choice then. I followed her to make-up, my mood worsening with each step. This was going to be a long day. And an even longer six months if I couldn't figure out how to make her quit or bend.

Now *that* was an image I could get behind.

Not ready to say goodbye to the Kings of Screen men? Turn the page for a sneak preview of *Married Blind*. Two strangers tie the knot for a reality tv

show: playboy actor and an everyday woman. What could possibly go wrong?

Or grab it now
books2read.com/MarriedBlind

ABOUT MARRIED BLIND

Will it be love at first sight, or are they fated to hate?

Abi

I'm busy. You're busy. We're all busy.

But it doesn't seem to matter how many hours I work, or how many coffee dates and drinks with friends I skip, there's never enough to go round.

I never expected that getting my sister out of debt would be this hard. So, when I cross paths with an easy way to earn big bucks fast, how can I say no?

Finn

Unpredictable. Loose canon. Playboy. Or, at least, that's what they say.

It's an issue; the image. One that I've apparently pushed too far.

A reality TV show was never on my agenda but it's this or nothing, how can I say no to that?

They're both in it, and there's just one question left on both their minds. Three months married to a stranger can't be that bad… can it?

Married Blind is a standalone marriage-of-conve-nience Hollywood romance set in the Kings of Screen world.

Turn the page for a sneak peak...

MARRIED BLIND EXCERPT

FINN

"C'mon, Charlie. You can't be serious."

"I'm sorry, Finn, but you knew the consequences." My agent sighed on the other end of the phone. "I don't enjoy playing the bad guy. Honestly, I don't."

"Then don't."

Ordinarily, I would work to keep the slightest hint of desperation from my voice, but all bets were off in this situation. I needed out, ASAP. Otherwise, I'd be putting a ring on a stranger for America's reality-TV-loving masses in just two weeks.

Finn McCarthy didn't do reality TV.

Finn McCarthy had multiple awards under his belt, and he didn't stoop to cheesy gimmicks.

He also didn't talk about himself in the third person.

Jesus. I'm losing it.

"You knew the deal, Finn. I warned you the last time, and you still—" A hushed voice cut him off, and I sank deeper into my sofa while he argued with his assistant.

"Take your time, Charlie. It's not like you've tied my life to a ticking bomb or anything."

He sighed again. "How long have I looked after your best interests in this town?"

"Five years, but clearly you've lost your damn mind. Making me marry a gold-digging stranger and broadcasting it to millions is not looking after my best interests."

My heart pounded and sweat beaded on my forehead. The longer I let the situation spiral, the more it made me panic. How could a TV show require you to legally marry someone? The entire industry had gone insane, right alongside my agent.

"Seriously, Charlie, what if they pair me up with a right eejit, and she tries to fight the prenup?"

Not to toot my horn, but multi-award-winning actors raked in the cash.

When they weren't caught in the bathroom with the studio head's twenty-year-old daughter.

Okay, so I'd fucked up royally, but did that mean they should punish me with potentially life-alternating consequences because a pretty woman offered herself to me?

Hell no.

"Next time you decide to make an ass of yourself in public, you'll remember the next three months," Charlie said. If his voice held so much as a grain of remorse, he hid it well. "I'm doing everything I can to make sure you have a long career, Finn. How about you get on board and help me?"

"Okay." I blew out a breath, a small fizzle of hope springing to life inside of me. "What about one of those survivalist shows? That's got to be better for my rep than this."

Charlie chuckled. "I like the image, bud, but the world already knows you as the macho man."

I'd even eat a spider if that would help me get out of tux fittings and ring shopping.

"It's not good for a well-rounded career actor." Charlie let those words drop like the dagger they were. "You told me you wanted to be the next Ryan Reynolds. Is that still true?"

I chewed my lip and wished I hadn't picked Charlie for a second. I should have picked a ruthless American. Someone born in LA. Hell, keeping my British agent might have worked more to my favour. Instead, I went for a Canadian transplant.

The second passed fast, unfortunately.

"Yes," I grumbled.

"Then trust me to do what's good for you."

I dragged a hand through my hair, biting back the desperate 'no' sitting at the tip of my tongue. I did trust him. Usually.

The thought of marrying someone for damage control put a sour taste in my mouth. Add cameras, producers, and undoubtedly awkward questions to the mix, and I would turn feral.

I'd seen the original of this show. After working extra hard to keep my personal life as personal as possible in this business, I did not want it painted all over billboards.

"I hate talking to reporters, Charlie. How am I meant to handle the producers?"

My best friends were taking bets on how fast I tanked the whole thing; honestly, they weren't wrong. I'll be standing at the altar, feet tapping and my eyes on the wrong door while I worked out my fifth exit strategy.

The point is, it made me feel dirty, and I was not in the business of doing things that aligned me with the lowest tier of Hollywood scum.

"Like you do everything else, Finn." Charlie's faith in me rang loud in his words. Given my knee's uncontrollable bouncing or shaky hands, I didn't deserve his misplaced faith. "It's a role."

Everything froze: my breath, my frazzled thoughts, my hands. "Say that again."

"You're an incredible actor. Just pick a persona and give

them that. There's no reason they have to see you unless you want them to."

Pick a persona.

Just another job.

"Let's say, hypothetically, I can do that," I whispered, a temporary calm flowing through my body.

"There's that confident Irish attitude I expect from you."

I snorted. "And there's that full of Canadian bullshit I expect from you." Shaking my head, I collapsed back against the sofa cushions. The leather whined beneath me. "There's really nothing I can say to talk you out of this?"

"You'd need a time machine, my friend. Suck it up and take your punishment, McCarthy," Charlie said, a thread of steel in his tone. "Next time a pretty woman comes on to you, you might think better of fucking her in a very public bathroom."

"What if my new wife is one of those pretty women?"

Charlie's heavy sigh rattled the phone.

ABI

New Email.

Subject: The solution to ALL your problems.

I snorted. Solutions to my problems wouldn't fit in an email. I needed a time-turner and a fourth job to help my sister clear her medical debt. It didn't matter how many pretty vintage garments I flipped or how much commission I made as a travel agent; we needed a miracle.

Despite my doubts, I clicked on the email, a tiny grain of hope worming its way to the forefront.

Did I mention the solution came with a total hottie attached?
Click the link and thank me later... with all the details.

Ros x

I frowned at the glaring neon blue web link. *Why did Ros think Infinity Productions could help me?* A small thread of common sense shouted at me for even thinking about clicking on a strange link in an email.

Maybe someone had hijacked Roseline's account… although she usually communicated in links and memes.

Throwing caution to the wind, I hit the link. The page loaded and my head cocked to the side, considering the brightly coloured advert before me.

TV SHOW SEEKING BRIDES FOR A BRAND-NEW MARRIAGE EXPERIMENT.

She can't be serious.

I had my cell in hand in a blink. *What the hell are they after?*

"Abi! Did you get my email? Omigod, isn't it amazing?" Roseline said, her words merging into one excited whoosh of breath.

"Uh, possibly, but Ros, I don't know what I'm reading." I chewed my lip, scanning the limited details again. "What is it?"

"You know that TV show, *Married Blind?* I used to force you to watch before I moved out."

"Yes…"

"They're making a celebrity edition." She paused, expecting a gasp of awe, I imagined. We'd been best friends since college. We were predictable to each other at this point. "And they want perfectly normal people to match them with…" She waited again, and this time I smirked, sensing her frustration. "Get a little excited, Abi. They'll pay you to marry a celeb and take part in the show for three months. It's perfect."

"What's the catch?"

Roseline snorted. "No catch beyond the obvious, honey."

"The obvious being what? Spell it out for me."

"Well, for starters, you'd be marrying a stranger."

"Got that part." I brushed it aside as if she could see. "Next?"

"They're celebs, so you'll probably have to move for the duration of the show."

I swallowed hard at that.

Sure, Eva had been back on her feet for nearly a year now. She'd even returned to her job, and her gorgeous red hair had grown back. She was happy, almost like before the diagnosis and chemo, but did that mean I stopped worrying?

Of course not. I'd nearly lost my sister and my best friend. The thought of leaving her now, of vanishing to the other side of the country, even to help pay off her substantial medical bills… How could I?

"Stop the internal debate," Ros said. All the excitement drained from her voice. "You can talk to your sister, Abi. She'll understand. Heck, I think she'll beg you to go."

"You don't know that."

"Hmm…"

"You already talked to her."

"Maybe…"

Maybe? "Ros!"

"Alright! She sent *me* the link."

I gasped. Every eye in the travel shop shot toward me, customers and colleagues alike. Roseline always had the worst timing. My boss's brows rose in question, genuine concern flickering across her face. I shook my head at her and pushed back from my desk.

"Why wouldn't she talk to me herself?" I hissed as I rushed to the backroom and away from curious ears. "Why are you the messenger?"

"How should I know?" Her attempt at innocence fell flat, and she sighed. "Fine! Eva thought you'd feel pressured into saying yes if she asked."

I rolled my eyes. "That's not true."

"Isn't it?"

"No."

Ros sighed again, her exasperation exploding in my ear. "Think about it for a second, Abs. I'm telling you about a fun thing, an exciting experience. Bonus, it just comes with a nice paycheque."

"What's your point?" My brows furrowed.

I sank into an uncomfortable plastic chair, my mind spinning enough that I didn't really feel the pinch of the seat. We only really used the backroom to store our coats and bags, but the bosses had set it up with chairs, a table, a fridge and a microwave. With the lack of windows, none of us ever wanted to spend too much time inside with the door shut. Far too depressing.

"Imagine how you would have taken my pitch if Eva asked."

I would have filled out the form already.

I dragged a shaking hand through my hair.

"So, now that you've listened to the specifics, are you going to do it?" The excitement returned threefold.

I blew out a breath, indecision a heavy weight in my chest. "How much money are we talking about?"

"I don't know. You'd have to fill in the form and hope you get picked to find out."

I nodded, even though she couldn't see me.

Right at this moment, the decision had to be about me. Could I marry a stranger? Did I want to leave my family and friends for three months?

It had been a tough couple of years, and as much as I hated to admit it, New York didn't have the same happy hold on me anymore. Too many bad things had happened within the city, including my sister's battle with cancer. Working three jobs also robbed any of the joy from my life.

Even if I had the hours to fall in love with the city again, constant exhaustion didn't allow for much.

Maybe a brief break from the city and my normal life would revive me somehow. I could get in some excitement and shake off the shadows while hopefully earning enough to pay off my sister's debt for good.

How could I say no to that kind of opportunity? The answer was simple. I couldn't.

"I'll do it."

If you'd like to know what happens next, *Married Blind* is available on all platforms and can be requested by most bookstores. Check it out here: books2read.com/MarriedBlind

Or request it from your local library.

ALSO BY MORGANA BEVAN

True Platinum Series (Rock Star Romance)

(Rhiannon)

Chasing Alys – Ryan (Resistant to Love)

Charming Daphne – Matt (Force Proximity)

Winning Nia – James (Second Chance)

Enticing Mel – Dan (Secret Baby)

Needing Emily – Emily (Accidental Marriage/Runaway Bride)

Defying Ella — Jared (Close Proximity / Snowed-in)

(The Brightside)

Braving Lily - Lily (Opposites Attract)

Daring Ceri - Alex (Second Chance)

Marrying Olivia - Lewis (Accidental Marriage)

Craving Leah - Andy (Best Friend's Sister) - Coming 2025

Kings of Screen Series (Hollywood Romance)

Between Takes (Enemies to Lovers)

Married Blind (Marriage of Convenience)

Acting Counsel (Close Proximity, Forbidden)

Fashionably Fake (Fake Dating)

Lights, Camera, Baby! (Accidental Pregnancy)

Sign up for Morgana Bevan's mailing list: https://morganabevan.com/mailing-list/

ACKNOWLEDGMENTS

With thanks to my best friends for putting up with my constant chatter about indie publishing and various marketing techniques. I'll talk about something else one day.

Big thanks to Meaghan and Janey for their endless support: keeping me sane and accepting all my requests for last-minute help.

Also thanks to Amy for being my second pair of eyes, catching any non-industry slips and my assumed knowledge.

To my amazing editor, Kristen, a massive thank you for supporting me through the start of my author career. Your encouragement has been invaluable and essential for boosting my confidence. Bet you didn't see this one coming when I was your intern?

Also thank you to my brilliant cover designer, Kirsty, and your incredible ability to create the perfect cover with very little direction from me. You nailed it in one try!

Moreover, I must say a huge thank you to my incredible PA, Tracey Leck. I'm not sure I'd have gotten to release day with my sanity intact without your support.

To the readers, thank you for reading this book and taking a chance on me as a new author.

ABOUT MORGANA BEVAN

Morgana Bevan is a sucker for a rock star romance, particularly if it involves a soul-destroying breakup or strangers waking up in Vegas. She's a contemporary romance author based in Wales. When Morgana's not writing steamy celebrity romances with gorgeous British rock stars and movie stars, she's travelling the world, searching for inspiration.

She enjoys travelling, attending gigs, and trying out the extreme activities she forces on her characters.

Find Morgana online at morganabevan.com.

Morgana's Facebook Reader Group: facebook.com/groups/4989193364708263

facebook.com/MorganaBevanAuthor

x.com/MorganaBevan

instagram.com/morganabevan

goodreads.com/morganabevan

bookbub.com/profile/morgana-bevan

www.ingramcontent.com/pod-product-compliance
Lightning Source LLC
Chambersburg PA
CBHW061521210726
48287CB00006B/1772

9 781916 719002